GROUND

OF THE

RICHARD REZENDES

PAGE PUBLISHING, INC.
New York, NY

First originally published by Page Publishing, Inc. 2019

ISBN 978-1-64424-644-3 (Paperback)
ISBN 978-1-64424-645-0 (Digital)

Printed in the United States of America

CHAPTER 1

The Haunted House

WEST TWENTY-ONE NORTH STREET IN Moodus, Connecticut, is where it's at, the Haunted House, on April's night. Police drove around the haunted house all night because people were getting ready to move in the next day. The next day, workers were fixing and cleaning around the three-floor tenement, which has been ascended for over fifty years, because people believed that this house was possessed by the devil. The new owner's name was Earl Davies. Earl rented an apartment on the first floor to this young couple, Jose and Tanya. "Are you the two people who's renting this apartment?" said Earl.

"Yes, sir, my name is Jose, and she is Tanya."

"Pleased to meet you. My name is Earl Davies, your landlord. Your rent will be $300 a month. Your rent includes heat, hot water, and gas cooking. Now come in and I will show you the apartment. This building has three floors and a large basement. Sorry, this building is run-down a little, but my workers are going to fix it up, and it's going to look nice after. Yours is the last one in the back of this building over an old garage. Come with me. You see, this garage used to be a morgue years ago. This building has been ascended for fifty years or more. You will see spiderwebs in the hallways, but your apartment is clean. This house will be restored into condominiums in a few years.

3

The town of Moodus has to fix this area because north street used to be a ghetto," said Earl.

"Sir, we're gonna live over an old morgue!" Tanya laughed.

"The garage under your apartment has not been used for years. It used to be a morgue years ago, but it's a garage now. This part of the building is the only rebuilt section, and this door leads to your apartment. Come with me and I will show you your apartment. Your address is Twenty-One North Street Apartment number 6, the last apartment in this building. Apartments 1 and 2 are on the third floor, 4 and 5 are on the second floor, 5 and 6 are here on the first.

"Look at your key ring, the first key enters this building, the second unlocks the dead bolt to your apartment, the third key is your house key. Your first key will also let you into the basement and the garage. Now this apartment needs a little fixing up. My work crew will take care of that for you. We just bought this property yesterday. Here is your kitchen. The first floor is in kind of a bad shape but we'll have fixed within a week. Now here's your living room, you don't have any windows in here. Let me turn on the lights," said Earl Davies. *Click.* Earl turned on the lights. A rat ran across the floor into another room.

"*Ahhhhh!* was that a rat!" Tanya screamed.

"No, Tanya, that was just a thick ball of dust," said Earl.

"Let me move the couch, I will see if it was a rat or not," said Jose.

Earl and Jose moved the couch. Nothing was under it. Earl then continued showing the apartment.

"You have a large fireplace in the living room, with a lot of ashes in it. Don't mind that, the chimney just needs to be cleaned."

"Earl, I thought you told me this apartment was cleaned?" said Tanya.

"I thought so too, Tanya. I will have my cleaning crew come in tomorrow to clean the rest of your place. I guess they haven't finished cleaning in here yet," said Earl.

"What's that tree doing in that comer?" asked Tanya.

"Oh! That's an old Christmas tree, it's been there for a while. I will take it out of here tomorrow," said Earl.

"This is a nice little room," said Jose.

"Okay, let's go to the next room now. This room is the dining room, overlooking the water. This room is the best room in this apartment. You also have a big fireplace," said Earl. Jose and Tanya do not know this house was haunted. "This room is the bedroom. You have a furnished king-size bed, with a double canopy on top and a curtain that goes around the bed. The bedframe has iron bars."

"It's lovely," said Tanya.

"Let me show you the big walk-in closets, it needs cleaning."

Earl was showing the walk-in closets in the bedroom, and a rat jumped out of the closet onto the bed, then it leaped off the bed into the fireplace. No one saw it.

"You have a large fireplace in the bedroom too. Now come with me and I will show you some more. This room here is your spare room, you can use this room for storage or an extra bedroom.

"This room has one door leading to the basement, the other leads to outside. The door on the left leads to the basement, the one on the right leads outside, but this door is bolted shut. This room has to be refinished, the plaster is peeling off everywhere. Will fix this room within a few days. Just keep the door closed in this room for now. Here is the bathroom, you have blue and gray tiles with a little tinted green coloring and drapes to match," continued Earl.

"Earl, do you mind if I interrupt you?" said Tanya.

"Sure," said Earl."

"Look at these drapes closely, there's spiders running all over them and webs all over the place," said Tanya.

"Tanya, don't worry, I will get you some new drapes tomorrow, and I will see that this place gets good and cleaned up. I will have all the spiders removed first thing in the morning. Now in your bathroom, you have an antique Jacuzzi, the Jacuzzi is fairly new. You turn the middle faucet on, the water will bubble at one hundred degrees. The tub automatically fills up with water and starts bubbling. The faucets on the right and left is your hot, cold water. If you want to take a shower, pull the middle faucet out, the shower will come on. You people will love this Jacuzzi! It's called the 1945 love tub. Enjoy your apartment, and I will see you tomorrow," said Earl.

Jose and Tanya finished the day moving in. By nighttime, Jose pulled his car up to the garage with his last load. He left his headlights on, and he got out of his car. He tried to use his key to get in the garage. He couldn't open it, so he drilled a hole in the door to get it open. The drilling did no good. The garage door was still jammed shut. Tanya was watching TV upstairs, while Jose was fixing the garage door. Jose finally gave up, and he went back inside his apartment by the back way. While he was going upstairs to his apartment, he heard a weird noise outside. Jose stopped for a minute, then he went inside. Jose and Tanya were taking a bubble bath in their Jacuzzi. Three rats was running around in the apartment. The rats hid under the bed. Jose got out of the tub to go to the toilet, and when he flushed the toilet, the rats ran like a bat out of hell into another room. Jose and Tanya were talking in bed.

Tanya said, "This apartment is spooky."

Later in the night, Jose and Tanya fell asleep. At midnight, Tanya woke up. She heard something running across the room. She was scared, and she woke up Jose.

She said, "Jose, listen, I hear something running around."

"I heard it too!" he said.

"We have rats!" Tanya cried.

"Tanya, you stay in bed. I'll get my flash and look," said Jose.

Jose grabbed his light, and he went looking for rats. Jose searched the whole apartment. He even flashed the light up the fireplace, but he still couldn't find any rats. He went downstairs in the basement, and he yelled, "Is anyone down here?" Jose then went downstairs into the basement, and he looked. He flashed his flashlight all around down there. He flashed the light on the cellar floor to see if he could find any footprints. He found nothing, so he went back upstairs to bed.

Tanya woke up when she heard water gurgling in the radiators, then she heard a big bang! She screamed.

Jose said, "What's wrong, Tanya?"

"Listen," she said.

"That's only water coming up through the radiators because the heat's coming up," said Jose.

"Are you sure?" Tanya said.

"Yes, Tanya, now don't worry. Let's go back to sleep," said Jose.

At 3:00 a.m., Jose got up to go to the bathroom. He heard something running around again! He turned the light on in the bathroom and the bedroom. He heard the running noise again! He said to himself, "That's a fuckin' rat!" Then he began pulling furniture out all night long, looking for rats. After Jose searched the apartment again, he put down rat traps, then he went back to bed.

Tanya woke up when Jose was putting down the rat traps. She said to him, "What's going on here?"

Jose said, "I was putting down rat traps. I fear that we have rats, but I haven't found any yet!"

"What!" Tanya cried.

"Tanya, don't worry about it. If we have rats, we'll find out pretty soon. When you get up in the morning, watch out where you walk," said Jose.

At 6:30 a.m., Jose and Tanya were taking a shower. While they were taking a shower, the rats were exploring the house. A big rat came down the fireplace, and it jumped up onto the bed. It ran under the pillow and stayed there! Tanya went into the bedroom to get a comb for her hair. While she was combing her hair, she saw the pillows move on the bed. She screamed hysterically.

"What's the matter, Tanya?" said Jose.

"I saw the pillows move on the bed!" she cried.

"You're kidding," said Jose.

"No, I'm not kidding!" Tanya cried.

Jose ran out of the bathroom with a baseball bat, and he tossed the pillows off the bed with the baseball bat. Nothing was there.

"Jose, I saw the pillows move, my right hand to God!" said Tanya.

"I believe you, Tanya, don't worry about it. We'll find out what's going on here when Earl gets here," said Jose.

At 8:00 a.m., Earl Davies and three other men came to clean the apartment. Earl rang the doorbell.

"Is that you, Earl?" said Tanya.

"Yes, ma'am, it's me. Good morning," said Earl.

"Good morning, Earl. It wasn't a good night for us last night. We have rats. I don't know where the they are, but we have rats! I woke up all night hearing them running around the house. Jose heard them too," said Tanya.

"Tanya said she saw the pillows move on the bed, and I heard them trampling around all night too! I put down rat traps, but I haven't caught any of them yet," said Jose.

"Okay, I have three people here with me today, and we're gonna go through this place and clean it up. If you have rats, we'll find out pretty soon. Jose and Tanya, this is Fred, Jimmy, and Larry. These people are going to clean here with me today."

"Pleased to meet you, gentlemen," said Jose and Tanya.

Jose and Tanya went to work. They worked at some factory out of town. Earl's workers were about ready to clean Jose and Tanya's place. Earl's men began cleaning the kitchen area, washing and waxing the kitchen floor. Then they cleaned the living room, dining room, bedroom, and the bathroom. The men washed and waxed every floor in the house and steam-cleaned the fireplaces and chimneys. When the men were cleaning, they found dead birds, rats, squirrels, and bees by the thousands. The men were taking all the dead animals out of the house in wheelbarrows. Later the men worked on the spare room.

"Hey, Larry," called Earl to one of his workers.

"Yes, sir!" he said.

"I want you to go up in to the attic in the spare room because something up there is knocking plaster down on the floor from the ceiling," said Earl.

"What could it be, Earl?" asked Larry.

"It could be bats or pigeons up there," said Earl.

"Okay, Earl, I'll go up there." Larry grabbed a ladder, and he opened the latch leading to the attic. When he got into the attic, something hit him in the head and knocked him off the ladder, and he fell to the floor, screaming.

"Larry, are you all right?" asked Earl. Earl ran to the spare room where Larry fell. Larry was unconscious. Another man came to help. Jimmy was the other man. Earl said to him, "Jimmy, call for a rescue right away!" The rescue came and took Larry to the hospital. A short time later, Earl was sweeping the floor in the spare room, and a decomposed dead body fell from the attic onto the floor.

Jimmy was outside with Larry, waiting for the rescue. Fred, Earl's other worker, was out to lunch. When the dead body dropped from the attic, Earl got the hell out of there as fast as he could! Then he called the police. The police arrived with two rescue wagons and a fire truck. One rescue took Lenny to the hospital; the other was on standby. After the first rescue left, Earl came running out of the house after he called the police.

When police got there, Earl was yelling, "There's a dead body in the house I'm working in! It fell from the attic, come right away!" The police, the firemen, and the paramedic of the second rescue ran to the scene. Fred came back from lunch. Earl said to him, "Fred, take another hour or hour and a half for lunch. I don't want anyone in the house right now!" Earl went back to the scene.

The policeman said to the paramedic, "John, go in the kitchen and get a large plastic garbage bag and remove this ugly, stinking body!" The police was writing out a report when Jimmy arrived from the hospital.

Earl said to him, "Jimmy, why don't you take an extra hour for lunch. I'm going to be with the police for a while."

"Why, what happened?" asked Jimmy.

"I'll tell you later," said Earl.

The firemen came in the room where the dead body was, and they said, "What the hell happened here?" The police was writing up the report and asking Earl some questions.

The police said, "What's your name?"

"My name is Earl Davies, the landlord of this house."

"What exactly happened here?" said the police.

"I was sweeping this room, suddenly a dead body fell from that hole up above onto the floor," said Earl.

"Please leave the room," the police told Earl. The police searched the apartment upstairs and downstairs. The firemen were up in the attic, checking it out. The rescue took the body away. The firemen were in the attic, flashing their flashlights. They saw dead rats, bats, bones, and skeletons by the hundreds.

"Oh my good god!" one firemen said to another.

One of the firemen went to get Earl. He said, "Earl, could you come with me, please?" The fireman took Earl up to the attic to show him the horror.

Earl exclaimed, "Oh my god, Jesus Christ, if Jose and Tanya ever saw this, they would drop dead!"

Tanya and Jose arrived home from work. Earl was sitting in the kitchen, drinking coffee. Tanya said, "Hello, Earl, were there any problems?"

"No problems, dear, your apartment is nice and clean. The only thing we got to do in here was clean the windows, some of your bedclothes, and finish the spare room. Don't go in the spare room because my workers have to come tomorrow to finish," said Earl.

"Earl, this place looks brand-new!" said Jose.

"I'm glad you like it," said Earl.

When Earl left, Tanya got dinner ready, and Jose checked the apartment, because they were having company coming tonight. A few relatives and friends came to visit Jose and Tanya. They watched TV and had a few beers. Jose showed his apartment to the guests. His dad said to him, "What made you pick Moodus to live?"

"Well, Dad, because it's close to work, and it's quiet around here," answered Jose.

"Jose, years ago Moodus, Connecticut, used to be a devil worship town. There's no Catholic churches, and you were brought up Catholic!" said Jose's dad.

Jose laughed, and he said, "Dad, this apartment is nice, and we live near the water. Tanya and I always wanted a place by the water, and this apartment is dirt cheap!" said Jose.

"Jose, let me tell you something. Moodus, Connecticut, is cheap to live because of the devil worships. I would never live in Moodus. Besides, I think this house is haunted. I can tell by the air, it's very heavy, and it's spooky in here. Believe me, Jose!" said Jose's dad.

At 9:00 p.m., Jose and Tanya took a bubble bath after Jose's dad and relatives left, then they went to bed. Around midnight, Jose got up, and he went to the kitchen to get some juice from the refrigerator. He opened the refrigerator door, and a gust of wind blew right at him. Jose said to himself, "Son of a bitch, what the hell was that! Maybe my father's right about this house being haunted!" Jose turned on the light in the kitchen, and the bulb blew out. "I swear this house is haunted!" he said. Jose lit a candle, and he went back to the refrigerator. He opened the door fast. No wind this time! Jose grabbed the bottle of juice out of the refrigerator, and he poured two glasses, and he drank them, then he put the bottle of juice back in the refrigerator. Tanya woke up screaming while Jose was still in the kitchen. Jose ran to the bedroom. He said, "Tanya, what's the matter?"

"I saw something in the mirror. It looked to me like the devil!" she cried, and she was shaking.

Jose looked in the mirror, and he said to Tanya, "You must have had a bad dream. There's nothing in the mirror."

"Jose, love, I'm not dreaming! I saw something in the mirror!" she said.

"You know something, Tanya, my father might be right about this house being haunted. I went to the refrigerator to get a glass of juice, and a gust of wind hit me in the face, then I turned the kitchen light on, and the bulb blew out! Then you saw something in the mirror. What do you think?" said Jose.

"Jose, I think we better sit up awhile to see what else happens," said Tanya. Jose and Tanya walked around the house for a few minutes to find the spooks. Everything was okay, and they went back to bed. Around 3:00 a.m., Tanya woke up and heard rocks falling in the fireplace in the bedroom. She shook Jose to wake him, and she cried, "Jose, Jose, Jose! Wake up!"

"What's wrong, Tanya?"

"I hear rocks falling in the fireplace!" she cried.

"Rocks!" said Jose.

Crash! Rocks came falling down the fireplace into the bedroom. "What the hell is going on here! We must be having an earthquake!" said Jose. Tanya was crying because she was scared. Jose moved the rocks from the bedroom back into the fireplace, then he went down in the basement to get some wood to board up the fireplace. Jose was downstairs getting wood when a pink ghost flew next to him, but he didn't see it. Jose boarded up the fireplace in the bedroom, and he moved the bed up against the plywood for support so the rocks didn't come tumbling in the bedroom again.

About 5:00 a.m., Tanya woke up to go to the bathroom. She heard a strange noise outside, so she screamed hysterically.

"What the hell's the matter now, Tanya?" said Jose.

"Did you hear that noise?" she cried.

"No, what was it?" said Jose.

"It sounded like a wolf howling outside," she cried.

"Tanya, it could be a wolf, because we have wolves in Moodus, Connecticut. Wolves won't bother you, they go after other animals and howl all night long. Now let's go back to sleep," replied Jose.

At 6:00 a.m. the horrors still continued. Jose woke up, and he went to the kitchen. The candlelight was burning. He said to himself, "I swear I blew that candle out last night!"

Jose blew out the candle and opened the shades on the windows to let the sunlight in. After, Jose went to the linen closet to get a tablecloth and a lightbulb to replace the one that burnt out during the night. After he replaced the new bulb, he turned around, and he saw the candle relight itself! Jose said, "Damn it, this must be a trick candle!" Jose turned the kitchen light on, he grabbed the candle with a wet rag, and he put it in the sink in some soapy water and left it there. Jose went to the refrigerator, and he saw blood coming from under it. Jose yelled, "Tanya, were you in the refrigerator during the night?"

"No, why?" she said.

"There's either blood or ketchup all over the kitchen floor dripping from the refrigerator," said Jose.

"Oh shit! I forgot to clean the fish we brought home last night," said Tanya.

"It smells like fish," said Jose. Tanya cleaned up the blood under the refrigerator, and she cleaned the fish in the sink, then she put the fish in the freezer. Jose was downstairs checking out the basement, then he went upstairs, and he searched the spare room, looking for rats or clues of last night's horrors. Jose had to bust the door down to get in to the spare room, because Earl did not want him in there. After Jose searched the spare room, the attic, and the doors that led here and there, he fixed the door and locked up the room. It was a Saturday afternoon. After a sleepless night, Jose and Tanya spent the rest of the day relaxing. Jose was watching the Boston Red Sox game on TV.

Jose fell asleep on the couch during the game on TV. Tanya was downstairs doing laundry. After she got finished, she went to bed for a nap. Three hours later, Jose woke up hearing a lot of yelling on TV. The Red Sox won! Jose shut the TV off, and he went outside. He searched the backyard and looked in a window in the garage, but he couldn't get in. It began to rain, Jose heard a rumble of thunder, then he went inside the house. The sky got dark as night. A thunderstorm was coming. *Crash! Bang! Bang!* the thunder sounded. Tanya woke up suddenly from her nap when the thunder came. She screamed!

"Tanya, everything is okay, it's only a thunderstorm!" said Jose. The storm moved quickly, then it was over, and the sky cleared up. It was a peaceful day. Jose tried to get a hold of Earl on the phone, but there was no answer. Jose said to Tanya, "Let's go on a picnic, go to the zoo to see the animals, and we'll take a ride by the water before it gets dark."

"Okay, Jose, let me get dressed and put the laundry in the dryer, then we'll go," said Tanya. Jose and Tanya went out for the rest of the day. The rats ran around the apartment while they were gone, snakes in the kitchen, rats running around in every room. Jose and Tanya went to a movie before they came home. The movie was about rats and snakes. Jose and Tanya got home about 9:00 p.m. They had a snack, took a bath, and went to bed early. Jose searched the apartment one more time before he went to bed.

At 10:00 p.m. the devil's powers began to take over! Scratching and rapping on doors, a weird scene. Jose and Tanya were sophisticated professionals, and they were strong and talented people. Jose owned a manufacturing company, and Tanya ran the place. They do not believe in such things as Poltergeists that would haunt their house with strange noises in the cellar and rapping on the door. Tanya woke up, and she looked at her digital alarm clock. The time was 11:02 p.m. She heard thunder coming up from the fireplace. Tanya was scared! She laid down on the bed and stood awake for a while; then she heard a faint noise of a baby crying in the fireplace, then she heard the thunder again! Then Tanya woke up Jose, and she said, "Jose, wake up!"

"What's the matter, Tanya?"

"I hear a baby crying, and thunder is rumbling through the fireplace," Tanya cried. Jose got out of bed, and he walked around the room. Tanya said, "Jose, do you hear the baby crying? It's crying now!"

Jose said, "I hear it too, it's crying in the fireplace!" Jose pushed the bed away from the fireplace and removed the wood he boarded up last night. They heard the baby cry nice and loudly. "Tanya, it's probably two cats in heat, because when cats are in heat, it sounds like a baby is crying," said Jose. Tanya laughed and laughed. She and Jose joked about the cats for a while, and they went back to sleep. Tanya woke up out of a sound sleep, and she heard the same noises of the baby crying, but this time, it was really loud! She jumped out of bed, and she turned the light on, and she looked at the time on her alarm clock. It was 12:02 a.m. Tanya was horrified. Jose woke up, and he said. "Tanya, love, what's wrong?"

"I heard the baby screaming this time!" she cried.

"Okay, Tanya, you go back to sleep, I'll go find out what it is," said Jose. Jose then heard the screams loud and clearly. Tanya was so scared! Jose said to Tanya, "That's not a cat, that's a child crying!" Jose went through the house, looking for the cat or child.

There's a graveyard in the backyard. No one knows about it. A baby was buried there, and the devil's spirit was in it.

Jose looked well and good around the house, and he found nothing. Jose said to Tanya, "I don't see nothing in the house or outside. I looked everywhere! If we hear it again, I'll call the police." Jose and Tanya went back to sleep.

Thump! Meow!

Tanya woke up again from a sound sleep. She yelled, "What the hell!" She turned the lamp on, and she looked at the alarm clock. The time was 1:02 a.m. She heard the thumping noise again; this time it was in another room. Tanya went in the dining room. She turned the light on, and she saw a tail wagging in the fireplace. Tanya screamed hysterically, so loud! Jose fell out of bed, and he landed on the floor.

Jose yelled, "Tanya, what the fuck's the matter now?"

"There's something in the fireplace, in the dining room!" she cried.

"Tanya, relax, it's only a cat! Here, kitty, kitty, kitty!" said Jose. Jose grabbed the cat hanging in the fireplace, and he threw it outside. The cat was covered with black soot. "Tanya, go to bed, I'll go outside to get a screen to cover the fireplace," said Jose. Jose went outside to find a fireplace screen. He found one near the trash cans in back of the garage. He covered the fireplace in the dining room, then he went back to bed. Tanya woke up about five minutes before 2:00 a.m., and she got up to go to the bathroom. After Tanya got out of the bathroom, she sat on the bed. She looked at the clock. It was 2:02 a.m.

Tanya said to herself, "It's 2:02 a.m. I've been haunted at 11:02, 12:02, and 1:02 now. It's 2:02, I am ready for you this time!" Then she heard three loud knocks on the door. "*Ahhhhh!*" Tanya screamed hysterically when she heard the knocks. She jumped right out of her bed and yelled, "This fuckin' house is haunted!" Tanya walked around the house hysterical. She couldn't determine just where the knocks were coming from. Jose woke up when Tanya screamed. Tanya said, "Jose, there's someone at the door!"

"Tanya, relax, I'll get it." Jose went out in the kitchen.

Knock! Knock! Knock! Knock!

Four knocks this time! Tanya screamed when she heard the four knocks, and she said, "Jose, the knocks are coming from the closed-off room!"

Jose was pissed off! He said, "Who in the blessed hell would bother us at two o'clock in the morning!" Jose got dressed, and he checked every door in the house to see who's knocking. He checked downstairs in the basement. He opened the bulkhead door and checked outside. No one was around. He went back inside and grabbed a flashlight and looked around the house. No one there! Jose then grabbed a baseball bat, and he went back outside near the garage. He shone the flashlight where the spare room was for a minute. Finally he gave up, and he went inside and went to bed; he put the baseball bat beside the bed, and he loaded a gun, and he put it in a drawer next to the bed. Just before 3:00 a.m., the curtains were blowing around in the house, just after Jose fell asleep.

At 3:02 a.m. *Knock! Knock! Knock!* The knocks were so loud it woke both Tanya and Jose up! They heard thunder and wind coming through the fireplace. Tanya looked at the clock. The time was 3:02 a.m. Tanya cried, "I don't believe this. At two minutes after every hour, we get haunted!"

Jose got up, and he got dressed, and he grabbed his gun, and he said, "Whoever's in this house, I'm gonna kill you!" Jose went searching, and he found nothing! Then he went back to bed.

Tanya cried, "Jose, where are all these knocks coming from?"

"I think it's the wind blowing the trees up against the house, because I can't find anyone outside," said Jose.

Scratch!

Tanya woke up quickly. She heard very loud scratching on every door in the house. Tanya screamed, and she screamed and screamed! The scratching was so loud and scary Tanya kept screaming hysterically; with all that screaming she did, Jose still didn't wake up! Tanya shook Jose to try and wake him, but she couldn't. She looked at the alarm clock. The time was 4:02 am. Tanya turned the lamp on, and the scratching went away. Tanya was still hysterical. She knocked the lamp over, and the bulb blew out. Suddenly a bright flash of lightning came through the windows, followed by a big bang of thunder; that woke Jose out of a sound sleep! Tanya was still hysterical.

Jose held Tanya because she was so scared, and he said, "It's okay, Tanya. It's only a thunderstorm."

Tanya cried, "Jose, I heard scratching on every door in this house."

Jose heard them too. He said, "Tanya, the scratching you hear is the tree limbs rubbing up against the house."

"Jose, the scratching was much louder before!" said Tanya.

"Tanya, the wind is not bad right now. It sounds like it's in the house because this house is not well insulated. Now go back to sleep," said Jose. Jose rolled over, and he went back to sleep.

Tanya couldn't go back to sleep because she was too scared. She sat on the edge of her bed, listening to the storm. *Crash! Boom! Bang!* The thunder was pounding away, and the lightning was flashing on and off like a strobe light. Tanya got up to go to the bathroom. When she came out, she left the bathroom light on; then she went back in to the bedroom and sat on the bed, watching the clock until 5:02 a.m. Tanya heard scratching in a corner of the bedroom, near the fireplace. Tanya cried, "I don't believe this, we have rats!" Tanya shook Jose to wake him once again.

"What's the matter now, Tanya, goddamn it!"

"I heard the scratching again, Jose. I think we have rats!" Tanya cried.

"I hear them too, and it's not from the storm. It sounds like It's coming from inside the walls! We might have rats!" said Jose.

"I thought that before we moved in here," Tanya cried.

"Tanya, let's get up and have some coffee and wait to see what happens at 6:02 a.m. If anything happens, I'm gonna call the police!" said Jose. Jose and Tanya were in the kitchen drinking coffee.

Knock! Knock! Knock! The knocks were coming from the back door. Jose grabbed his gun. He opened the door quickly and pointed his gun at a police officer. Jose said, "I'm sorry, I thought you were an intruder, Officer!"

"That's why I'm here, to find the intruder! Did you see anyone?" said the policeman.

"No, but I was interrupted all goddamn night with knocks on the doors and scratching in the walls! I also found a cat in my fireplace during the night," said Jose.

"Sir, could you come outside for a minute, please?" said the policeman.

Jose said, "Tanya, why don't you get breakfast ready while I'm outside with the policeman." Jose went outside with the policeman.

The policeman said to Jose, "Is this the cat you found last night in your fireplace?"

"Yes, sir, it looks to me some animal must have got a hold of it and tore it apart!" said Jose. Jose and the policeman went back inside. "Officer, we have complaints about being haunted, two minutes after hour. I've been trying to get a hold of Earl Davies, the owner of this property, all weekend. I called him by phone, and there's never any answer!"

"Earl Davies is a hard man to get a hold of! What things are happening?" said the policeman.

"Tanya and I heard scratching in the walls, loud knocks on the doors, a baby crying, rocks falling down the fireplace, and all kinds of weird noises keeping us awake all the time! Either someone is fucking around, or this house is haunted!" said Jose.

"I know who the man is. He's been arrested a few times for fraud and false information. He also tried sucking people in to paying extra rent and trying to be their friend. You have to watch this man," said the policeman.

"Officer, could you have this house checked to find out if we are really horny?" said Tanya. Jose laughed and laughed because Tanya said *horny* instead of *haunted*.

He said, "Tanya, you mean to see if our house is haunted!" Tanya caught on and she laughed.

"Personally, I don't think your house is haunted, but I can have someone look at it. If you can't get a hold of Earl Davies by tomorrow, let me know. Call the police station and ask for Jack," said the policeman. The policeman walked around the house with Jose. They went in the spare room and searched the room and the attic good. The policeman said, "I have to leave now because I have to find the intruder in the area. In the meanwhile, I'll try to find out where Earl Davies is." The policeman left; when he got in his car, he called into headquarters. "Ten four. Car number 3 Jack, over."

"Headquarters, car number 3 go head."

"Could you call Earl Davies and send him to Twenty-One North Street apartment number 6. His tenants are complaining that they're house is haunted! Car number 3, Jack, over."

"Ten four, will do. Headquarters, over."

The policeman went on with his business.

Sunday morning at 8:00 a.m. Earl Davies, the landlord arrived at Jose and Tanya's apartment.

Knock! Knock! Knock!

"Who is it?" said Jose.

"It's Earl Davies, the landlord."

"Come right in, sir! Where in the hell were you, I've been trying to get a hold of you on the phone for the last three days?" said Jose.

"I was in New York over the weekend," said Earl.

"Well, we have a serious problem here at Twenty-One North Street starting last night. Tanya and I were haunted two minutes after every hour! At 11:02 p.m., we heard strange noises in the fireplace. At 12:02 a.m., we heard a baby crying in the corner of our bedroom. At 1:02 a.m., we heard thumping noises in the house. I got up and checked around the house and found a cat in the fireplace in the dining room. I removed the poor cat covered in soot and threw it outside. The cops came this morning and found the cat all cut up in pieces out in the backyard. Some animal must have got a hold of it!"

"At 2:02 a.m., we heard knocks on the doors, they were so loud. I got up to check the house and found nothing! At 3:02 a.m., Tanya woke up and heard scratching on the doors. At 4:02 a.m., Tanya heard them again, then I heard them! At 5:02 a.m., we heard the noises again. Finally we got up at 5:30 a.m. The police knocked on the door. I grabbed my gun, and I went to the door thinking it was an intruder. I pointed my gun to a police officer. I told him that I was sorry. He wanted to know if I saw the intruder he was looking for. I told him no. Then he showed me the tortured cat out in the backyard," said Jose.

"The police sent me here. They told me you had some problems about a haunted house and intruders broke into a barn down the road, about seven o'clock this morning. The intruders must have been a good part of your noises last night, because they broke into a few empty summer homes dressed like animals and scaring people, down by the water. They broke windows and did a lot of damage. I got about twenty rat traps you can use in case you do have rats. I forgot to tell you that this building is kind of old. It's a possibility you may have rats. If you do, I will take care of it. Don't forget, you live near the water, water attracts rats! Just put one rat trap in every room. These rat traps are a special kind that kills any rat or mouse and keeps others away!" said Earl.

"Earl, let me tell you something right now. If you don't get rid of these fuckin' rats, I want my money back, and I'm getting the hell out of here! That's simple as that, okay!" said Jose.

"Jose, I promise, I will get rid of the rats tomorrow, if you have any. I will get my work crew here in the morning and steam clean your apartment. Believe me, Jose, you won't have to worry about being haunted anymore. You can rest assured on that. When you come home from work tomorrow, your place will be like brand-new!" said Earl.

"Earl, let me say this. If Tanya or me gets bitten by a rat, believe me, I will own your property, your house, your car, and your whole fuckin' life, do I make myself clear?" said Jose.

"Jose, if you get haunted any more, just let me know," said Earl. Earl left Jose and Tanya's apartment. He heard something outside the apartment building hissing! Earl checked the area for a while. He drove around north street looking for intruders. Tanya went to take a shower. She saw blood on the sink. Tanya screamed, and she said, "Jose come here quick!"

"What's the matter, Tanya?" said Jose.

"Jose, what's this?" Tanya cried.

"It looks like blood," said Jose.

"Where did it come from?" said Tanya.

"I don't know. Wash it down the sink and see if it comes back!" said Jose.

Tanya washed the blood down the sink, then she took a shower. While Tanya was in the shower, Jose searched the house to see what was haunting them. Jose went in the shower. Tanya got dressed, and she cleaned up around the house, then Jose and Tanya went to church. After church, they went out to eat. They had to go out of town to go to Mass because there were no churches in Moodus. Late Sunday afternoon, Jose and Tanya came back home. Tanya watched TV, while Jose searched the whole apartment building; he went upstairs and downstairs, checked outside, and he went out in to the woods, and he found nothing! Jose went back home to watch TV with Tanya.

"Jose, the news on TV said we had gusty thunderstorms last night, and people were complaining that their homes were haunted because of loud thunder, strong winds, and heavy rains. The lightning was so bright and that the storm was so close it made unusual noises during the night," said Tanya.

"Tanya, that's maybe why we were haunted last night, because of the bad storm!" said Jose.

Tanya laughed, and then Jose went outside to rake leaves. Tanya joked, "The storm shook the house all night long!" While Jose was out raking leaves, Tanya switched the channel on TV to watch a movie.

After Jose finished cleaning up in the backyard, he joined Tanya watching TV. Just before 8:00 p.m., Tanya went downstairs to put a load of laundry in the washer. Tanya was putting her clothes in the washing machine, then she sat in a chair near the washer to read a book. Tanya read one page, and then she looked at her watch; the time was 8:02 p.m. She was breathing heavy and getting nervous because she was wondering if the horrors were going to continue from last night. The time on her watch was 8:03 p.m. Nothing happened. Tanya took a deep breath, then she sat down and continued reading her book. After the wash was done, she put the clothes in the dryer. Later, Tanya finished reading her book. She looked at her watch, and the time was 9:02 p.m. Tanya sat down, and she said the rosary. Nothing happened. She walked around the basement for a while before she said the rosary. Everything was okay. Then Tanya left the dryer going, and she went upstairs. Jose and Tanya went to bed shortly after 9:30 p.m.

During the night, Jose got up to go to the bathroom. He felt cold. After Jose came out of the bathroom, he went down in the basement to check the boiler, because there was no heat in the house. Jose was fixing the boiler when suddenly he heard a knocking sound in the cellar. Jose stopped for a minute after hearing the knocking. He looked at his watch. The time was 11:02 p.m.

Jose said to himself, "Oh my dear god, not another night like last night!"

The knocking noise sounded again. Jose grabbed his baseball bat from behind the furnace, and he ran to the stairs. Jose heard the knocking sound again from a corner of the stairs. Jose hit the corner of the stairs where he heard the knocks with the baseball bat. The knockings stopped. Jose went back to fix the boiler. He saw a flash. He stopped for a minute, then he finished fixing the boiler. Finally he got it working. Jose looked at his watch. It was half past midnight, then he went upstairs to bed, and he read Tanya's book for a while.

Jose was reading Tanya's book when suddenly he heard the knocking noises again. This time the knocking sounds were coming from a corner in the bedroom. Jose got up, and he looked at the clock; the time was 1:02 a.m. He went over where he heard the knockings, and he stomped on the floor, then the knocks stopped. Jose put rat traps in every corner of the house, then he stayed up until 2:02 a.m. to see what would happen next. Tanya was sound asleep. She didn't hear nothing. Jose said to himself, "I guess it's my turn tonight!" At 2:02 a.m., the house filled up with smoke quickly. Jose looked at the clock, and he said, "Goddamn it!" Then he ran down in the basement to check the boiler. The boiler was okay. He went back upstairs and opened all the windows to let all the smoke out, then he walked around the house to find out where the smoke was coming from. He couldn't find anything! Jose searched the apartment up and down stairs. At 3:02 a.m., Jose heard three loud knocks coming from the front door.

Jose grabbed his gun. He opened the door quickly, and he pointed his gun when he opened the door. A pretty blonde was there. She said, "Hey, baby, are you alone? Do you want to have some fun?" Smoke was coming out of the apartment when the girl was propositioning Jose.

Jose said, "Screw it, bitch! I'm married." Then Jose went back to bed. After Jose went to bed, a big rat ran around the house, but he didn't see it. At 4:02 a.m., Jose heard three loud knocks at the front door again! This time he called the police. Before the police came, Jose cocked his gun, and he ran to the front door and opened the door quickly and pointed his gun! No one was there. Then the police arrived. Tanya was sound asleep. She didn't know what was going on. Jose saw the police coming, so he opened the door to let him in.

The policeman said, "What's the problem?"

"Officer, I had a visitor about three o'clock this morning. Some broad kept knocking on my door, wanting to go to bed with me. I told her to screw because I was married! Then I heard knocking sounds all fuckin night. I haven't slept in two nights now because of these fuckin' noises!" said Jose.

"Let's go take a look around. There have been a lot of complaints of gangs hanging around at night causing trouble!" said the policeman.

The policeman and Jose looked around. The policeman took the report on the girl propositioning Jose. The cop and Jose searched the area and found nothing. After the cop left, Jose sat on the edge of his bed until 5:02 a.m. The house filled up with smoke again.

Jose heard something in the basement growling. It sounded like some animal. Jose quickly grabbed his gun, and he ran downstairs to see what it was. He said, "I know you're down here. Come out wherever you are, or I'll shoot! I know you're down here, and you're not going to get out of here alive!" Jose searched the entire cellar, and he found nothing. Jose then went upstairs to call the police; then he woke Tanya up. The police arrived. The apartment was filled with smoke. Jose said, "Tanya, get up and get dressed, we're going to a motel!!"

"What happened, there's smoke all over the place!" said Tanya.

"Tanya, don't ask any questions. Get dressed quick and let's go!" said Jose.

When the police came, the policeman said to Jose, "What's the problem now?"

"I heard some animal growling in the basement, and there's smoke all over the house, and I don't know where it's coming from!" said Jose.

"Maybe it's the devil," the cop joked. The policeman went downstairs to investigate. Jose and Tanya were packing up and getting ready to leave. The police questioned them outside their apartment. The policeman said, "When was the last time you had your furnace cleaned?"

"I don't know, sir." said Tanya.

"Well, you better get it cleaned out before you have a fire, because the smoke is coming from the furnace through the fireplace and smoking up the apartment. Now the growling noise is the furnace is clogged up, and it needs to be cleaned out right away," said the policemen.

"Okay, Officer, I'll call Earl to come and clean the fuckin' thing later this morning!" said Jose. Jose and Tanya left the house. More policemen arrived later to search the house some more. At 6:02 a.m., the smoke in the house disappeared. The police left the house at 6:45 a.m. Jose was driving down the road a little ways, when suddenly his car broke down. Jose tried to get the car started, but he couldn't. Tanya was standing out in the road, trying to flag down a motorist to help. At 7:02 a.m. Monday morning, the house blew up! The explosion was so loud Jose and Tanya thought it was their car! Jose and Tanya saw the house in flames after they heard the blast. It was one big ball of fire!

The Haunted House 2

Jose said to Tanya, "God was with us. Something was telling us to get the hell out of that house!" said Jose.

"I knew that something was going to happen too, Jose," she said.

"Tanya, last night, the spooks happened to me at two minutes after the hour while you were sleeping! It was my turn last night!" said Jose.

"I didn't hear nothing. I was sound asleep," she said.

"I didn't get any goddamn sleep at all last night," said Jose.

The police and the fire department arrived shortly after Jose and Tanya's house blew up. A police car pulled up alongside of Jose's car, and the policeman said, "Are you having troubles?"

"Yes, Officer, double trouble. My house blew up! Now my car broke down!" said Jose.

"You people come with us. I'm not blaming you for any damages, but it seems kind of funny that your house is burning to the ground, and you're sitting in your car watching it, when all I did is turn the key to your ignition, and your car started," said the policeman.

"Officer, we did not do anything to the house, we were trying to get away from it!" said Tanya.

"Like I said, I'm not blaming you for the damages, but I'm taking you two down the police station for questioning!" said the policeman.

Three apartments burned to the ground. The only thing that was left was Tanya's color TV showing cartoons on it while the house was burning down; the flames didn't touch the TV. The firemen watched the cartoons while they were fighting the fire! The fire was under control at about 8:00 a.m. Two days later, the police and the fire department investigated the cause of the fire; the police held Jose and Tanya in jail until they found out. "The cause of the blast was a failure in the boiler," a fireman was telling a police officer. The police unlocked the jail and let Jose and Tanya go.

Earl Davies gave them their money back, and he said, "I'm sorry this happened!"

"Mr. Earl Davies, sir, I think you better get your boilers cleaned out before you kill someone next!" said a policeman.

Many people were in a local bar watching the news on TV. Ben and Rose were there for a bowling banquet. "Good evening, this is the Monday night evening news on channel 13 here in Hartford, Connecticut. The town of Moodus, Connecticut, has been haunted out of their homes the last few nights, police say. Neighbors in Moodus reported to police that they've been hearing strange noises and seeing things move. Seismologists reported strange rumblings such as sounding like thunder coming up from deep in the earth, firing of guns, the popping of popcorn, the rumbling of trucks going down highways, trains going by or airplanes flying by, etc. Other seismologists, geologists, and scientists reported these noises are caused by small earthquakes in caves under the ground. Other reports say that the noises could be caused by water eroding a network of shallow underground caves, causing rocks to be ripped off walls and ceilings and hurled against the cave. The Connecticut Indians believed the noises were the devil over two hundred years ago. If you hear any of these noises, call toll-free hotline at l-800-GOOD-EVIL. This toll-free number will give information on the noises in Moodus. The National Guard now has issued a possible earthquake watch for Moodus, Connecticut, and other communities. Seismologists said not to worry about any serious earthquakes or any dangers. This is Maggy Green reporting."

Three days later, Jose and Tanya got a new house and new furniture; their car was in the garage being fixed. They lived happier and slept well after! Ben and Rose were driving through Moodus, Connecticut. They knew nothing about Moodus; they were newcomers. They stopped at Twenty-One North Street, wanting to rent an apartment near where Jose and Tanya's house burned down, but they decided not to. Then Ben, who was driving, stopped at a local bar for a drink. They watched the news on TV.

Food was being served at the bar Ben and Rose were at. Suddenly everyone heard rumblings right after the news was over. The ground shook and shook. People were screaming! Then the lights went out, and the ceiling in the bar was ready to cave in. People were hysterical. The noises rumbled for hours!

"May I have your attention please. This is the owner of Taft's Pub speaking. We have an earthquake going on right now at the present time. I wish everyone would slowly leave the area. Thank you."

People were panicking while leaving the pub. The police, the fire department, and the rescue arrived at Taft's Pub, picking up people who passed out panicking from the earthquakes.

Bang! Bang! Bang!

The ground opened up near the pub. Rumblings were heard everywhere! People were running toward the rescues when the ground opened up from the earthquakes. A bus came to pick up the rest of the panicking people, taking them to area hospitals for treatment. At 8:02 p.m., the manager was downstairs, putting stock away to keep safe from the earthquakes.

Crash!

The noise was so loud it sounded like a bomb going off! "What the fuck!" the owner of Taft's Pub said to himself. Then he ran upstairs, and he saw part of the roof had caved in over the bar. He said, "Jesus fuckin' Christ! This whole place is falling down!" Then he went outside; the rumblings were still being heard. He saw parts of the bar torn off by the quakes. "Oh my god, it's the end of the fuckin' world!" the owner of the bar cried. At 9:02 p.m. the rumblings were really heavy, and things were shaking and moving around. Windows were braking, people were running from their homes. At 10:02 p.m. the earthquakes got worse and worse! Stores were falling to the ground, windows were braking in homes, and fires were braking out! The police and the fire department were out all night long rescuing people from the quakes and putting out fires.

At 11:02 p.m. great big fireballs were popping up from the ground in areas where the ground had opened up from the earthquakes. Fir was a policeman on the Moodus Police force. He was driving down a road, and he spotted a burned cat. He called back to the station to report it. Meanwhile a group of baseball players came in to Taft's Pub to order drinks and snacks after the game. They watched the 11:00 p.m. news on TV.

"Good evening, this is the Monday night news on channel 13 in Moodus, Connecticut. The news is late tonight because of the earthquakes. The time now is 11:39 p.m., and here's the news: A major earthquake hit Moodus, Connecticut, at 8:02 p.m. this evening. The quake measured 7.6, causing the ground to open up and shoot fireballs from the ground. Windows in several homes were reported broken. Some homes were destroyed by this quake. Moodus Police reported seeing a burned cat in the middle of the road. State police has reported fireballs soaring in to people's homes in the Moodus, Connecticut, county from manhole covers, blasted through from the earthquake. No major injuries were reported from the quake, but fifty-seven people were taken to area hospitals. The national weather service is issuing severe thunderstorms to move in to the central Connecticut area after midnight, with strong winds, static lightning, heavy downpours, and a possible tornado watch! That's all we need now is a tornado after having earthquakes all night long. In other news tonight, two people were driven out of their homes early this morning, at Twenty-One North Street. A fire swept through a home there. No one was injured. Police say the boiler had failed.

"When firefighters arrived, the only left was a color TV resting on a rooftop, showing cartoons, believe it or not. Freaky ha! Why did the fire leave a TV set? I guess the fire wanted to watch the cartoons while it burns everything else, ha, ha! This is Maggy Green reporting on 13 news in Hartford, Connecticut."

Ben and Rose were sitting at the bar, laughing about the news. The next day, Ben and Rose went for a second look at Twenty-One North Street, the same house where Jose and Tanya lived that burned. Ben and Rose walked around the area for a while, then they left. The next day, Ben and Rose bought a house in town. Earl Davies sold Ben and Rose a home in Moodus, the same landlord who rented out the haunted house.

Later that day, Earl Davies rented an apartment to a young couple with a baby; the couple was waiting for Earl. He arrived in a short time. The guy said, "Are you Mr. Earl Davies?"

"Yes, sir. My name is Earl Davies, the landlord."

"Hello, my name is Ted, and she is Nancy. We would like to rent an apartment for us and our child."

"Okay, the apartment won't be ready until May first because we had a fire yesterday in another building, and I have to clean things up a little. The address is Twenty-One North Street. Nice meeting you two, we'll see you in a month," said Earl.

One month later, the haunted house was looking pretty good. Ted, Nancy, and their child was all moved in. Earl did such a good job the apartment looked like a mansion. For over a month, the earthquakes in Moodus had stopped. Ted and Nancy loved their new place. Everything was quiet and normal for about a week later. Ted and Nancy were friends of Jose and Tanya; they invited them to a belated mayday breakfast at their new apartment one morning. It was a weekday, then they spent the weekend together. Jose rang the doorbell.

Ding-dong!

Ted came to the door, and he said, "Jose, Tanya, welcome back to your old home!"

A baby was crying upstairs when Ted let Jose and Tanya in the house.

"How is your new place, Ted and Nancy?"

"Earl did a pretty good job fixing this place so quickly!" said Tanya.

"Yeah, Earl rented us your old apartment, then he told me it was the one that burned down last month!" said Ted.

"Whose baby do I hear crying upstairs?" said Tanya.

"That's my baby, Tanya," said Nancy.

"Nancy, I didn't know you had a baby! What's its name?" said Tanya.

"His name is Dameon. I better go upstairs and change little Dameon's diaper, that's why he's crying," said Nancy.

"Dameon! That's the name of the devil, Nancy!" said Tanya.

"Shut up! Don't tell me that!" Nancy screamed, and she ran upstairs.

"Tanya, I think we better go," said Jose.

"Don't worry, Nancy will be okay. Ted named the baby, not her!" said Tanya.

Nancy was upstairs, taking care of the baby, changing him and feeding him. Ted, Jose, and Tanya were downstairs talking.

"Ted, how come you have two floors here? When Jose and I lived here, we only had an apartment," said Tanya.

"Tanya, when your apartment burned down, Earl made a duplex out of this one, and he expanded this home much bigger, he told us," said Ted.

"He did a great Job fixing this place up. You'll probably have good luck with this home. They say when a person moves in to a house that had burned down before, it's good luck, etc.!"

Nancy finished feeding the baby, then she went downstairs to her company. A gust of wind blew black soot out of the fireplace, and it covered the baby's face, the baby started crying again. Nancy ran upstairs when she heard the baby crying again; she saw the mess, black soot all over the room.

"Goddamn you, Ted, last week you said you were going to have the fireplace cleaned, and you never did, now there's black soot all over the place, and it got all over poor Dameon's face!" said Nancy. Nancy cleaned the baby's face, and she brought the possessed little devil downstairs! "Tanya, would you like to hold this little devil?" said Nancy.

"Sure!" Tanya said.

While Tanya was holding the baby, Nancy went upstairs to clean up the mess and vacuumed up the soot. Suddenly Nancy heard a big bang, and then she heard rumbling sounds, then it stopped.

Ted said, "What the hell was that?"

"It sounds like we're getting more earthquakes!" said Jose.

"Oh my god, not again!" Tanya cried.

Nancy was upstairs screaming. Nancy came running downstairs, and she said, "Don't worry, everyone, we get them noises sometimes. It's coming from the caves!"

"It sounds like thunder," said Ted.

Later in the day, Nancy took the baby from Tanya's hands, and she put him to bed, and then she made a pot of coffee and put donuts out on the table. Everyone sat down and enjoyed the snacks Nancy made.

Tanya was eating her donut, and she began to feel sick; she left the table, and she went to the bathroom, and she threw up! She closed the bathroom door after she got sick. The bathroom was directly across the baby's bedroom upstairs. Tanya felt a bump in the back of her head, because she had a bad headache, then she looked at herself in the mirror; her vision was getting blurry. Then she ran downstairs, and she said to Jose, "Jose, let's go home, I'm feeling sick."

Jose and Tanya left, Ted went to work, and Nancy was all alone with the baby. Nancy was sitting in the kitchen, drinking coffee, then her baby started crying again; she ran upstairs to the baby's crib, and she saw the baby turning red. The baby was screaming very loudly! Blood was dripping under the crib and running in to the fireplace. Nancy did not see it. Nancy picked up the baby; she burned her hands when she picked the baby up, then she dropped the baby in the crib, and the baby was screaming very violently! Nancy looked at her hands after she dropped the baby in the crib; her hands were smoldering and burning, then she began to shake. She was in such pain she was too frightened to notice. Nancy cried, "I hope my baby's not the devil!" Nancy was in shock. The baby was getting red, red, and it started bouncing around in the crib, then it was throwing up blood! Nancy watched the horror, then she got sick, and she was throwing up green! Nancy was ready to pass out from fright. There was blood all over the room. Nancy screamed and cried hysterically, watching the worst nightmare of her life. It's not over yet! The baby bounced out of the crib on to the floor, full of blood, then the baby bounced around like a basketball around the room, then the baby stopped bouncing around, and the blood was flowing down the stairs as Nancy watched in shock. She turned around, and she saw her baby beginning to turn into the devil. When she saw the baby turn in to the devil, she passed out! Then the baby burst in to flames; the heat from the flames woke Nancy up, and she quickly ran down the stairs, crashing through the door, and she ran outside screaming.

"*Help! Help! Help! Help! Help!*" Then she passed out again when she got far enough away from the house.

Just before evening, Nancy woke up, and she ran down North Street, yelling for help. A thunderstorm was coming. Nancy ran to the nearest house in the woods. Just before she got there, the devil grabbed her!

About 8:00 p.m., Earl Davies was driving around Twenty-One North Street. He noticed Nancy's apartment had a fire. "What the fuck!" he said to himself. Earl went into her apartment, and he saw the fire burning inside the house and not much on the outside. Earl said to himself. "That's strange, something fishy is going on here!" The phone was working in the apartment, so Earl called the police. The police and the fire department arrived there in minutes. Earl said, "Officers, something's going fishy around here. My fuckin' property has burned up again!"

"Boy, this is weird, the entire house burned from the inside and not outside!" said one of the firemen. The firemen was searching upstairs where the baby's bedroom was; the burned little devil had disappeared! One fireman noticed a mirror with diamonds all over it.

31

Ted came home late from work, about 10:00 p.m. He saw the police and the fire trucks out in front of his house. "What the hell happened here?" Ted said to himself.

One of the policemen said to Ted, "Are you the owner of this house?"

"No, sir, I rent this place. Earl Davies is the owner," said Ted.

"Ted, you're the one we want to talk to. Your wife or girlfriend placed a belt of diamonds around a mirror. The sun was reflecting on them, causing your apartment to burn. Those diamonds she had is ultra violet, and it caused rays from the sun beating heat in a closed area, and it made your house blow up! Let's go, you're under arrest until Nancy shows up at the police station!" said the police. Ted struggled with the police, denying he had anything to do with it. The police took Ted down to the police station.

"Where's Nancy and the baby?" said Ted to a police officer.

"I don't know, they got away, or they got killed, you'll find out soon!" said the police officer.

CHAPTER 2

The Brown Barn

*A*NN AND HER SON WERE ready to move in to a house in Moodus. Her relatives and friends were helping her. Ann got divorced a short time ago, and she moved to Moodus; she says Moodus is a quiet place to live, but she knew nothing about Moodus. She moved in a brown-white house. Alongside the house, there was a brown barn called the Brown Barn. She lived near Pickerel field, a dangerous area. The movers were moving Ann and Tony into the house during a thunderstorm. Ann had money; she wanted a house with a barn because Tony had a horse. Earl Davies owned the house, and Ann was renting the house from him. The movers just finished moving her in. Earl Davies stopped by.

Ding-dong! Earl rang her doorbell.

"Who is it?"

"It's Earl Davies, the landlord."

"Come in, nice to meet you. I just moved in. My name is Ann, and he's Tony, my son."

"I am pleased to meet you and Tony. How do you like the house?" said Earl.

"I love it, it's beautiful!" she said.

"Ann, the reason why I dropped by is because there's a few rules and regulations you have to follow to rent this house. Number 1, you pay the mortgage at the first of every month. You come to my house and pay me cash, not by check. I will not accept any checks, money orders, credit cards etc. Number 2, my house is located in Lyme, Connecticut. The address is 6502 North Main Street apartment no. 6 in downtown Lyme. I live just nine miles away from here. Number 3, you have no mail coming to this house. You have to pick up the mail at my house. If you got important mail, you give me a call at my house. Here's my business card. Nice meeting you, have a nice day," said Earl Davies. Then he left.

Ann was standing at the door after he left. She said to herself, "That man is weird!"

Tony laughed and laughed. Later Tony was watching TV. Mommy was washing dishes in the kitchen. Suddenly she saw a ghost flying by the kitchen window outside. She screamed three times very loudly!

"Mommy, Mommy, what's the matter?" Tony cried.

"Nothing, Tony, I just saw a bright flash of lightning, and I got scared."

Tony later was doing his homework, while Mommy went down to the cellar to do a load of laundry. She saw a quick glimpse of the ghost again! The ghost went in to a wall. Mommy was in fright washing the clothes. "That's not lightning, it's something else!" she said to herself, and she ran upstairs!

Later, Mommy went downstairs with a broom. She put the clothes in the dryer, then she went over to the wall where she saw the ghost, and she rubbed her hand in circles. She turned her hand over, and she smelled her hand. Her hand was black from rubbing the wall, then she stepped back, and she watched for the ghost to come back. After a while, she waited and waited, then finally she went back upstairs with the broom. Mommy finished cleaning the kitchen, then she got Tony ready for bed. Mommy was washing up in the bathroom. Tony was in bed early. Suddenly the lights went out. Tony and Mommy screamed! Tony was crying.

"It's okay, Tony, Mommy's right here!"

The lights came back on. Mommy went back downstairs with the broom. She took the clothes out of the dryer, and she went upstairs, and she went to bed. The night was quiet. Next morning, Mommy got Tony up for school. It was seven thirty in the morning. Mommy asked Tony what he wanted for breakfast.

"Tony, what kind of cereal do you want this morning? CoCo Puffs, Cornflakes, or Froot Loops?"

"I will have the Froot Loops, Mommy!" he said.

Mommy had her breakfast with Tony, and then she went downstairs without the broom this time. She waited for a few minutes, watching the wall. Tony came downstairs, and he saw Mommy staring at the cellar wall, and he said, "Mommy, what are you doing?"

"Nothing, Tony, I'm just checking for leaks down here from last night's storm," she said.

Later Mommy took Tony to school. Mommy was driving Tony to school, and she said to him, "Tony, you're going to a new school today, Greenhill Elementary School. You will like this school, and you will meet a lot of new friends here."

"Mommy, will there be horses there?" he said.

"Maybe!" Mommy said. The principal came to get Tony. Mommy introduced herself to the principal, they had a brief conversation about Tony, then off to school Tony went! Later in the day, Tony's horse was delivered to the new house.

In school, the principal took Tony to his teacher. The principal said, "Tony, this is Mr. Hive, your teacher. Mr. Hive, this is Tony. He's a very smart boy. He loves horses."

"Tony, nice to meet you. I'm Mr. Hive, and welcome to Greenhill School. You're in the third grade now, and God bless you! Please have a seat anywhere here in the room, and I will get you started. Okay, kids, first we're going to start with math. In your math book, the title reads arithmetic! Please turn to page b-10. Okay, kids, you'll be adding and doing divisions to day in class," said Mr. Hive, Tony's teacher.

While Tony was at school, Mommy was home preparing books, clothes, pens, papers etc., for Tony to use for school during the school year. Noontime, Mommy went outside to hang some blankets, and she stepped on a black cat.

"Oh, I'm sorry, little kitty, I didn't mean to step on your feet!" Mommy said. Mommy bent over to pet the cat, but the cat ran off. After Tony's mother hung the blankets, she walked between them back to the house. Before Mother went in the house, she turned around, and she watched the blankets flapping in the wind; it appeared, to her, very strange. Suddenly Mother saw a flash of the ghost flying by. Mother screamed, and she ran into the house; the ghost disappeared! The horse saw the ghost too! Outside, it was going crazy. Mother ran out to the horse, and she put the horse in the barn. She gave it some water, then she closed the barn doors, then she went over to the clothesline again, where she hung the blankets. She felt the blankets, then she went back into the house to get more clothes to hang outside. The wind started to pick up when Mother came out to hang more clothes. After Mother hung another batch of clothes, she walked through the blankets, and her hair stood straight up in the air like Christmas tinsel! The wind was blowing really hard. Mother got scared. She screamed and ran into the house, and she closed the door quickly! Mother ran to a nearby window inside the house to watch the blankets and clothes flap around in the wind. Later in the day, the sun came out, and the wind died down; she kept saying to herself "Please no ghost! Please no ghost! Please no ghost!" as she looked out the window.

Mother was in the kitchen, making a sandwich to eat, crying. "God, please let this house not be haunted!" Mother was eating her sandwich when suddenly she heard rocks falling in her house. "Oh dear God, please help me!" were the first words she said to herself before she went searching the house for the falling rocks. Mother searched the house upstairs and downstairs. She checked the fireplace, the whole house, and she didn't see anything out of place. She didn't see any rocks! Then she went down in the basement with a baseball bat, and she waited for a while. She didn't see nothing! Mother went back upstairs, and the phone rang; she answered the phone. "Hello!" No one answered. "Hello!" No answer. "Hello!" Still no one answered the phone! Mother put the phone down, and she went out to get the blankets on the clothesline; then after she took the clothes into the house, she went back outside to check on the horse to see if it was all right. Then she went back into the house, and the phone rang again! Mother answered the phone.

"Hello!"

"Ann, is this you?" Ann is Tony's mother.

"Yes, Mom, how are you?"

"I'm not doing too well. Your father just passed away." Ann's mother cried over the phone.

"What! When did this happen?" Ann cried.

"Just now, he just dropped dead!" her mother cried.

"Mom, we'll be over the soon as Tony gets home from school," said Ann.

Ann and her mother talked on the phone for a while about the death. Meanwhile, Tony was in his last class of the day in school. He was in art class. He drew a picture of the devil on a large piece of paper.

Mr. Hive came over to Tony, and he looked at his drawing and he said, "What's that?"

"It's a funny-looking man!" said Tony.

"It looks like the devil to me! You can draw better pictures than that!" said Mr. Hive.

"Sorry," said Tony.

The bell rang; school was over for the day. Tony took the bus home. A short ways down the road, the bus got a flat tire. Tony ended up walking home. He didn't have too far to go. He was walking along a field near his home when he saw a white ghost flying through the cornfields. Tony was so scared he ran like a bat out of hell home screaming and crying! Tony crashed through the screen door at his home, screaming, "Mommy, Mommy, Mommy! I saw a ghost in the field coming home from school!" Tony cried.

"Oh my god, did you! I saw something too, Tony, but there's no such thing as ghosts. Maybe it's some kind of a spirit flying around, I don't know.

"Tony, I have good news for you and bad news. The good news is I bought you a horse. The bad news is Papa passed away early today. Nana told me over the phone that my father died."

"Oh my god, Mommy, he did?" Tony cried.

"Yes, he did. Tony, listen to me, I don't mean to scare you, but Nana told me over the phone that sometimes when family relatives die, we sometimes see things like white ghosts flying around, but they're not. A death in the family is so shocking you see things that are not there! Tony, whatever you saw out in the cornfields is the same thing I saw. A white sheet flying by means someone is going to die in the family. The sheet won't bother you, it's just your vision going funny because of the death. Don't worry about the ghost you see, it will not hurt you!" said Mommy.

"Mommy, does this white sheet have a mouth, a nose, ears, eyes, and arms?" Tony said.

Mommy laughed, and she said, "Tony, Papa's dead now. You will not see the ghost's sprit anymore! So don't worry about it."

"Mommy, I'm going outside to ride my horse for a while," said Tony.

"You do your homework first!" said Mommy.

Tony finished his homework, ate supper, then he took his horse for a ride.

"Tony, you get home before dark!"

"I will, Mommy!" And off Tony went on his horse. He had a ball riding his horse. He went through the woods, and the horse jumped over hills, streams, rocks, and fences like nothing! Tony rode the horse through the open field, riding good and fast. Tony was loving it! Then he rode the horse back home, and he put it away just before it got dark.

Mother called, "Tony!"

Tony came running out of the barn into the house all excited!

"Mommy, I love my new horse. I went through the fields, the horse jumped over trees, rocks, water, and everything! I love my new horse, Mommy, and I'm going to name it Brownie!" said Tony. Tony hugged Mommy, and he kept thanking her for buying him a new horse.

"I'm so glad you like your horse. Did you feed him before you left the barn?" said Mommy.

"No, I forgot!" Tony ran outside to the barn, and he fed the horse, brushed it down, and gave it a bath.

Mommy called, "Tony, come in the house now, it's getting late!"

Tony finished with his horse, and he said, "Brownie, you be a good horse now. Good night!" Tony closed the barn door, locked it, then he went in the house to watch TV. About 9:00 p.m. Tony and Mommy went to bed early. Mommy checked the house to make sure all the doors were locked, the windows were shut, and no strange happenings were going on before she went to bed.

At 2:30 a.m., Mother heard someone coming up the stairs. She turned the bedroom light on, and she grabbed a baseball bat from the bedroom closet, and she ran over to the stairs. She yelled, "Who's there!" No one answered. Mommy was petrified, and she was shaking! She checked Tony's room to make sure he was all right. Tony was fine. Mommy searched upstairs first, then she went downstairs, looking around. She looked outside, and she didn't see anything; then she searched down cellar, nothing was there! Mommy then searched the barn to make sure the horse was okay then finally went back to bed after searching the house for an hour. She put the baseball bat alongside her bed while she slept.

About 4:00 a.m., blood was dripping in back of the furnace down cellar. The furnace was making funny noises. After the noises stopped in the furnace, that was when Tony woke up. He went outside to visit his horse. Mother went to get Tony up for school, but he was gone. Mommy went out to the barn to get him.

"Tony, what are you doing out here at six thirty in the morning, when you're supposed to be getting ready for school?"

"Keeping Brownie company!" he said.

"Get your butt in the house and get ready for school, you know better than that!" said Mommy. It was a rainy day. Mommy drove tony to school in her car; she said, "Tony, you be a good boy in school today."

"Mommy, I saw the ghost right there in that field on the way home from school yesterday. The bus had a flat tire, so I walked home," said Tony.

"Bye, Tony, be good," said Mommy. Mommy dropped Tony off at school, and she drove home, and she cried about her father's death on the way.

Tony was in school. Mr. Hive was talking to the class, when suddenly Tony saw something move. He jumped out of his seat, screaming! Mr. Hive turned around, and he said, "Tony, are you all right?"

"I saw something move!" he cried.

The bell rang, and it was recess period. Tony went out in the schoolyard, and a gust of wind came. Suddenly he saw the white ghost again! He quickly ran back into the school, crying! Tony ran down the hallway, calling Mr. Hive.

Mr. Hive ran out of his room, and he said, "Tony, what's the matter?"

"I saw a ghost outside," Tony cried.

"A ghost!" said Mr. Hive.

"Yes, a ghost! I saw it yesterday too, getting off the bus on the way home last night," Tony cried.

"Tony, follow me, I'm going to take you to see the nurse. Just wait here, the nurse will be right back," said Mr. Hive.

About five minutes later, the nurse came. She said, "Are you Tony?"

"Yes, nurse, I'm Tony."

"Tony, what happened outside during recess?" said the nurse.

"I just saw a white ghost outside. I saw it yesterday too!"

"Tony, there's no such thing as a ghost! Your mother called the school a few minutes ago. She wants me to ask you a few questions. Have you been having strange thoughts and seeing strange things lately?" said the nurse.

"Yes, I saw that ghost two or three times. I saw flashes of light and something move in class this morning," Tony cried.

"Tony, can you describe the flashes of light and the thing you saw move in the classroom this morning?" said the nurse.

"I saw pink-colored lightning, and I think I might have seen a rat run across the floor in the classroom," said Tony.

"Tony, you're giving me the answers I need. Did anyone die recently in your family?" said the nurse.

"Yes, nurse, my Papa, my mom's dad," said Tony.

"Tony, the reason why you're seeing weird things could be because you have a death in the family. Your home maybe haunted for a few days, but it's nothing to worry about, because you will not get hurt. The excitement over your grandfather's death is a good reason for your home to be haunted and play tricks on your mind. When people close to you die, your mind acts differently. Tony, strip down and get up on the examining table, a doctor is coming in to exam you," said the nurse.

Tony's mother came to the school to pick him up after the doctor examined him. The nurse came in, and she put a thermometer in Tony's mouth until the doctor came. The doctor came in, and he examined Tony. After Tony's mother arrived, the nurse said to Tony's mother, "The results on Tony's examination will be here in a week." Mother took Tony home. The doctor called the nurse into the office.

"Ms. Farntain, I personally think that Tony is possessed by the devil. I can tell by his examination he's a schizophrenic," said the doctor.

Tony was at home crying. His mother then asked him some questions.

"What happened at school today, Tony?"

"I saw that white ghost again, and I saw something strange move in class. I saw the ghost in the school yard, Mommy!" Tony cried.

"Tony, here's some soup Mommy made for you. Have some crackers, then I will fix you a cup of tea, then I want you to go upstairs and take a hot bath and go to bed."

"Mommy, I don't want to go to bed!" Tony cried.

"It's the doctor's orders. You're sick, and you have to get some rest!" said Mommy.

"But, Mommy, what about Brownie?" Tony cried.

"You can ride Brownie tomorrow, I promise! The doctor gave me orders to put you to bed and get plenty of rest because of the strange things you've been seeing lately. Now go to bed and get some sleep and the horrors will go away. Brownie will make sure that nothing happens to you, okay?"

"Okay, Mommy!" said Tony.

About 1:30 p.m., Tony went to bed. Mommy was downstairs watching TV. She left the coffeepot on, so she poured a second cup of coffee, then she went back into the living room to watch TV. Suddenly a bird crashed right through the living room window. It flew around the house, then it fell in front of the TV set. Mother screamed and she screamed! Then she opened the front door, and she chased the bird out of the house with a broom, then she called the landlord to come and fix the window.

Ding-dong!

Mommy let Earl Davies in the house. "What happened here?" said Earl.

"A big bird came crashing through my window while I was watching TV. I had to get a broom to chase the goddamn thing out of here!" said Mother.

"Ann, what kind of bird was it?" said Earl.

"It looked like a giant, big black bird with scary-looking wings on it!" she said.

"Ann, we had this problem a couple of times before. It's nothing to worry about. It was just a wild bird, and I will have a new, thicker window put in right away, okay!" said Earl.

"Thanks a lot!" said Ann.

People came to fix the window for her within a few minutes. Later in the day, Mother went upstairs to check on Tony. He was still sleeping, so Mother took a nap for a while. A few minutes later, the devil ran across the yard, about three times. Tony's horse was going crazy! Mother woke up. The horse outside was making all kinds of noises, so she went outside to check on the horse. She brushed it down, and she calmed it down, and she put Brownie in the barn. Ann said to herself, "Maybe she saw the white ghost, or she saw something!" Later in the day, a man Ann knew came over the house to see her. Minutes later, they were loving it up on the couch.

Tony got up, and he ran outside to see his horse. Tony opened the barn, and he went in to see the horse. "Brownie, you're a nice horse. I love you very much, you're such a good little horsey." As Tony was talking to the horse, the horse was rising its head up and down, greeting Tony, then Tony fed the horse some hay. Tony closed the barn door, and he went back into the house very quietly. He peeked in the living room, and he saw Mommy making love to some guy. Tony went upstairs to get a better view. He watched through the railings on the stairway. The man was taking Mommy's clothes off! They were naked! After Tony watched the show, he went back to bed.

Mommy and the man came upstairs after and went to bed. About an hour later, Mommy brought some hot tea to Tony in bed. At the same time, the man Mommy was with left. Mommy said, "Tony, do you feel better?"

"Yes, Mommy."

"Do you want some chicken for supper?"

"Yes, Mommy, I love chicken!" said Tony.

After dinner, Tony said, "Mommy, who's that man you were with this afternoon?"

"What man are you talking about, Tony?" asked Mommy.

"Mommy, I saw everything you and him were doing. You can't fool me, Mommy!" Tony laughed.

Mother was embarrassed, and she said, "Tony, you weren't too sick to watch that, were you? You're not supposed to be sneaking up on Mommy when I'm with someone. I told you about that before!"

"Mommy, is he your new boyfriend?" said Tony.

"No, he's just a friend. I invited him over for coffee and watch TV," said Mommy. Mommy was watching TV while Tony went outside to ride his horse. Tony rode his horse through town, and a truck almost hit it, then he almost rambled a house, then he nearly hit a tree! He was riding his horse too fast! A cop chased the horse down the road. Brownie jumped over the side of the road, and he leaped into the woods, and it got away. It was dark when Tony arrived with his horse. He put the horse back into the barn, he brushed it down, fed it, and he went back into the house to do his homework, then he went to bed.

Mommy didn't know Tony was out. She shut the TV off then she went to bed. About an hour later, Mommy woke up, and she saw an orange coloring outside. She didn't pay much attention to it, then she went to sleep. Minutes later, Mother heard *roar!* Mother looked out the window, and she saw nothing. The devil was right around her house. Later, Mommy got up with a stick, and she went downstairs. Bats were flying around down there. She ran back upstairs, and she looked the cellar up. Mommy was in the kitchen when suddenly she saw flashes of lightning, then she heard more thunder. Suddenly she saw a bolt of lightning just missing her house, and she heard a loud crack of thunder. The storm got worse and worse as the night went on. Tony was horrified; he slept with Mommy all night!

The next day was a delightful day. It was beautiful! Tony got up nice and early. He fixed his own breakfast, and he left the dirty dishes in the sink, and he took a joy ride on his horse! When Tony went out, he left the door wide open. A big dog came in the house. It jumped up on a table, and it ate the roast Mommy was going to prepare for the next day; she left the roast on the counter so it could thaw out after she took it out of the freezer last night. The dog ate the whole thing! Mommy came downstairs just after the dog finished the roast. There was blood all over the table, and she said to the dog, "Get out! Get out of here! *Git!*" Mommy chased the dog around the house with a broom. The dog ran upstairs, and Mommy chased it from room to room, whacking it with the broom a few times. Finally she was able to get the dog out of the house, and she closed the door.

At 7:00 a.m., Tony's alarm went off. It was ringing, ringing, and ringing. Mommy said, "Come on, Tony, it's time to get up for school!" Mommy went upstairs to get Tony, but he was gone. "Goddamn that kid, I'll kill him!" she said to herself. Then she went out to the barn, and Tony was in there with his horse. He was feeding it and petting it. The dog was in the barn too! "Tony, what the hell are you doing out here, didn't I tell you many times before not to go outside without my permission? You left the damn door open, and that damn dog came in the house and ate the roast I planned to have for supper tonight! Now get your ass in that house, and don't you go outside without me telling you, you understand!" said Mommy.

"Sorry, Mommy, I won't do it again," said Tony. Then he ran into the house.

Mommy chased the dog around the barn with a baseball bat she carried from the house. "Come here, you little fuck, I'm gonna kill you!" Mommy said to the dog. She wacked the dog with the baseball bat several times before the dog ran out of the barn and into the woods. The dog looked something like the devil. Mommy went in the house. She was upset.

Tony said to her, "Mommy, can I ride my horse to school today?"

She said, "*No!*" in anger. Then Mommy took Tony to school; on the way, she said, "Tony, you be a good boy in school today. When you get home, you have to do your homework right away because we have to go to Grandpa's wake, do you hear me?"

"Yes, Mommy!" said Tony. Tony went off to school. He had a great day! Mommy had a great day at home with her new boyfriend; they were in bed most of the day. Mommy had been going through a lot of stress lately; she needed the rest! Tony was winning spelling contests all day in school. Tony was coming home from school. He just stepped off the bus near his home. He picked up a big stick because he feared he'd see the ghost again. He had his books in the other hand.

A big black cloud was overhead, and a bad storm was coming. Tony walked along pickerel field, looking for the ghost. It started thundering very loudly. Tony ran home like a bat out of hell! He kissed Mommy, then he did his homework.

"Tony, did you have a nice day in school today?" asked Mommy.

"Yes, Mommy, I had a fantastic day. I met a lot of new friends, I won all the Greenhill spelling test today, and I found a new girlfriend in school! Did you have a nice day, Mommy?" said Tony.

"I had a great day today too, Tony!" Mommy laughed.

Crack! A big thunderstorm was overhead! During the thunderstorm, Tony did his homework from school. After he went outside to take care of his horse, it was still pouring! Tony saw a bolt of lightning shoot across the sky, then he heard a big crack of thunder. He got scared, and he took Brownie, his horse, into the barn. He fed the horse, brushed it down, gave it plenty of hay, then he loved it, and he said, "Brownie, you be a good horsey. I have to go somewhere." Tony went back into the house to get ready for the wake tonight.

Tony and Mommy were eating dinner. After dinner, mother saw a swirl of leaves go up into the air with the wind. "Tony, we better leave now because I think we're gonna get some more storms," said Mommy. Sure enough, on the way to Grandpa's wake, Mommy drove through a violent thunderstorm! Mommy and Tony screamed and were frightened because the lightning was so bad in the storm. Mommy arrived at Wilson's Funeral Home.

Grandma came to the car, and she said, "Hi, Ann, how have you been?"

"I'm in shock to hear this!" she said.

"I know, it's too bad, but things like this happen! I don't think it's a good idea to take Tony to the wake. I better take him to my house until you're ready to leave, then you can come pick him up," Grandma cried.

"Okay, Tony, go with Grandma," said Mom.

"Bye, Mommy!" said Tony.

Mommy waved bye, then she went into the funeral home. Ann went over to say some prayers over her father, then she broke down, screaming and crying. Her relatives cooled her down. Dad's body had blood on his shirt, and some blood had dripped from his mouth laying in the coffin. Tony fell asleep at Grandma's while the wake was going on. A bolt of lightning struck a big tree, and it went through the window again at Mommy's house, then another bolt struck the brown barn, setting the barn on fire, killing Brownie, Tony's horse. The barn was burning away! The horse was inside, suffering, covered with flames, screaming, yelping and jumping around. The horse was toasting like a marshmallow. Then a gas can exploded, and the barn blew apart!

Heavy rains put the fire out before the fire department knew what happened. After the wake, Mommy went to Grandma's house to get Tony. Tony was sound asleep. "Ann, you better stay here tonight. The storm outside is too bad," said Grandma. Grandma was Mommy's mother.

"Okay, Mom, if you really don't mind, thank you." Mommy talked to her mother for a while before she went to bed. The next day was beautiful. Mommy and Tony left Grandma's house early. Mommy took Tony straight to school.

"Mommy, can I see Brownie before you take me to school?" said Tony.

"No, Tony, we're late now!" she said. Then she dropped Tony off to school, kissed him goodbye. "Tony, you be a good boy now."

Mother was driving home. "Jesus Christ! Did we have a tornado last night or something? All these trees knocked down... Oh my god!" Mother parked her car on the street. She went in the house, the back way, and she saw the tree through the window. "You son of a bitch! A fuckin' tree went through my window!" Mother called the landlord on the phone.

Earl picked it up, and he said, "Hello!"

"Hi, Earl, this is Ann calling from the brown house near Pickerel. My front window is broken again. Lightning must have hit a tree, and it went through my window!"

"Ann, I will take care of it as soon as I can, because I have a lot of problems from last night's storm. Hang tight, I'll be there shortly," said Earl.

"Oh, thanks, Earl!" Mother was happy. Ann went upstairs to take a bath, dress up, and she came downstairs to put a load of laundry in the washer, then she made some breakfast, then she went outside to check on Brownie. Mother went outside, and she saw the barn burned to the ground. The horse was dead! All you could see was the skeleton of the horse—charcoal! Ann screamed, and she cried, and she screamed hysterically before she passed out!!

"I heard someone screaming, Junior, did you?" said Officer Reid, a police officer.

"Yes, I did, do you know where it could be coming from?" asked Junior.

"It might be coming from Pickerel field. Let's check it out," said Officer Reid. The two police officers got in the police car and went cruising.

Earl Davies, the landlord, came to fix the window at Ann's house. Ann was on the phone, calling the police. She was hysterical! Earl said, "What happened?" The police came right away, with a rescue, a fire truck, and about four police cars. Earl's workers came to help him replace the broken window and remove the fallen trees, while the police was writing up a report from the storm damage. The police was trying to talk to Ann about the damage. She passed out. The rescue took her to the hospital, along with a police officer. The police was still writing up the damages while Ann was in the hospital. Later in the day, Earl's workers cleaned up the debris and broke up the horses skeleton, raked it up, and threw it into a dump truck. Back at the hospital, Ann gained consciousness.

"Ann, my name is Lieutenant Licker, from the Moodus Police Department. Can you remember what last night's storm damage did? Please don't cry."

"Yes, I remember very well! I came home from my father's wake. I stayed at my mother's last night, and I came home early this morning, and I found a tree had gone through my front window. Then I saw the barn in the back of my house had burnt down, killing my son's horse. I could see the bones. Nothing was left with the horse. I couldn't take it anymore, I was too frightened!" Ann cried.

"Ann, I'm very sorry to hear about your father's death," said Lieutenant Licker.

"Ann, my name is Richard Brown, I'm a friend of Earl Davies, your landlord. For a couple of weeks, I have a place where you and Tony will stay until Earl builds a new barn, and the state will get Tony a new horse because of last night's storm. Don't tell Tony what happened for a few days, just tell him his horse got sick, and it will be in a horse hospital for a week."

At the end of the day, Mommy picked Tony up at school. Richard Brown was with her. "Tony, did you have a great day at school today?" asked Mommy.

"I had a great day, Mommy!" he said.

"Tony, listen, we're not going home for a few days because lightning hit our house last night. The barn got struck too, but Brownie is going to be okay. He was taken to a horse hospital," said Mommy.

Tony started crying. "Tony, this is Richard Brown. We're going to stay at one of his houses until ours is fixed," said Mommy.

Pine Green Hotel. It was beautiful. Tony and Mommy loved staying there! The next day, Earl Davies and his workers started building a new brown barn.

A week later, the new brown barn was built. Ann and Richard Brown went in to town to pick up the new horse. Ann was standing near a horse trailer, where the new horse was in. It started to get windy, and a storm was coming. Ann was getting cold while she was waiting for Richard Brown. The trailer shook from the strong winds. Ann was standing at one side of the trailer, and her father's spirit was standing on the other. When she turned around, the spirit disappeared! A little while later, Richard Brown drove the new horse to his home. Ann later went home to wait for Tony to get home from school.

Tony was coming home from school. A storm was coming, so he ran when he got off the bus. Tony was running by the cornfields, fearing that he would see the ghost again! He ran home as fast as he could because the sky was getting dark, and it was beginning to rain. He went to the front door, but the door was locked. Mommy met him before he ran to the back door and took him to the Pine Green Hotel, where they were staying. At the hotel, Mommy talked with Tony.

"Tony, I have bad news. Brownie's dead!"

"My horse died… Brownie's dead! There's no horsey like Brownie! How did he die, Mommy?" Tony screamed, and he cried hysterically.

"Lightning hit the barn, and it burned to the ground, and Brownie died too!"

Tony went hysterical, crying, "My horsey is dead, oh no! My horsey is dead, oh no! Brownie is dead!" Tony cried, and he started throwing his school books around and ripping up pages in his books. Mother calmed him down, and she said to him, "Let's have some supper now because I have a big surprise for you after!"

Richard Brown came home to Pine Green to have dinner with Ann.

"Richard, my horse died," said Tony.

"I heard, Tony, your mommy was telling me. After we eat, do you and Mommy want to take a ride to the house, because I got you a new horse, Tony, a big one too!" said Richard.

"You did?" Tony yelled.

"Eat your supper, Tony, then we'll go," said mommy.

Richard, Mommy, and Tony went to the house. As soon as Richard stopped his truck, Tony jumped out, and he ran to the back of the house, and he saw his new horse and barn. He jumped for joy! Tony ran over, and he pet the new horse, and he kept saying, "My new horsey, my new horsey, my new horsey!" Tony was so excited.

Mommy said to Tony, "Do you like it?"

"Mommy, thank you so much for my new horsey. It looks just like Brownie!"

"What are you going to name it? She's a female," said Mommy.

"I think I'm going to name her Doo Doo!" said Tony.

Mommy laughed and laughed. "Tony, why Doo Doo?"

"Because she looks like a big brown Doo Doo!" Mommy and Tony laughed hysterically. "Mommy, do you want go for a ride?" said Tony.

"Yes, I'd love too!" she said. Tony and mommy went for a nice long ride with the new horse.

Mommy and Tony got back from the ride. Tony put the horse in the barn, fed her, brushed it down, and gave it a bath. The horse loved all of Tony's attention. She was very friendly. Next day, Tony went to school, and he told Mr. Hive about Brownie. Mr. Hive felt so sorry about that he gave Tony a bag of candy. Tony was filled with smiles!

While Tony was at school, Mommy was at home, cutting branches off trees that were hitting her house. Later she went out to talk with Tony's new horse. After Tony got home from school, he and Mommy went for a ride on it. The horse was so happy to see Tony when he got home from school she jumped up on her back legs to greet him! Tony said, "Wow!" Then he took Mommy for a ride.

Doo Doo stopped at every brook to get a drink of water. It was a thirsty one! The horse was a live wire; it jumped over fences, bushes, streams, rocks, etc. Mommy and Tony had a blast riding it. After they were through riding, Tony brushed the horse down, he fed it, gave her some bay. The horse was in lots of glory. It gave Tony its paws. it kissed Tony in the face. Doo Doo accidently knocked Tony over a bucket of water, and she was licking Tony's face. Tony tried to get up, and Doo Doo was still licking him to death!

"Doo Doo, you are such a friendly horse. You have a good home here!" said Tony. Tony talked with his new horse for a while, then he gave her a bath and put her in her stall, then he closed the barn, and he went into the house. The horse was crying in the barn. Tony was taking a bath, when he heard Brownie, his old horse, laughing! Tony put his pajamas on, and he quickly ran to his bedroom, and he yelled out the window, "Brownie, is that you?" He saw nothing out there, so he went to bed.

At 3:00 a.m., Mommy woke up hearing a howling noise. She got out of bed, and she went to the bathroom. The howling noise stopped. She went back to bed, but she heard the howling noise again! She got up, and she grabbed the phone, and she called the police.

"Moodus Police."

"Hi, I hear some animal howling outside my house."

"I know all about it. It's a wolf. It may have broken loose from the zoo. Make sure your doors are locked and windows are closed. We're trying to capture it now," said the police.

"Thank you, sir," Ann said. Mother checked all the doors and windows in the house before she went back to bed.

The howling noise was the devil! Next day, Mommy got Tony up for school. Tony had breakfast, and then he went for a ride on his horse before Mommy took him to school.

"Mommy, can I ride my horse to school?" said Tony.

"Sure, let's go and I'll ride her back home!"

Mommy and Tony rode Doo Doo to Tony's school. When Tony arrived at school, Mr. Hive was waiting for him. "Mr. Hive, see my new horsey!" said Tony.

"Wow, Tony, what a nice horse. When did you get that?" said Mr. Hive.

"I got it yesterday. My mommy's friend Richard brought it for me!" said Tony.

"What's the horse's name, Tony?" said Mr. Hive.

"Her name is Doo Doo. I named her Doo Doo because she looks like a big Doo Doo!" said Tony. Mr. Hive laughed and laughed. Mommy laughed too.

Mr. Hive said, "Well, congratulations on your new horse, Tony!"

Tony went in school, and Ann rode Doo Doo back home. Class was about to begin. Mr. Hive told the class about Tony's new horse.

"Good morning, children. Today's a special day. Tony has a new horse, her name is Doo Doo!"

Everyone in the class laughed hysterically. Doo Doo!

"I asked Tony, 'Why did you name the new horse Doo Doo?' He said, 'Because she looks like a big Doo Doo!'" said Mr. Hive. The class roared! Tony had a great day at school, telling everybody about his new horse, while Mommy was at home, fighting the devil's horrors. It was 12:34 p.m. on a Friday afternoon. Mommy noticed a beagle dog laying in her backyard. She was eating a sandwich and watching TV. She got up, and she got some ham out of the refrigerator, and she threw some out to the dog. The dog didn't move. She went outside to pet the dog and talk to it. The dog still didn't move!

Then at 1:23 p.m., the dog howled three times, then it ran around in circles, and it took off! Ann started crying. "When a beagle howls three times, that's a sign of death. My father died, and Brownie is dead, that's strange." Ann took a short nap, and then she grabbed her laundry, and she went downstairs to put a load in the washer. She saw a quick glimpse of the ghost. She screamed and screamed. She dropped her clothes, and she ran upstairs like a bat out of hell. Then she closed the cellar door, and she put a heavy chair in front of the door, then the phone rang twice. No one answered both times, so she called Richard to come over.

"Hi, this is Ann, can I speak to Richard?"

"Hi, Ann, this is Richard, what's up?"

"Richard, could you come over for a little while? I think my house is haunted, because I'm hearing all kinds of noises and seeing weird things. I need someone to be with!" Ann cried.

"A haunted house, this I got to see! I'll be right over!" said Richard.

Ann fell asleep on the couch while she was waiting for Richard to come over. Richard was on his way over to Ann's house, but his car got stuck way out in Pickerel Field somewhere! At 2:30 p.m., Ann finally woke up. Her friend Richard was supposed to be there at that time. She heard three loud knocks coming from the back door. She said to herself, "That don't sound like Richard's knocks!"

"Who is it?" No one answered. "Who is it?" she said. No one answered. "Who is it?" Still no one answered! Then she heard three loud knocks coming from the front door. "Who is it?" No one answered. Now Ann was getting mad! "Whoever you are, better answer, or I'm gonna call the police. Now stop fucking around and tell me who's out there!" Ann opened the front door, and no one was there! Minutes later, Ann heard someone going upstairs. "Richard, is that you?" she said. No one answered. "That's it, what the fuck!" She went out the front door, and she went to the barn to grab a stick, then she went in the back way, and she went up the stairs. "Whoever's in here better answer me, or I will kick your fuckin' ass! I know you're in here, stop fuckin' around! Richard? Richard? Richard! Jesus Christ!" Ann cried.

No one answered. The house was quiet for a few minutes. Then she heard a voice that sounded like her father say, "Come to me!"

"Richard, stop playing games!" Ann was crying, and then she searched every room upstairs. She checked all the closets and drawers. She made sure all the windows were shut and locked. She checked the bathroom, she looked in the shower, then she grabbed her baseball bat from her bedroom, then she went downstairs. Ann was shaking like a leaf because of the haunted horrors. Mommy called the police to tell them about the horrors, then she called Tony's school.

Mr. Hive said to Tony, "Tony, your mother called. You better take the bus home, because she's not feeling too well."

"Okay!" said Tony. Tony took the bus, and he got off at Pickerel Field, to walk the rest of the way home. The sky got dark. It was ready to rain. Tony heard a rumble of thunder in the sky. He stopped, and he looked in the cornfields. He saw two big red eyeballs looking at him, then he started running. This weird animal (the devil) came running out of the cornfield and chasing Tony home. Tony screamed, "Mommy! Mommy! Mommy! The devil's chasing me! *Help! Help! Help!*" Tony jumped up on a tree, and he climbed this sucker as fast as he could, all the way to the top. He looked out at the cornfields. He lost sight of the thing. Tony was crying for help—"Mommy, help me please!"—a number of times, but Tony was too far out in the woods to be heard.

Minutes after the police left, Ann could not get a hold of Richard. She was beginning to get worried because Tony was not home from school yet. It was getting dark. Mommy called Tony several times. He was still not home from school. "What am I going to do?" she cried.

After the sun set, Tony looked all around at the top of the tree he was in. He broke off a big branch, and he climbed down the tree slowly. He didn't see the devil-like animal anywhere. He jumped down from the tree, but he lost sight of his house, so he had to walk through the cornfields again. Tony was moving the stick through the corn starches in case he would see the animal. The poor kid was still a long way from home. Tony was as quiet as he could be. He turned his head behind him, and he saw the eyeballs again way out in the corn. He ran through the cornfields as fast as he could, away from the red eyeballs; he slipped and fell on a rock, and he landed in the corn!

Tony got up to run, and the devil was right there in back of him. Tony screamed, "No, no, no! Please, God, help me!" Tony tried to run away from the devil, but the devil grabbed him from behind, ripping off Tony's shirt, then the devil slipped. Tony got away, and he ran as fast as he could. Suddenly the devil caught up with him, and it plowed in to him like a football player. The devil grounded its teeth into Tony's abdomen, and it ripped poor Tony alive! Tony screamed and he screamed until the devil ate him up.

Mommy heard Tony screaming; she opened her bedroom window, and she yelled to the top of her lungs, "*Tony! Tony! Tony! Tony! Tony! Tony!*" After she couldn't hear Tony's response, she cried hysterically. Then she ran to the top of the stairs, crying, "Tony, please come home!"

Then she heard her father's voice again. "Come to me!"

Ann screamed, and she said, "Dad, that can't be you, where's Tony?" Ann started to go down the stairs. Her hair stood straight up in the air. She screamed and screamed, and she cried, "Tony, help me, please! Tony, help me, please!" Ann's hair was blowing straight up in the air, like a hurricane was taking her away. She screamed and cried hysterically. The wind stopped blowing Ann's hair straight up in the air. She turned around, and she saw her father's spirit at the top of the stairs. She screamed and screamed and screamed. Her hair stood straight up again, then she fell, tumbling down the stairs, hitting her head on the fireplace, where she died. (They were possessed.) Then her body disappeared.

CHAPTER 3

Pickerel Field
The Devil's Work

*E*ARL DAVIES OWNED PICKEREL FIELD. He rented a house on Pickerel Field to six college students, Dameon, David, Omen, Carry, Chrissy, and Dona. The six of them were waiting for Earl Davies to come. He was supposed to arrive at four o'clock. Chrissy was with Dameon, Dana was with David, and Carry was with Omen. It was September the first, and it was a hot day. The kids were ready to go to school. Earl Davies arrived in a 1984 Chrysler Fifth Avenue car, a real beauty!

"Are you Mr. Earl Davies?" said Omen.

"Yes, I am. Are you the people renting this house?"

"Yes, sir, we would like to see it first before we decide for sure," said Omen.

"Okay, ladies and gentlemen, come this way. Here is the living room, dining room combination. Then you have a lounge and a large kitchen. You can use the lounge for your dances, and you can put a bar in here if you want to. You have a big fireplace in the lounge and the living room. Downstairs, you have a big basement. You have a washer and dryer, a workshop, and here you have an extra room in case you have other people staying with you. Also you have a fireplace-woodstove combination. It's pretty warm down here in the winter time, with all these fireplaces. Come upstairs and I'll show you the bedrooms.

"Here on the second floor, we have three bedrooms and one large bathroom, plus you have a large porch. Now on the third floor, you have two great big rooms, each with fireplaces in them, a large bath, and a balcony porch. Also you have a skylight and a watch-out tower. This building used to be an old church, years ago. You people will be blessed for good!

"The rent is $2,000 a month, plus utilities. I will be here the first of every month to collect your rent, right here at this house. Each of you will be paying $333 a month, plus $2. Thank you very much. If you have any problems, just call me at my office," said Earl Davies.

Everyone who rented the house went out to a baseball game, except Omen. Omen didn't mix in with the crowd too often. Omen stayed home. He saw this weird-looking animal outside, eating something out of the garbage cans located in the back of the building. Omen locked all the doors and windows in the house, then he called the police minutes later. The police arrived. They knocked on the door three times before Omen answered.

"Hello, Officers, I'm calling about some strange-looking animal that was in the trash. This animal looked like the devil. It has a long tail, funny-looking face, and I've never seen anything like it before," said Omen.

"I know this animal you're talking about. You saw a giant wolf, there's a lot of wolves around Pickerel Field," the police said.

"Officers, will these wolves bother me?" said Omen.

"Don't worry about them, wolves won't bother you. Just don't go near them. Wolves are more afraid of you than you are of them!" said the policeman. The police left, and they searched Pickerel Field.

Nighttime came, and the other five students were back from the ballgame. They had food, wine, and plenty of beer, so they decided to throw a big party. Omen hooked up kegs of beer to the refrigerator; the rest helped out with the party. A little while later, a storm was coming. The party was going on, when suddenly *ba boom!*

"What the hell was that!" said Carry.

"That's thunder!" said Omen.

"Omen, don't say that. I have to go out and shut the windows in my car!" said Carry. Carry went out in the rain. Dana ran out too because she left the windows open in her car too. She was closing the window in her car when suddenly she saw a bolt of lightning hit the ground, and sparks flew all over the place. Dana and Carry ran back in the house, screaming their heads off.

"What happened, Dana, did something blow up?" asked Carry.

"No, I saw this vicious bolt of lightning hit the ground, and sparks went flying all over the place!" said Dana.

"I saw it too here in the house. I thought it was the end of the fuckin' world!" said Chrissy.

Suddenly the lights went out, followed a big crack of thunder! Everyone in the house screamed and was frightened, but they partied anyway!

"Good night, everyone," said Omen.

"Omen, don't go to bed, let's party!" said Dana. Omen went upstairs. "David, go upstairs and get Omen to come down," said Dana.

"Dana, if he doesn't want to party, fuck him!" said David.

About midnight, Omen lit one of the fireplaces in one of the big rooms on the third floor. He stared at the flame. He stared at the fire for hours, until it started making weird shapes and turning colors. Finally the fire went out. Omen then heard strange noises in the fireplace that sounded like cracks and squeaking noises, and it was still thundering and lightning outside. Then Omen went up on the roof through the skylight to watch the thunderstorm. He was acting strange, talking to himself. (Omen was on drugs.)

About two in the morning, everyone was going to bed. Omen came down from the roof after the storm was over. He lit another fire in the fireplace in the room he was in before. He overheard David and Dana talk about him through a heating duct near the radiator.

"Dana, you know something, Omen is really strange. His girlfriend, Carry, is a little weird too! I think Omen's on drugs, and he tells people that he sees things that are not real and tells everyone that he's possessed by the devil because his name is Omen!" said David. Dana laughed and laughed.

"He told me he belonged to a devil worship and brutal organizations! And he has no faith in God at all! He's thirty-five years old, and he's the oldest man here living with us. As a matter of fact, I think he's the oldest student at Connecticut College," said David.

"He scares me, David, for some reason. He's a funny-looking guy, and he talks weird sometimes! I don't trust him," said Dana.

About 4:00 a.m. the fire went out. Omen went downstairs in the living room, and he lit that one, and he sat in front of it for the rest of the night. His face looked weird! Everyone else was in bed. About 6:15 a.m. in, Dameon and Chrissy went out for breakfast. "Bye, Omen," they said. Omen didn't answer. David and Dana woke up, and they were talking upstairs, while Omen was downstairs in the process of getting possessed! Carry woke up, and she went downstairs to talk to Omen.

"Omen, what are you doing?" she said.

Omen was sitting in front of the fireplace, popping drugs. He said in a funny voice, "Mind your own fuckin' business!"

Carry was stunned. She ran upstairs to David's room. "David, Dana, you gotta help! Omen just ate a bottle of pills!" Carry cried.

"Carry, stay up here, I'll go down and talk to him. Dana, you stay here too!" said David. Then David went downstairs to talk with Omen.

"Omen, what the fuck you doing?"

Omen was inside the fireplace while the fire was going. He came out of the fireplace burning!

"*No! No! No!*" David cried, then he grabbed a blanket, and he rolled Omen in the blanket to stop him from burning! Then David looked at his face; his face was all burned, and blood was pouring from his melted face! "Oh my fuckin' god!" David cried.

Carry ran downstairs, and she saw Omen's face. "Aahhhh!" Carry screamed and ran out of the house.

Dana came running downstairs, yelling, "What's going on down here?"

"Dana, get upstairs and call the police right away!"

"What happened, David?" she said.

"Just do what I said, please!" David threw a bucket of water on Omen.

Then Dana saw the body. She screamed and screamed and cried, "What did Omen do, David?" Dana cried.

"Dana, just get out of the house until the police come!" said David. David and Dana ran out of the house to flag down the police. Just before the police came, David heard something in the house. "You girls stay here and wait for the police. Something must be happening to Omen!"

"David, don't go in there!" the girls yelled.

David ran back into the house, and he saw Omen lying in front of the fireplace moaning and crying, then David walked out of the house. The police came; the girls were outside, crying, "Police, police, there's a burning body in the house!" Carry and Dana cried. The cop ran into the house and saw Omen sprawled out on the floor in front of the fireplace.

"Jesus Christ, I have to waist this guy!" The policeman grabbed his gun from his holster; he cocked it twice, and he fired one shot and blew Omen's head right off! Omen's head flew up the chimney! The policeman stepped outside to take a report on this accident. Here comes Omen, with no head, crashing through a window and falling to the ground. The police fired several shots at him to make sure he was dead. The girls and David watched the horror in shock.

"What the fuck! Do we have the devil living with us or what!" said hysterical David.

Omen started spraying fire after he was shot several times. The police fired more bullet holes into him. Dana was coughing and crying. Carry was throwing up. The police took David, Dana, and Carry to the police station for questioning. A short time later, the house burned down. Dameon and Chrissy were out for the day. They never knew what had happened until later on! The fire trucks, the rescue, the police, and Earl Davies were there at the fire. Dameon and Chrissy went out for breakfast since early this morning, then they went bowling, visiting, camping, and they went to the other side of town. At the police station, Lieutenant Licker took David, Dana, and Carry into his office.

"Mr. David Kesler, who committed the murder?" asked Lieutenant Licker.

"Omen did, sir. He killed himself on drugs. He overdosed, and he fell into a burning fireplace," said David.

"You see, Omen is a tough kid to get along with. He's always in some kind of trouble. He's always spending time here at the Moodus Police Station! Before we talk about this nut, how did this happen?" said Lieutenant Licker.

"I woke up about 6:3 a.m., I went downstairs, Omen was doing drugs. I asked him, 'What are you doing?' He spoke to me in a funny voice, telling me to mind my own fuckin' business, so I ran upstairs to get help, and it was too late!" Carry cried.

"I saw Omen burning, so I wrapped him in blankets, then Dana called for the police. After, we waited for the police," said David.

"Well, I give you three a lot of credit. The good news is you saved a lot of lives. Omen was a very bad man. He had a police record about five hundred pages long. I mean, this guy was pathetic! According to our records, this guy hasn't committed any murders as far as we know of, but I think he has. But I can't prove that! This man is very dangerous. He has special powers. He was a master of black belt karate. Omen was heavy into drugs. We arrested him on drugs by the books! Another thing the Moodus Police proved on the lie detector screen, that Omen is possessed by the devil! Go out in the hall and grab a cup of coffee for a short break and I'll finish telling you about the rest of Omen in a few minutes," said Lieutenant Licker.

"Okay, I'm back. Omen's major possession power is that he can burn things by looking at them. This man has been booked for drugs, arson, and other weird shit! This man has been locked behind bars I don't know many times, and he always finds a way to burn his way out! Omen has burned down police stations, jails, prisons, you name it! He once burned his way out of a jail. The police locked him inside a tomb, and he burned his way out of that too! Police had to let the bastard free! I really don't know how the hell you people lived with this man, he was nuts! I'm glad this fuckin' mental case is dead, I really do! Because I was ready to kill the bastard myself!" said Lieutenant Licker.

"Are you Carry Phillips?" said some man dressed up.

"Yes, I am," she said.

"Hi, my name is Detective Ty-Tino, from the Supper Investigations Group, and I would like to talk to you about Omen. Have a seat in my office, and I will be with you in a minute. Ms. Carry Phillips, could you tell me a little about Omen?" said the detective.

"I have been with Omen about a year now, and we never had a problem. He liked me. When we're together, we get along fine. When he's alone or with his friends, I don't know what goes on. I heard from my friends that he does a lot of drugs—cocaine, LSD, and he does acid. He did acid in front of me once. I was really scared, but he didn't do anything. He just acted weird! My friends tell me that he's an asshole, and he used to belong to the Ku Klux Klan. Is that some kind of karate?" said Carry.

"No, it's a devil worship organization. They hate Catholics and blacks. They kill them in favor of the devil. Just like us, we worship God, but the KKK is the opposite, they pray for the devil," said the detective.

"Can I leave, Detective?" said Carry.

He nodded his head and said, "Yes."

Carry, Dana, and David left the police station to go get something to eat.

"Good morning, Lieutenant."

"Good morning, Junior. What's happening?"

"I have further results on the bloody massacre at the old white inn on Pickerel Field. Omen, the body found there, his autopsy said he was loaded with so much drugs, which must have made him look like the devil. He took horse tranquilizers, LSD, mercury pills, and a lot of booze. The booze and the mercury pills may have caused this man to turn into some weird-looking creature that sprays fire! A human that sprays fire, that's strange! Mercury pills and the booze activating together may have caused this man to turn into something we don't know about. The result of this autopsy is going to the head medical books! Lieutenant, where are Carry, Dana, and David?" said Junior.

"They went out to get something to eat, they'll be right back," said Lieutenant Licker.

"Good, hold them, because we have more questions to ask them for the Moodus Police Department," said Junior.

Just about noontime, Junior drove the witnesses back to the house at Pickerel Field where the horrors happened. Lieutenant Licker was with them.

"Lieutenant, this is a bad place!" said Junior.

David, Dana, and Carry were the witnesses. Lieutenant Licker took the three of them around where the damages were. "Jesus Christ, the house burned down to the brick! Is this your car?" said Lieutenant Licker.

"Yes, it is, and the blue car is Omens," said David.

"Okay, Omen's car is going to be towed. Can you three leave the area in one car?" said Lieutenant Licker.

"Yes, we can. Carry will come with us," said David. Then they left. Earl Davies, the owner of the house, showed up. Dameon and Chrissy were still out. They never knew what had happened.

That night, Dameon and Chrissy were walking through the cornfields back to the house where they were staying at Pickerel Field. A gust of wind came, blowing leaves around and around; then a fuzzy ball was flying overhead, and it landed on the other side of the road. Dameon and Chrissy saw it—they were scared! Then they ran into the woods as fast as they could. Then the fuzzy balls started flying around through the trees.

"Oh my god, I see a witch flying around the moon or something!" said Chrissy.

"Chrissy, that's someone flying a kite, it's not a ghost." Dameon laughed, and he said, "Come this way and I'll show you a shortcut to the house."

Chrissy and Dameon got lost, and they ended up back at the cornfields to some road. The road was foggy and dark; the wind was blowing hard. They walked for a little while. The fuzzy balls were still flying around.

"Hey, Chrissy, we made it without getting attacked by something!" said Dameon. Dameon laughed.

"Shut up, Dameon, you're scaring me!" said Chrissy.

"Oh my god, where's the house, Chrissy?"

"I bet Omen burned it down, Dameon! Omen did this, the asshole!" said Chrissy.

"Chrissy, we have to try to get Carry out of the house because she's a lot of trouble too. Every time we're with them, they somehow cause trouble!" said Dameon.

Chrissy yelled, "Carry! Carry! Carry! Omen! Omen! Omen!" No answer!

The devil was roaming around the cornfields in Pickerel Field.

Dameon and Chrissy walked out into the street. Dameon called for his other friends. "David! David! David!" No answer. "Dana! Dana! Dana!" Still no answers! Dameon and Chrissy walked down the road a little more. Chrissy tried calling their friends again.

"Omen! Carry! David! Dana! Where the hell are you?" Chrissy yelled as loud as she could. Still no answers!

Awoooo!

"What the hell was that?" said Chrissy.

"I don't know, it sounds like a wolf to me," said Dameon.

"Oh my god, a wolf!" she said.

"Don't worry, Chrissy, wolves won't bother humans. Those go after other animals," said Dameon.

Awooooo!

"Oh my god, there it is again, and it's getting louder and louder!" Chrissy cried.

"It's okay, Chrissy, let's go find our friends," said Dameon.

Awooooo!

"Ahhhhh!" Chrissy screamed.

"Chrissy, stay on the road so the wolves won't get near us. Walk in the middle of the road, wolves don't cross the street," said Dameon.

Aawwooooooooooo!

"Let's get the hell out of here before we get eaten!" Chrissy cried.

"Chrissy, just stay in the middle of the road. The wolves will leave," said Dameon.

"Dameon, do you think it could be some other animal?" Chrissy cried.

"No, Chrissy, it's wolves looking for food."

"Yeah, us! Dameon, are you sure that wolves won't attack?" said Chrissy.

"Chrissy, the only way a wolf will attack us is if we tease it. Just stay away from them, that's all!"

"Dameon, stop, I see something!"

"Chrissy, what is it?"

"I don't know what it is. I saw it running across the street. I thought wolves don't cross the street!" said Chrissy.

"Maybe it's something else, but I'm pretty sure it was a wolf," said Dameon.

Dameon and Chrissy were walking down the road. The road was getting narrower and narrower, which led to a bridge. They walked over the bridge back on the road again and out of the woods. The road came to an end. There was a rotary leading to paths. Pickerel Field was on both sides of the paths. Dameon and Chrissy both walked into the horror zone.

Awoooo!

"There it is again, Dameon!" Chrissy cried.

"Chrissy, love, it's only a wolf, don't be scared!"

"Dameon, let's go back the way we came!"

"No, Chrissy, let's take this path, it leads to another road."

Awoooooo!

"It's coming closer, Dameon!" she cried.

"Come on, Chrissy, don't worry about it or we'll never get out of here!"

A deep fog formed while Chrissy and Dameon were walking.

"Help! Help! Help!" Chrissy cried.

"What's the matter, Chrissy?"

"Just look behind you!" she cried.

Dameon turned around, and he saw two big red eyeballs in the corn stalks. "Jesus fuckin' Christ!" he said. Then he grabbed his gun, and he fired two shots at the eyeballs, and it disappeared.

"Dameon, did you see the eyeballs?"

"Yes, I did, they're gone now, let's go!"

"Ah! I see something, Dameon!"

"I see it too, and it's not a wolf! Let's be very quiet and go back the way we came from. That animal, whatever it is, it's a lot bigger than a wolf! Let's go!" said Dameon.

The horrors were about to begin!

Suddenly, the ground shook. Chrissy screamed. Dameon held his hand over Chrissy's mouth so she won't scream.

"Chrissy, try not to be afraid, because I have a gun. When the creature comes near, I'll blow its fuckin' head off!"

Chrissy then laughed. The devil started howling away. Dameon saw the red eyeballs in the cornfields again.

"Oh my god."

"Chrissy, please don't fuckin' scream!"

Then Dameon and Chrissy hid behind a tall tree. Dameon watched the red eyes get a little closer. He jerked his gun, and he said, "Chrissy, you stay here, I won't go far." Dameon crept closer to the eyes until he was ready to shoot. When he pointed his gun, the eyes disappeared! Then he ran over to where the eyes were. The devil attacked Chrissy from behind the tree!

"Help! Help! Dameon! Help! Dameon!" Chrissy screamed to death as the devil grabbed her, and it was pulling Chrissy into the ground. Dameon responded quickly. He saw the devil attack her and pulling her into the ground. He fired six shots at the devil with his gun. The devil disappeared! It happened so fast.

Dameon walked backward to the tree where the devil attacked Chrissy. He saw something moving under the ground, and then he saw Chrissy's head rolling from behind the tree. Her head rolled over to Daemon's feet. Dameon was about ready to pass out! When Chrissy's head rolled over to his feet, it looked at him. There was blood all over the place! Dameon was breathing very heavily, and he was dizzy. He couldn't move! Finally he was able to run. Dameon was running down a path, screaming for help. The wolf howled again. Dameon was crying hysterically. Then he saw a bright flash of lightning. The wolf cried again.

Awooooo!

Really, really loud this time! Dameon turned around, and he saw a quick flash of a ghost flying over Pickerel Field. Dameon started running like a bat out of hell after he saw the ghost. He found a house in the cornfield, so he jumped up on the porch, and he looked around to see if the devil was coming near. He couldn't see much because it was dark and foggy. Dameon rang the doorbell; no one answered the door. Dameon ran around the house, looking for lights. No lights! Dameon heard the wolf cry three more times—the devil was near! Some of the wolf cries sounded like those were in the house. Dameon ran to the front of the house, and he banged on the door several times; still no one answered!

The wolves sounded again.

Awoooooo!

The wolf cries got louder and louder! Then Dameon kicked the door in, and he went in the house. A big black Doberman pincher went at Dameon, and it chased him down the street! Dameon pulled out his gun to shoot the dog, and he missed! The dog grabbed Dameon's leg. Dameon lost control of his balance, dropped the shotgun, and the dog dragged him down the road. The dog kept pulling at Dameon's leg until it tore his leg off. Then the dog went on its business. Dameon screamed and screamed he was in such pain. Dameon's leg was laying in the street. There was blood all over the place. Dameon watched his torn-off leg hop around in the street! A few minutes later, the devil came to finish him off. The devil finally found some flesh in the street. It grabbed Dameon's torn-off leg and started eating it like a chicken bone. The devil ate the flesh on that leg in seconds, as Dameon watched in shock! Dameon was in such shock the devil came over to him and it bit his other leg off, and it did the same thing, then the devil finished him off for supper! Dameon screamed and growled as the devil ate him piece by piece. There was nothing left but a little blood in the street after the devil got through eating him alive. David and Dana arrived at the burned-down house in Pickerel Field after the police told them not to go there. The reason they went there was they heard screams and cries, and they needed a quiet place to make love. They were coming from a Halloween party. David and Dana were in the middle of having sex in David's car when the devil was eating up Dameon.

"Dana, did you hear someone screaming?" said David.

"Yes, I did!" she said.

"Let's go find out what it is!" David drove a short ways down the road, and his car stalled. He tried to get his car started, and it wouldn't start; he messed with his car for an hour, and he still couldn't get it going.

The wolves started to cry again.

"Dana, roll up your windows and lay down in the car!" said David.

"What's that noise, David?"

"It's only wolves!"

David was working on his car. Dana wanted him to stop, but David wanted to get this car started so they could get the hell out of there.

"I can't get this motherfucker to start, we're gonna have to walk!"

"Walk, David, are you crazy!" said Dana.

"Don't worry, I have a gun, let's go!"

Awooooooo!

"Oh dear god!" said Dana.

"Dana, it's just a wolf. Stay in the street, wolves won't bother you, just stay in the middle of the road and keep walking."

David and Dana walked around Pickerel Field until they got to Dameon's aunt and uncle's house. They were walking alongside of the road overlooking the big cornstalks in Pickerel Field, when suddenly David saw a bright white flash, and he looked up in the air, and he saw a white ring flying over his head. Then David heard a popping sound; he said to his girl, "Dana, look up in the air!"

"Oh my god, it looks like a smoke ring from a giant sager!" she said.

The ring flew directly lower over David's head, then it shot a fireball right at him! It happened so fast. David turned white, flashing in lightning rods! Dana turned around, and she saw the horror, she screamed hysterically! Then David was a ball of fire; he just lit up like a flash of lightning. While Dana was watching her boyfriend burn, she passed out. Later the devil came along, and it ate David's burned body, then it went under the ground. After the devil dug its way into the ground, Pickerel Field burned up. The fire overcame Dana too! Fire trucks all night long were putting out a major alarm forest fire at Pickerel Field. The next day, police found Dana's body. It looked like the devil!

"Good morning, this is the WMCN radio news. Four people are believed to be missing from last night's Halloween parties. Police found a body burned from last night's fire. Also, bones were found on Pickerel Field road. We'll have more after this message."

Chapter 4

Ben and Rose

*E*ARL DAVIES WAS ON VACATION while the horrors were going on in Pickerel Field. Earl just rented this home to a couple near the center of town; their names were Ben and Rose. After he rented the home to Ben and Rose, he went to the police station. He walked in the door, slamming it shut, and he said, "May I speak to Lieutenant Licker, please?"

"You're looking at him."

"I am Mr. Earl Davies, new in real state here in Moodus."

"Yes, sir, I heard all about you. You're not the most honest man in town, but the most handiest! Every time something happens, you take off! I believe you rented a house in Pickerel Field to Omen, Dameon, David, Chrissy, Carry, and Dana. Where are they? Four people were found dead near that house you just rented to them college students. One of them was a fuckin' asshole! Omen is dead, but the other five is unknown. That house, by the way, burned down," said Lieutenant Licker.

"I saw it, sir. I'm just getting back from vacation, and I'm trying to get things back together," Earl said.

"Well, mister, you better get it together pretty soon because you're in a lot of trouble, you know that, don't you? Bodies were found burned, tortured, and heads chopped off! Can you tell me what the fuck is going on?" said Lieutenant Licker.

"Sir, there are wild animals in Pickerel Field!" said Earl.

"Earl, we have a serious problem to solve between you and the Moodus Police Station. Are you aware of the north street incident about a month ago?" said Lieutenant Licker.

"I think I have a report on it back at my office," said Earl Davies.

"Earl, you better go back to your office. As a matter of fact, let me go with you. I want to see this report," said Lieutenant Licker.

Ben and Rose were moving in to their new home. Relatives came to help. They seemed very happy.

Lieutenant Licker drove Earl Davies in the police car to his new real state office to see the report on the brown house. Lieutenant Licker was reading it.

"Jesus Christ, I can't understand this report at all!" said Lieutenant Licker.

"Sir, I heard the house burned to the ground, killing Ann, her horse, Tony, her son, was reported missing," said Earl.

"Here's my report. Ann burned up in her home, the fire was unknown, her son, Tony, was reported missing, still we don't know if he's dead or alive! She had two horses, one is dead, the other belongs to Ann's boyfriend, Richard. Something is screwy, Earl, and I'm going to lock your fuckin' ass up!" said Lieutenant Licker.

"Lieutenant, I would never hurt anyone. I must be renting homes to the wrong people," said Earl. The chief of police came in the lieutenant's office. He grabbed Earl Davies by the hair and locked him in a jail cell!

At nighttime, Ben and Rose finished moving in. They were eating and drinking wine, watching the news on TV.

It was getting cool outside, so Ben lit the fireplace. The wind was starting to pick up, and Rose shut the doors on the pantry. The fire went out in the fireplace. Ben lit it again. Ben went outside to the barn to get a bunch of wood for the fireplace. He brought it inside, and he put some in the fireplace, and he got a good fire going. Ben said, "Okay, Rose, let's sit down and watch TV, ha!" *Click!* Ben turned the TV on. "Here's a good movie on HBO, how about this?" he said.

"Ben, I still feel a draft," said Rose.

"Maybe it's the fireplace. You got to give it time to warm up, or the damper might be stuck closed," said Ben. Then Ben got up to go to the bathroom. While he was in the bathroom, the fire in the fireplace went out, and the room filled with smoke.

Rose screamed, "Ben, open the doors quick and let this goddam smoke out!"

Ben opened all the windows and doors to let all the smoke out. The fireplace went out again. He relit it. Ben moved the logs around in the fireplace to get a better fit, and then he lit the fire again. The fire went out again, then black soot fell into her living room.

"Holy shit! I'll bet the gramper isn't closed right," said Ben. Sure enough, it wasn't. Ben had to fix it. Rose vacuumed up the soot. The fireplace went out again! All of a sudden, the pantry doors blew open! The fire went out again.

"For Christ sake's, Ben, why didn't lock the doors!" said Rose. Ben locked all the windows and doors in the house. The fire in the fireplace went out again! Ben shoved a lot of wood under the fire to keep it going. When he got the fire going, he said, "Now come on, fire, burn, goddam it! For the fifth time!" Then the fire almost went out again, but he was able to keep it up, and he said to Rose, "Look at that fire burn now!"

"I wonder if this town is possessed by the devil!" Rose laughed.

"Maybe it is!" Ben joked.

The movie on HBO was almost over; the fire in the fireplace was getting low, smaller and smaller. Suddenly a big bang sounded! Ben and Rose got scared.

"What the hell was that?" said Ben. Then Ben and Rose started hearing weird noises. The noises got louder and louder until the dishes and glass started rattling and breaking all over the place.

"Ben, what's going on here?" Rose cried.

"I don't know, we're probably having an earthquake!" said Ben.

While the rumbling sounds were going on, the fire in the fireplace blew out again. Then an ugly flame appeared in the fireplace.

Rose screamed. The fire came back, and it framed a devil-shaped face, as Rose watched in shock. Then blood started dripping down the fireplace into the house. Rose was screaming hysterically! Then the fire blew out again, The damper or something blew out of the fireplace through the chimney, then a strong wind came down the fireplace into the house.

Rose, cried, "*Help! Help!* God, help us, please!"

Ben was standing there, watching the horror show; he couldn't believe what was going on, but he was scared! The wind outside died down for a few minutes. The fire came back in the fireplace, forming that ugly flame again. The flame showed the devil's picture. Ben went over to the fireplace, and he took the poker, and he was messing with the flame.

"Ben, what's the matter with you, get away from that fireplace!" said Rose.

The fire went out again when Ben was poking around with it, then a gust of wind picked up, sucking papers and some trash up the fireplace. Ben said, "There's something wrong here!" Ben went down in the cellar to get a piece of plywood to put in front of the fireplace to stop the wind. He put the plywood in front of the fireplace. He started to nail the plywood to the fireplace, but the wind got so strong it sucked Ben and the plywood up the chimney! Rose screamed hysterically in shock. The fright was too much! A fire started up again in the fireplace, showing the devil's picture. Rose was watching the horror. The pitch fork poker flew off the fireplace at Rose, but it missed! The fire got bigger and bigger; the devil's flame got worse and worse! Rose was so frightened she couldn't move.

"*No! No! No!*" Rose screamed when the devil's flame was coming close to her, then she dropped dead!

The next day, Ben's uncle Danny came over. He promised to do some work on his house.

About 8:00 a.m. on a Saturday, it was pouring rain outside. Ben's uncle Danny parked his car on the other side of the street. He reached under his car seat to get his umbrella, and he walked toward the house. The front door was wide open. Danny was walking slowly to the house. He saw a bright flash of lightning, then he heard a loud crack of thunder. He knocked on Ben's door three times, and no one answered.

"Hello! Hello! Hello! Hello! Hello! Anybody home?" Danny yelled, but no one answered. Danny heard a loud crack of thunder, then he went in the house. He saw a fresh pot of coffee already made; he made himself a cup, and he waited forty minutes, thinking maybe Ben was not up yet, or he might have stepped out for a while, so he grabbed another cup of coffee. Finally he had a third cup, then he went into another room.

Danny saw Rose lying on the floor near the fireplace covered in black soot from the fireplace—*dead!* Danny cried, and he cried, and he cried! He said to himself, "What did she do, commit suicide?" Then he went out of the house, staggering and crying of fright! Danny fell on the ground, crying. When he got up, Ben slid off the roof covered with blood! Danny choked, and he dropped dead!

A policeman was riding around, making a routine check in the pouring rain, listening to country music on his car radio. The policeman saw a car with the driver's side door open. He got out of his car, and he went over to the other car to search it, then he went over to a house across the street. The policeman saw Ben's and Danny's bodies lying outside near the front stairs. He pulled his gun out of his holster, and he went into the house. The cop searched the house. First he had a cup of coffee too, then he saw Rose's black body. The policeman threw up. He couldn't take it anymore! Then he searched the entire house for more bodies. He found those three! The rookie cop radioed to headquarters, then other cops came. The police took the reports: Danny and Rose died of a heart attack, and Ben committed suicide. A week later, Earl Davies passed the murder test at the Moodus Police Station, and police let him free.

CHAPTER 5

The River

Two people were rowing a canoe down the Moodus River. John and Mike were the campers' names. They camped in a wooded area near the river. It was late May, just before the break of summer. It was beginning to get dark, and there was a full moon tonight; fog was forming around the moon, then it came down to the water from the sky.

"John, feel this water, it's warm," said Mike.

Minutes later, a big orange cloud appeared, then it started thundering. John and Mike started unpacking at their camp site. They saw an orange glow near the water. The water started bubbling and turning colors.

John said to Mike, "Wow! Look out there, I didn't know we had hot springs in Connecticut waters!"

John and Mike were putting up their tent, when suddenly a storm was coming. They just finished in time. The storm moved through quickly!

The bubbling water was a meteorite that had fallen from space some time ago, which had the devil in it! People didn't know too much of this thing. This rock had so much power to generate to power off other things from its gasses, then it boiled the water and caused severe thunderstorms.

Roar!

"Did you hear that, Mike?" asked John.

"Yes, I did. It sounded like some animal roaring!" said Mike.

Around midnight, John and Mike were sound asleep, but they woke up hearing strange noises during the night, mainly howling noises and wolf cries.

"Mike, did you hear that?" said John.

Mike was half asleep. He was dreaming. The river looked like lava from a volcano, and the water was bubbling, and it was making a loud hissing sound. The hissing sound was the meteorite floating under the river, and it floated to the end of the river, where it rested. Finally the river cooled off, and the fears ran away. John and Mike went back to sleep. Later on, a storm was coming. John and Mike were in a deep sleep.

Baboom!

John and Mike woke up fast! All that was happening was the rock was settling in the water at the end of the river. John and Mike both got out of their tents to see what happened upon hearing the loud bangs! They saw continuous flashes of lightning, heard loud cracks of thunder. John and Mike were scared to death watching this. Some lightning was brighter than useful. It was scary.

"John, I have to go for a wicked shit!" said Mike.

"Go out in the woods, don't shit here!" said john.

Mike had to wait until the storm was over before he went out into the woods. When Mike was in the woods having his shit, he looked up into the sky; the sky was crystal clear. There was a nice, bright full moon outside. The moon was shining brightly through the trees in the woods. When Mike came out of the woods, he saw some patches of fog and weak flashes of lightning. Mike went in his tent to go to sleep. Just a half hour later, a sonic boom came, shaking the ground. The ground started moving, then a gust of wind picked up, and it blew a big tree in front of the tent. Mike found a silver sparkling chain near where the big tree fell; he shined it up at the moon, and the wind stopped, but the ground started moving again. Mike said to himself, "I must be seeing things or something. I know I had five beers, but that's not enough to go senile!" Clouds formed overhead. A storm was coming, and it was beginning to rain. Mike looked up at the sky. He saw the clouds moving fast, covering up the full moon, then he saw a bright flash of lightning followed by a big crack of thunder. Then after the thunder sounded, Mike heard a roar.

"John, is that you?" Mike said. John was sound asleep. "What could that roaring noise be?" Mike said to himself. Mike got dressed, and he went for a walk in the woods.

Mike was heading back out into the woods, until he saw the ground move. "Fuck this, I'm going back to the tent before the devil grabs me!"

The devil was under the ground, where everywhere it moved.

Mike yelled, "John, help! John, help! John, help me!"

John woke up when he heard Mike's screams. John got up, and he got dressed fast, and he went looking for Mike in the pouring rain and thunder and lightning. John went way out in the woods, and he hollered, "Mike! Mike! Mike! Mike! Where the hell are you?" No one answered. John stayed in the woods for a while to see if he could spot Mike through lightning flashes.

A rock exploded at the end of the river because it was activated every time it moved. It was like a mine blowing up. The rock shot bolts of lightning in all different directions, shooting out smoke and puffing steam, then it shot like a geyser sky high into the night, all lit up like a Christmas tree! The geyser was water getting sucked into the rock and exploding high into the air. While the rock was making all these things happen, it made vicious and very loud thunderous sounds, thunder that sounded much worse than a normal thunderstorm. John watched the spectacular horrors in fright in the woods. John was so scared he hollered, "Oh shit! Mike! Mike! Mike!" Still no answer. So John had to go looking for him.

He heard something, and then he saw a flash of lightning, and he saw Mike lying unconscious, trapped under a big tree. John ran over to where Mike was, and he helped him. John had to lift the tree just enough so Mike could free himself.

"John, thank God you saved me! I got caught in a ditch, lightning struck a tree, and I got trapped. If that tree fell on me, I'd be dead!" said Mike.

Then the lightning was flashing again, and it flashed constantly, then the rain came down in buckets.

"Mike, let's get out of here now before we get stuck again!" said John. On the way, Mike passed out again. "Oh shit!" John said, then he took off his shirt, and he dipped into the water, and he put it above Mike's head so he'd wake up. Then John's shirt fell into the water. He went in the water to get it, and he saw a bolt of lightning split a tree in two, then he got a vicious shock from the lightning strike. He screamed and got out of that water as fast as he could. He left his shirt in the water.

Roar!

"What the fuck is that!" said Mike.

"I don't know, let's get the hell out of here fast!" said John.

Finally John and Mike made it back to their tent. They watched the woods for a while until the storm was over. The lightning flashed, and Mike saw something out in the woods. He said, "John, did you see that?"

"No, why, what was it?"

"John, I saw something strange out in the woods."

"Like what?" said John. The lightning flashed again.

"There it is, John!" said Mike.

"Where is it, Mike?" he said. The lightning flashed on and off about six times.

"There it is, John, it's right near us, can you see it?" said Mike.

"Yes, I see it now. It looks like some kind of rock or a meteorite from outer space. It looks like it might be still burning. Let's take a walk closer to it so we can get a better look at it!" said John.

John and Mike went for a walk. The lightning flashed again. The devil's face appeared on the rock, but John and Mike didn't see it. John and Mike walked down to where they saw this thing, and the rock was making a rumbling sound. Then the rock moved, and strange-looking faces appeared in the rock. The lightning flashed several times. then the rock rolled away from them, and it went rolling into the woods.

"Well, John, I think we got a meteorite!" said Mike.

"Think so too, Mike, an active one!" said John.

The sun was about to rise John and Mike were out all night long exploring this rock. John picked up a big stick, and he whacked the rock several times.

"It's a rugged one!" said Mike.

"Mike, let's roll this meteorite down a little hill against them trees so it can't fall into the water," said John, so they did.

"Let's get some sleep and we'll paint that rock later on," said Mike.

Then John and Mike went back to the tent to get some sleep. About three hours later, John went for a walk out into the woods. All the birds were singing. John went over to the rock. He noticed bright rays shinning on the rock coming from the sun, then it started to turn colors. The sky was pretty and colorful, then a rainbow formed. John enjoyed watching it!

Fast-moving clouds started to move in again. John ran back to his tent. John woke Mike up.

"Mike, Mike!" said John.

"What do you want, John? I'm trying to get some sleep, god-damn it," said Mike.

"Come outside for a minute and look at this!" said John.

"Wow, all these colors, where is it coming from?" said Mike. John and Mike watched the colored rays shinning on the meteorite in the woods. John and Mike ran down to the rock. They heard popping noises and the rock was smoking.

"Mike, let's get some sticks and roll this rock into the water. It might be dangerous, so watch out!" said John. John and Mike grabbed a big stick each and pushed the rock back into the water. The rays were still shinning on it.

"Let's go back to the tent before something else happens. I'm gonna get some more sleep," said Mike. John and Mike went back to the tent. They had something to eat, then they went to sleep for a while. After, John got up, and he went for a canoe ride down the Moodus River. He noticed some crystal-clear water at the mouth of the river and a sandy patch too; the water was beautiful! The sand at the bottom of the river looked like crystals! The rays from the sun

RICHARD REZENDES

were still shinning down in the river this time. The rock had moved again. The rock wasn't far from where John was.

John went swimming. The water was cold, but he found a rock to dive off. The water was about twenty feet deep, and it was refreshing! John swam for two hours while he was watching the rays still shinning from up above into the river. John rowed the canoe up to where the rays from the sun was shining in the river. The rock was directly below him underwater, then he rowed his canoe back to the mouth of the river. John saw the rays started getting brighter and brighter. The brightness was raising the rock out of the water, and it rolled into the woods, and it disappeared for a few minutes. Then suddenly the rock rolled down a riverbank, bouncing off another rock, and it splashed into the water, then it sunk.

The meteorite blew up! Water shot straight up in the air like a geyser! The meteorite-like rock raised from the water and floated to a rock near the river's edge, then it rolled up on the riverbank and stayed there. John watched in shock. The rays from the sun were still shining on the meteorite everywhere it went. John said to himself, "I don't think I'll get out of here alive. I cannot believe what I'm seeing. This can't be true. This is weird!" John watched the meteorite very closely. Suddenly the rays on the meteorite started getting brighter and brighter, then it was really bright! John kept watching the meteorite. Suddenly a bright flash of light blinded John. John turned around, and he cried, "I'm blind! I'm blind!" Finally he got his vision back.

John turned around, and he faced the meteorite. The rock was puffing smoke out of it. John was getting scared, then the meteorite blew up again, bursting into flames! The rays were still shining on the meteorite when it blew up. John watched the rock burn as he tried to get away. John was rowing the canoe away from the meteorite, but instead, the meteorite came toward the canoe. The rays came down from the sun, and it started burning John. John screamed, "Help me, God! Help me, God! Please don't let the devil take me! Help me please!" The rays from the sun were burning him. Then John had a flashback about how he tried to murder a coworker back in the sixties. The rays started burning John painfully. He screamed and he screamed, but there was nobody around to hear him. Well, as John was screaming to death, a big chunk of rock flew off the meteorite and struck John in the head and killed him. John fell off the boat, and he sank to the bottom of the river. The devil's got him now!

Mike woke up to go for a swim. He never knew what had happened to John; he slept through it. At four in the afternoon, when John wasn't back, Mike wondered, so he went looking for him until six o'clock. Finally he gave up. He cooked some fish to eat, then he went looking for John later on. Mike kept looking for John until 9:00 p.m. before he went back to his tent; John still didn't come back!

Mike was getting his things organized in the tent, then he cooked some more fish, and he grabbed a big flashlight, and he tried looking for John again. "John! John! John! John!" Mike didn't hear nothing. Mike went for a walk along the river, looking and calling for John.

Aawwoooooo!

"What the hell is that!" Mike said, then he ran back to his tent, and he went to bed. About midnight, John still didn't show up. Mike said, "Midnight, John's not back yet, something must have happened! Mike was carving a stick about one thirty in the morning, and he went looking for John again. Mike was shining his flashlight into the woods, and he saw something move! He turned his light off, and he said, "What the fuck!" He shined the light on the ground again, and he saw ground movement a second time. Then Mike backed up a few steps, and he flashed the light on the ground a third time at the same spot; he saw the movement again! He shined the light again. He saw the movement good and clear this time. It had legs. Suddenly it disappeared! "I must be going out of my mind, I'm seeing weird things!" Mike cried, and then he called John for the last time. "John! John! John! John! Fuck you, man, I give up!" Then Mike went back to his tent.

Mike went to bed finally. An hour later, he heard a loud bang! Mike woke up quick, and he looked down the end of the river, and he saw an orange cloud, then he heard thunder; colorful rays were shining on the orange cloud, coming from the moon, then the rays from the moon disappeared, and the orange cloud formed a thunderhead; the wind started to blow, and a storm was coming. The sky completely clouded up, and it started pouring rain, just like that! Mike was calling John from his tent. A giant bolt of lightning struck a tree, and it landed in front of Mike's tent. A gust of wind came and blew his tent and belongings all over the place. Mike was so scared. The lightning was flashing constantly, and the thunder got louder and louder.

Mike grabbed his sleeping bag, and he found a hole he could run for cover so he could he could stay dry until the storm was over. He grabbed all his belongings to safety. He almost got struck by lightning! The big rock Mike found to hide from the storm was cutting off the strong winds. After the storm died down a little, Mike went to finish finding the rest of his belongings to put under the big rock. Mike packed everything he found together, and he put it to one side, then he set the tent up under the big rock so the wind couldn't get to it. Mike had heavy-duty duffel bags, where most of his clothes stayed dry. Finally he went to sleep.

At 2:30 a.m. the wind started blowing hard again, then by 3:00 a.m. the storm finally ended! The moon was out, shining beautifully over the river. It looked like there never was a storm in the middle of the night! At ten the next morning, Mike woke up. There was still no John! It was a crystal-clear day, not a cloud in the sky. Mike went fishing, then he went swimming for a while, then he cooked some fish for lunch. After that, he went back in swimming. By noontime, it started to get hot. By 1:00 p.m. it was hot! Mike came back from swimming briefly to put some of last night's wet things out in the sun to dry for the day, then he went back in swimming; he swam down the length of the river, to the mouth, which was where the deepest water was. He swam to a waterfall that led into an extension of the river. Mike saw John's canoe at the bottom of the waterfall lying on the riverbank. Mike called for John four times, "John! John! John! John!" No answer! Mike saw a cliff directly over the river on the other side of the waterfall. He jumped thirty-five feet into the lower river. Mike swam to shore. He got John's canoe, and he rowed down the lower part of the river. Mike was rowing the canoe through the woods. All you could see was a pack of trees and the river, then he got back out into the open waters, then he saw the meteorite resting up on shore.

"Oh my god, how the hell does this rock move around so much!" Mike said to himself. Mike rowed the canoe to shore, where the meteorite was. He got out, and he grabbed a big stick, and he pushed the rock into the water. A minute later, the rock rolled back out of the water and back where it was! "This rock has got to be a fuckin' meteorite!" Mike said to himself, then he went over to the rock, and he saw blood pouring out of it! Mike said to himself, "What the hell is this...blood! Blood, what the fuck is in this thing!" Mike pushed the rock back into the water; the rock started puffing steam from underwater. "It's a fuckin' meteorite! I don't believe it! A fuckin' meteorite!" Mike said to himself; he couldn't believe what he was seeing. He was having fun! He was playing with the devil's home.

The rock rose from the surface of the river. It made a popping noise, then a big bang, like a bomb going off, then it finally sunk! Mike stayed by the river for a while to see what the meteorite was going to do next. A big black thunderhead formed from under the water, rushing up into the air. It scared the shit out of Mike; he got in his canoe so fast, and he rowed it away as fast as he could. The meteorite followed Mike everywhere he went. Underwater, it made a hissing noise, then a big bang. The river started getting a little choppy. Suddenly a big bubble was forming in the river; the meteorite made a giant wave about thirty feet high. It knocked Mike off his canoe, as he watched in fright! When the wave hit, mike went under. The wave tossed Mike's canoe, slamming on a big rock, and it burst in millions of pieces. Mike was a good swimmer; he managed to get out of the wave and swim to shore. The rock followed Mike underwater, and it stopped near the shore. Then the rock came above water, floating to shore. It made a big loud bang, then a black cloud came out of it. Mike ran like a bat out of hell into the woods. Mike was running in the woods, and rays came down from the sun and followed him. Mike hid behind a tree, then he started running again. He found a brook, so he followed the brook, which led to a bridge. He stopped on the bridge for a brief rest. The rays were shining on Mike again, and it was burning him.

Mike ran to a shady tree to avoid getting burned from the strong rays. A cloud covered the sun, and Mike went back onto the bridge, and he looked in the pretty brook. The sun briefly came out. Mike could see an eclipse of the sun looking in the water in the brook. Mike said to himself, "No wonder I'm getting burned by the sun's rays, we're having an eclipse!" Minutes later, the sky was overcast. Mike noticed some blood on the bridge. He saw more blood on a rock in the woods, then he walked on the other side of the bridge, and he looked over into the water, and he saw John's body all bit up! The body had no head, and the arms and legs were torn off! One of John's leg was lying on a rock covered with flies and maggots eating the flesh. Mike went into shock when he saw that. He was going hysterical, then he passed out on the bridge. When Mike regained consciousness, he crawled to the end of the bridge, crying. Mike got up, staggering at the end of the bridge. He saw a rock filled with blood, and there were thousands and thousands of giant bloodsuckers swarming all over the bloody rocks. Some of them were flying bloodsuckers too. Mike was hysterical. He ran as fast as he could away from there, out into the woods. Mike was running through the woods. He heard a big crack of thunder as a storm was coming fast. Mike fell a few times while running because it was getting dark in the forest. The storm was on its way. Suddenly the sky opened up and filled the deep forest with heavy rains. Mike found a tall tree to escape getting drowned in the heavy rains! Bolts of lightning was chopping through the forest. Mike was up in a tree! He managed to climb down from the tree and run to a big rock before the rains got too bad. Then a bolt of lightning struck the tree he was in! Luckily, Mike got out of the tree in time. Mike saw this weird-looking animal on the rock he was on. Its tail slapped Mike in the face. Mike was able to get up and run. The lightning flashed; Mike saw blood on a rock. Mike started screaming, then the lightning kept flashing and flashing. Mike kept running. A bolt of lightning struck a tree, and it landed in front of him, he slipped under it, and he was screaming in fright.

Mike struggled, and he broke loose, and he was running through the woods. Another bolt of lightning struck a tree, and it just missed Mike this time. Mike was running in the woods, then he heard a zap! Then he saw branches flying everywhere. As Mike kept running in the woods, a bolt of lightning struck right through the ground. Mike first heard a big bang then roar! Mike didn't stop to find out what the roar was, just kept running. Mike was practically having a heart attack, but he just kept running. Suddenly the lightning flashed about six times very, very brightly, followed by cracks of thunder as loud as an earthquake. The ground was moving, rumbling, and cracking. The lightning was flashing very brightly and constantly. Mike was going hysterical in fright, and he ran headfirst into a tree. Something grabbed Mike by the foot, and it was trying to pull him into the ground. Mike screamed and he screamed and he screamed and he struggled to break free. Finally a bright bolt of lightning struck, blinding the devil's vision. Mike was able to break loose and run! The lightning flashed. Mike saw that animal—the devil. When the lightning flashed again, the devil disappeared! Suddenly the devil grabbed Mike from behind and dragged him to the river. Mike was watching this animal dragging him, but he didn't know what it was. He was too frightened to know! Then Mike was wrestling with the devil, trying to break free. The lightning flashed brightly again, blinding the devil momentarily, and Mike was able to break free again! Then the devil suddenly clawed the back of Mike's shirt while it was chasing him and ripped his shirt off! Mike scrambled to get away from the devil by crisscrossing in the deep forest, but the devil got a peace of him by tearing his arm; finally, Mike broke loose when he saw a foggy patch, where he ran into. The devil lost track of him! Mike was running in the fog, holding his arm. It was full of blood. He made it to the brook he saw before. He dived into the brook, and he swam to the river.

Mike was swimming in the brook, heading toward the river. He saw John's head all mashed up under a bridge. "Jesus fuckin' Christ!" Mike screamed when he saw John's bashed up head under the bridge. Mike ended up where he started from; he swam away from the bridge into a tunnel that led to a shack. Mike ran to the shack, hoping the devil wasn't going to be there. He made it to the shack, and he found some towels to cover his bloody arm. He rapped a few towels to hold for a while.

Roar! The devil roared five times, and it was near. Mike was in the shack, crying when he heard the devil roar. The devil went in the shack where Mike was. Quickly Mike leaped out a window to a fire escape. He climbed the fire escape to the roof, then he climbed up a chimney on top of the roof, and he got inside the chimney to hide from the devil. The devil then wandered off into the woods, roaring away! A few minutes later, Mike jumped off the roof, and he went back into the shack. He had a brick in his hands. The devil came back! The devil was somewhere close, roaring away out there. Mike found some gasoline in the shack, then he found a stick. He put one of the towels he found around the stick to make a wick, then he dipped the stick in the gasoline, making a torch out of the stick. The devil was coming closer, making all kinds of noises out there. It came right into the shack. Mike surprised the devil. He poured gasoline where the devil came in, and when the devil entered the shack, Mike lit the torch, and he threw it, chasing the devil out! Mike grabbed the can of gasoline that was in the shack out of a window, then he made a second torch, and he stuck it in the ground.

Mike poured the gasoline around the shack, then he grabbed his torch, and he tossed it to the shack. The shack went puff, and it burned to ashes. The fire started burning in the woods too! Mike thought the devil was gone. Mike ran as fast as he could through the woods, then he jumped into the brook, and he swam to the river. Mike thought a forest fire should kill the devil, but it attracted the devil more than anything! Mike was swimming to the river. The brook was getting wider and wider. Soon he was in the river. He swam to the waterfall, then he climbed up the waterfall. He did that so the devil couldn't see him. Mike made it to the mouth of the river, the deepest part. He swam up the river until he got back to the camp-site. Finally he made it back to the campsite. He put his gun right in front of the tent, in case the devil came. Then Mike cooked lots of fish to eat for supper. After Mike was all done eating, he threw the scraps of fish into the river. He shouldn't have done that because it attracted the devil. Mike closed his tent, and he went for a nap after supper.

After dark, the devil surprised Mike. It ripped a hole in his tent, then it grabbed him by the throat and threw him up and down on the rocks. Then the devil started tearing Mike up; it ate up his guts and left some of it on the rocks, then the devil bit Mike's head off and ate it! The devil tore his legs off, his arms, and ate the flesh and left the bones. Then it went on its business. The next day, Boy Scouts were hiking through the Moodus River. They found Mike's body, then the Boy Scouts notified the police. A half hour later, the police came and saw the mess. Junior and Lieutenant Licker were at the scene.

"Lieutenant, something is fucked up around here. Whoever or whatever is doing these murders in Moodus likes chopping off heads!" said Junior.

"I think it's some kind of unknown animal that comes out at night, killing these people. Who would brutalize a human body like this! It's got to be some animal!" said Lieutenant Licker.

About ten police cars came to the body. The police closed the park where the river was located.

CHAPTER 6

The Hunter

MAN WAS CARRYING A SHOTGUN, hunting on a beautiful afternoon in the Moodus Connecticut woods. The man came across this big black furry thing in the woods. Rays from the sun was shining on it. The man cocked his gun twice, and then he shot at it; the bullet bounced off it and went through a tree. The hunter went over to the black thing. It looked like a rock with bird feathers all over it, then the rock jumped and rolled over. The hunter ran out of the way quickly, and he watched. He stood aside, and he said to himself, "Shit! I must be seeing things or something!" The hunter left that area, and he went on his business. The hunter heard something after he left that spot. He turned around, and he saw this strange-looking animal. (The devil.) The hunter shot at the animal, and it disappeared! The hunter went on. The rays were still shining through the trees in the woods. The rays were very bright. Later the hunter found some deer in the woods. He went way out in the woods to chase the deer. He was so far out in the woods, and suddenly, a fast-moving storm was coming. The sky blackened quickly. As the hunter watched the clouds move through, it started thundering, then came the lightning. Moments later, the lightning started striking; bolts were flying all over the woods! Lightning hit a tree stump, ripping it right out of the ground and tossing it way out into the deep forest! Then the rains came down so hard. The hunter ran for cover between two big rocks to wait out the thunderstorm. The storm passed through quickly, and the sun came back out. The hunter was walking through four feet of water in the woods. He noticed a pack of trees torn out of the ground from the storm. Maybe a tornado might have gone through. The hunter just kept hunting.

The hunter came across this graveyard, and fog was forming around the graves, and he heard weird noises. The noises stopped, and a gravestone fell over, and there was a dead black cat under it. The hunter kicked the dead cat out of the way, and he saw a hole from where the stone fell over. The hunter looked inside the hole, and he heard a voice, saying, "You're next!" The hunter thought the voice was someone playing games, so he cocked his gun twice, and he looked all around him! A weird substance started boiling under where the stone fell over, then suddenly a fire started. The hunter ran back into the woods. The hunter was hearing noises in the woods, so he had his gun ready to shoot; he saw two big eyeballs looking at him in a tree. The hunter laughed and laughed, then he shot the eyeballs in the tree. He blew a hole right between the eyes. The hunter laughed! The eyeballs in the tree disappeared. That was when the hunter got a good laugh, when the eyeballs disappeared! Then the ground started moving from under him. He heard all kinds of weird noises in the woods! Something was about ready to come up from the ground. The hunter said, "*Holy shit!*" Tentacles, worms, and snakes started rising from the ground all over the place. The hunter was so scared. The things started jumping at him and grabbing him. The hunter cut the snakes away and pulled the worms off him then he ran away from them. The hunter ran as fast as he could to get away from these things. Finally the hunter made it to a road. He saw a car with no one in it, so he blew the door open with his shotgun, hotwired the car, and he took off! While the hunter was driving, he saw something moving in the woods. The hunter stopped the car because he saw a big lump moving out in the woods. He got out of the car, and he grabbed his shotgun, and he shot at the movement; the movement stopped! Rays came down from the sun, and it shined on where the movement was. The hunter walked carefully over to where the rays were shining, and the ground was bubbling because the rays were so strong! The hunter ran back to the car he was driving. He drove down the road a little, and his car overheated. There was a pail in the back of the car. The hunter went for a little walk, and he found a bridge with a brook under it to get some water.

While the car was cooling off, the hunter filled the bucket of water, and he went over to where the rays were, and he threw the water where the rays were bubbling in the ground. When the hunter threw the water on the bubbling substance, it made a pop then a loud noise. A cloud formed; the cloud turned jet-black, as the hunter watched in fright. Suddenly, the devil was right behind him. The hunter turned around, and the devil kicked him in the face. He fell, and the fog covered him over. The hunter screamed in fright! While he was screaming, he could still hear the devil roaring in the background. Finally the fog had disappeared; the hunter was still trapped in a hole. He saw the devil sneaking up from behind him. He turned around, loaded his gun, and he fired three shots into the devil; quickly the devil disappeared! Then the hunter was able to break loose and run to the car, and he made it! "I'm not wasting any more time with this animal!" he said to himself. He locked the doors and put the windows up in the car, and he sat there and waited for a while. A few minutes later, the hunter filled the radiator with water, then he drove off! The hunter was driving down the road. He saw that animal he shot earlier running across the street, so he stepped on the gas, and he rammed into it! Then he hit a tree after ramming the devil; the impact threw him out of the car about a hundred feet sky high into the air, and he landed in the trees safe. He had a few cuts and bruises, but nothing serious. The car exploded! The hunter climbed down from a tree. He was in some field. He ran over to the burning car to get his gun. He got it! Then he saw a rock in the middle of the road. The devil was inside of it! The hunter cocked his gun, and he fired several times at the devil's shell, which was a meteorite. The meteorite rolled off the road, and it rolled down a hill into a field. The hunter said, "I got that motherfucker now!" The meteorite rolled and rolled until it went way out in the woods! The hunter was running through the woods to a rocky area, and he saw a cliff that led to water. He jumped fifty feet off the cliff into the Moodus River.

How quickly the devil responded! The devil ran over to the cliff where the hunter dove off. It looked down, then it went its own business! The hunter was swimming in the lower part of the river, but he lost his gun! Before nighttime, the hunter got out of the water, and he went back into the woods. The hunter had no protection now. He lost his gun, so he'll have to fight with his bare hands! The hunter went for a nap. Ehen he woke up, he saw eyeballs looking at him from a tree, then the ground started moving. The hunter scrambled, and he ran into a fog. He didn't know what to do, so he ran in the foggy woods. He saw lightning. A storm was on the way. The devil was following him. The storm was overhead now, with strong winds, bright lightning, and loud thunder. Also, the heavy rains came. As the rain got heavier, the fog lifted. After the fog had lifted, a severe thunderstorm was in progress. The lightning flashed on and off like a disco strobe light. The rain came down in buckets! The thunder was pounding away! The hunter noticed a burned building on his travels through the deep forest every time the lightning flashed. The hunter saw a well cover near the burned building. He moved it out of the way, and there was a well that had stairs leading down. The hunter got inside the well, and he closed the cement cover over the well. It was dark in there! The hunter pulled his flashlight from his knapsack, and he went down inside the well. The well's tunnel was spooky every time the thunder outside sounded! When the hunter reached the last step on the well's ladder. He almost broke it. He shined the flashlight on the well's floor, and he saw snakes and rats running around down there.

"*Ahhhhhh!*" the hunter screamed because he almost fell. The hunter said to himself, "What the hell am I going to do with all these rats and snakes!" The hunter had a blowtorch with him in his knapsack. He grabbed and he lit the torch; you should see those rats run around like a bastard! The hunter burned away the snakes below so he could have a place to sleep, then he put up flares to keep the rats and snakes away. When the thunder sounded, you should hear those rats make noises!

In the well, there were some cement blocks. The hunter placed the cement blocks over every rat hole in the well, and there he went to sleep. The hunter opened his sleeping bag, and he got inside, and he fell right to sleep. The rats and snakes made noises all night long, but it didn't bother him one bit! The rats and snakes were afraid of the flares. The next day the hunter woke up, and he packed up his sleeping bag. You could hear the rats under the ground! Breakfast time, the hunter torched a big snake, and he ate it! Then he left the well and went on his business. The hunter was walking through the woods. It was a dark, gray day. The hunter crossed a brook that led to the river, then he kept walking, and he got to a bridge. He thought he saw the devil under the bridge, so he ran like a bat out of hell over the bridge and into the woods, then he found a road. He ran down the road that led to the river. The hunter spotted another bridge with a brook under it that led to the river. He saw human bones under that bridge. "Jesus Christ!" The hunter was frightened.

The hunter was right back where he started from—the devil's picnic area! The hunter went through the woods to the river, where he spent the rest of the day fishing. The hunter caught a lot of fish. He had plenty to eat. It was better than eating snakeskin. The hunter was worried about that animal. Was it still around? After the hunter finished fishing and eating, it was dark, so he set up a campsite under a big rock to keep dry in case a storm came. He pitched up a big tent, then he took a nap. The hunter left his fish in a bucket outside his tent. Meanwhile, the devil jumped up on the rock the hunter was camping, and it ate all his fish! The hunter heard pots and pans flying around, but he didn't hear the devil. Later in the night, the hunter got up, and he set up a tepee, the worst thing he could have done since it attracted the devil. He picked up his belongings, washed them, and he put them back in the tent. Suddenly something clawed him from behind. The hunter screamed hysterically. Then he turned around, and the devil bit his head off and ate him alive!

CHAPTER 7

Camp Indiana

A BLUE MINTY BUS WAS RIDING through town to Camp Indiana. Ed was the scoutmaster's name. He was the driver of the bus, with three or four other campers camping here for the weekend. The names of the boys were Nick, Tom, Ray, Steve, and Ed, the camp master. The five of them camped at the Moodus, Connecticut, caves. Ed drove into the camp. There was a lady at the gate. She said, "May I have your name, please?"

"My name is Mr. Ed Evans, and I have four campers with me."

"How long are you staying?" said the lady.

"I plan to stay here till Sunday, miss."

"Okay, are you staying in tents or a cottage?" said the lady.

"We have our own tents thank you," said Ed.

"Okay, it is $6 a night to camp here with a tent, so there's five altogether, right. Okay, it's $60 to stay for two nights," said the lady.

Ed paid the lady. He said, "Do we have permission to camp at caves hill too?"

"No, Camp Indiana only!" said the lady.

Before it got dark, Ed and the boys were camping way up near the Moodus Caves on a hill. The campers went out looking for wood. They heard all kinds of noises out in the woods! Ed was at the campsite, preparing for a cookout, while the campers were out getting wood. The campers came across an Indian camp.

"Nick, look at this!" said Tom.

"It's an Indian camp!" said Ray.

The boys were taking a long time getting wood, so Ed went looking for them, and he caught up with them. "Hey, boys, don't go in there! It's an Indian camp, they'll chase us out. Let's get back to the campsite before it gets too dark!" said Ed.

"They won't bother us, Ed, let's go!" said Steve.

"Okay, let's stay on the trails," said Ed.

The campers went higher up in the woods and found the Indian camp. The Indians were cooking a big pig! One of the Indians ran down the hill and said, "Are you lost?"

"No, sir, we're just camping down the hill a little ways. We just came up here to see what's here. We're staying in Camp Indiana for the weekend," said Ed.

"Why don't you come and join us, we're cooking a pig!" said the Indian.

The Indians were talking mostly to themselves. They were talking about possessions of the devil. The Indian that invited Ed and the boys to eat with them said to Ed, "Beware of the devil, the devil lives in these caves!" Ed laughed. The Indian said, "Seriously, you will hear strange noises and see weird things here at camp Indiana. We believe the devil lives under the ground in Moodus, Connecticut. This town has been spooked for years, and the Indians are the only ones that know about the devil. The spooky noise has been here for over two hundred years. This town has been possessed then, and it still is now! You will see the ground move sometimes and see weird colors of fog forming. If you don't believe the Indians, you'll find out for yourself."

"What kind of drugs do you people have, can we have some?" Ed joked.

"Believe the most powerful Indians! You will hear trains, trucks, or thunder on a sunny day! Popping sounds and you will see the earth move!" said the Indian. Then all the Indians said, "The devil lives here!"

"Bullshit!" said Ed.

All the Indians laughed and laughed.

"It was a nice meal. Come down and visit us sometime, and thank you," said Ed.

"It was a pleasure!" said the Indians. Ed and the rest of the campers walked to their campsite very quietly; they seemed interested with their stories.

"Ed, I really believe in the Indians. Their stories are true, they don't tell tales!" said Tom.

"We'll see what happens," said Ed. It was getting dark, and a storm was coming. The campers made it back to their tents before the storm hit. Ed was giving the boys instructions before they went to bed. "Boys, if you need to go to the bathroom, it's up on the hill in a cabin about a hundred feet," said Ed.

Bedtime, at midnight, the storm outside was bad. The rain was really coming down. Ed got up, and he grabbed his umbrella, and he put his shoes on, and he went up to the restrooms in the woods. Ed was walking toward the restrooms in the foggy woods. The lightning flashed, and he saw a strange-looking animal way out in the woods. He caught it in the corner of his eye. He went back to his tent and grabbed his gun, then he went back out into the woods to the restrooms. While Ed was on his way to the restrooms, he kept getting shocks every time the lightning flashed.

"Ouch! Ouch! Ouch! You son of a bitch!" Ed was screaming when he kept getting shocks from the lightning. The thunder was so loud Ed was getting scared. Lightning bolts started hitting everywhere! Ed thought he saw something in the lightning, so he stopped and hid near a tree. The lightning flashed six times after that. He then saw that animal again! Ed made it to the restrooms alive. He did what he had to do, then he waited awhile.

Ed waited out the storm until it was all over, then the woods began to get foggy. Ed walked back to where he was staying, walking through the foggy woods. Suddenly he saw a bright light coming from the sky, and it nearly blinded him, then something came out of the woods and whacked him. Quickly the devil got him by surprise. The next day, the devil had attacked Ed, the camp master! Early in the morning, one of the campers got up to go to the restrooms out in the woods. He saw Ed all cut up and lying in a pool of blood out near the restrooms. Nick was the camper who saw him. He was hysterical. Nick grabbed Ed's gun, and he brought it back to the tent. Nick said, "Tom, Ray, and Steve! Get up, pack our stuff, and we're getting the hell out of here! Ed is Dead!" he cried.

Tom said, "What!"

"Ray and Steve, why don't you pack up all the gear, take down the tents, and put everything together, while Tom and I go over to the Indian camp," said Nick in a crying voice.

Nick and Tom went up to the Indians. The chief of the Indians saw them first, and he said, "Can we help you?"

"Yes, you sure may! What the hell is going on here? Ed, our camp master, is dead!" Tom cried.

"We have nothing to do with this buddy!" said the Indian chief.

"Bullshit!" said Tom.

"Don't you people know the devil might have something to do with him!" said the Indian chief.

Tom punched the Indian chief in the face, and he said, "Fuck off!" Then Torn kicked the Indian chief in the groin, and he punched the Indian chief in the face again, then he and Nick went back to their campsite to meet Ray and Steve. Earlier, Ray and Steve got help after they packed everything up ready to go. The police was there when Tom and Nick got back from the Indian camp.

Tom said to the police, "Officers, Ed, our camp master, was murdered up near the restrooms!"

"I have the report. A bear must have grabbed him!" said the police.

While Tom was talking to the police, Nick gave Ray and Steve a ride back home, then he returned to the camp. The police, Tom, and Nick searched the area. "Officers, I didn't know we have bears in the woods in Connecticut!" said Tom.

"We don't usually, but lately we've had reports of bears around here!" said the police. The police escorted Tom and Nick to their cars and asked them to leave the campground. Other police came in to check the area for any possible foul play. The police checked the log cabins in the camp; those were messed up!

Steve's Dream
The Orange Sand in Camp Indiana

Two weeks later, Nick, Ray, Tom, and Steve came back to Camp Indiana. They checked into log cabins this time. The log cabins had a private bath outside. The four boys camped here for vacation. The first day, everyone went to the caves to explore them. Nighttime, everyone was in bed. The devil's powers took over in this part of the story. Every one of these boys has a dream each night. Tonight was Steve's dream. Steve dreamed about the orange sand. Everyone was now camping in the caves now instead of log cabins! The four campers dug a hole and removed a stone in the Moodus Cave, and they were on their way to hell!

Nick said, "Tom, come here and look at this sand. It's red!" Tom grabbed a shovel, and he started digging. Tom dug a three-foot hole in the cave, and he fell in.

"Tom, are you all right?!" said Nick.

"I'm fine, come on down," he said.

Nick, Ray, and Steve jumped into the hole Tom dug. Ray said, "Look, a tunnel full of colors!" The four of them went through the tunnel of light, and it was cold in there. The four campers went exploring for an hour; they dug deeper and deeper.

"Hey, maybe we'll find some gold down here!" Steve laughed. The campers had knapsacks, knives, guns, plenty of food and extra tents, etc. The boys pitched up a big tent and slept in a tunnel for the night. The police closed the caves at 6:00 p.m. and reopened them by 9:00 a.m. The boys are locked in the caves. The caves were mostly for tourist people to go through, not for the public. The campers were locked in the cave, and the police never knew they were in there! From Friday afternoon, the campers followed the tunnel almost to the ice caves. The temperature was only thirty-five degrees. They were five hundred feet over the ice caves. The campers spent sixteen hours trying to find the ice caves. It was 4:00 a.m. before the boys finally crashed— to go to sleep, they had only a short ways to go.

"It's 11:00 a.m. Let's get on the move!" said Steve.

Nick was in charge. "Steve, let me take charge, I know all about climbing mountains, caves, trees, etc. My father taught me. It's a long winter down here, boys, so let's get on the move!" said Nick. The campers had breakfast first, then they were on their way!

The boys had their winter jackets on to keep warm. The boys had another big tent and plenty of camping gear to go on. Off the campers went, to the middle of the earth. By 6:00 p.m., the campers hit the center of the ice caves. There was nothing but ice crystals all around them. The temperature dropped fifteen degrees the farther they went down! It was negative fifteen degrees, Nick showed on his navy compass. The campers went down, down, and down! The ice was turning colors. The campers climbed the ice downward for about two hours, heading out of the ice caves. Nick looked at his navy compass. The temperature was twenty-two degrees, and he said, "It's getting warmer, and we're on our way to hell. Let's go!"

The colorful ice crystals were beautiful! Finally the boys were out of the ice caves about midnight. The campers ended up in a giant cave. There was a lake with hundreds of waterfalls flowing into it. Fog formed around most of the lake because the water was so cold. The campers kept going to their new world, where they saw the most beautiful rainbow ever. Then it was 2:30 a.m. on Sunday.

"Okay, gang, we're in the most beautiful part of the earth. Then we'll head to hell," said Nick.

"Nick, look over here!" said Steve. The boys read a sign: "38-hour walk to hell!"

"Okay, boys, we have thirty-eight more hours before we reach hell. Some us will make it there, some of us my not, it all depends on you, so let's take it easy for the rest of the night. Grab some steak, chicken, bread, or whatever you want to drink, and get some rest after, because we only have a week to see the orange sand," said Nick.

Then the campers were on their way to hell.

"We have almost thirteen hours to get to the devil's landmark," said Ray.

"How do you know, Ray?" said Nick.

"Because I saw a sign that said thirteen hours from the devil's landmark."

At 4:00 a.m., the boys set up tents and went to sleep. At 12:00 p.m. Sunday, the boys were ready to head for the devil's map. By 4:00 p.m. Sunday, the campers were miles under the earth, way past the ice caves and heading for hell! The temperature had warmed up to seventy degrees. The campers kept going down, and all they saw were rocks and waterfalls. They went swimming. The water was crystal clear! By 7:00 a.m. Monday, the temperature was already over one hundred degrees. It was so hot!

"I don't think we're going to make the orange sand. It's too fuckin' hot!" said Steve.

"Steve, we're six hours from hell, just six hours! If it gets too much hotter, we'll swim it out! It's hot down here, but the water is ice-cold! We'll make it, Steve, don't worry!" said Nick.

The campers dove into the cold waters and swam down waterfalls; they had a hell of a time! By 9:00 a.m. the temperature was one hundred thirty degrees in the caves near hell!

The campers took a rest at the bottom of the waterfall, then they went on. The boys swam for over fourteen hours straight before they stopped to eat and rest. It was 3:00 a.m. Wednesday.

"Okay, we're two miles from the devil's base station. Now let's swim to hell!" said Nick. Nick looked at his navy compass, leading the way, saying, "Boys, it is one hundred sixty-six degrees. Keep in the water because you'll burn if you don't! The water temp is eighty-three degrees. Stay in the water! We're heading west, to the devil," said Nick. They were finally five minutes from hell. The cave temperature rose to a steamy one hundred eighty, and the water temperature was ninety according to Nick's navy compass. Finally they were in hell, swimming in about thirty feet deep of water. You could see the crystal orange sand under the beautiful clear water at the devil's base stations floor as the campers swam into beautiful hell! Sparks of fire began to form in the cave, flaring off the stoned cave, showing orange crystals of the magic sand on the rocks. The campers swam to a cliff about one thousand feet below. You could see the real orange sand.

Nick said, "Boys, this is too nice of a place for the devil to live. Jesus, it's a palace! Let's go for the lake below and get closer to the great orange sand gang!"

The campers spent three hours climbing down the cliff leading to the real thing. The orange sand! Nick was the first one to dive in the devil's path, the water over the orange sand! A water spout formed and sucked Nick below the surface down under the orange sand. The last words Nick said were "This water is nice!" Then the water twister took him away. The other campers screamed and cried.

Tom said, "Let's go, boys, we're going back."

The three campers that left had fire suits on, and they climbed the walls of hell for fifteen hours straight until the cave got cooler. Steve had a navy compass on. The temperature dropped sixty-five degrees from one hundred eighty in hell to one hundred fifteen in the hot cave. The boys were so tired they had to crash there! It was 9:00 a.m. Friday before the campers started hiking again. By 10:00 p.m. Friday, the three campers were halfway between hell and the ice caves, where they crashed, ate, partied for two hours, then they went to sleep in the rocks; the temperature was down to eighty-five degrees.

At 10:00 a.m. Sunday, the boys woke up and had breakfast. It was going to be a scary trip back, the boys were thinking. By 11:00 a.m., Tom, Ray, and Steve were on their way!

"Let's not talk, let's climb and climb!" said Tom. The three campers enjoyed beautiful scenery heading up toward the ice caves. They spent fifteen hours climbing. The caves were quite cold. They were about five miles under the ice caves. The temperature was thirty-eight degrees before they crashed for more sleep. It was 2:00 a.m. Monday. By 11:00 a.m. Monday, the boys had something to eat, then they were on their way for another hike. The campers left at noontime; they lost track of the compass, and they were nine miles away. The cave warmed to fifty-seven degrees. Snakes, rats, and strange wild animals were running around. The campers were in fright!

"Listen, we have to go north, straight up to get to the ice caves gang," said Tom. By 3:00 p.m. the temperature was down to thirty-two degrees. "Okay, boys, we reached the ice caves. See it up ahead, put your ice cleats on, and start climbing!" said Tom. The boys had to climb nothing but frozen rock and ice caves for about thirty hours straight. The boys climbed for six hours. Tom slipped and he fell through the ice tunnel.

"Help me, I'm slipping! Ahhhhhhh!" Goodbye, Tom.

"Oh my god! Tom is gone!" Steve cried.

Ray was ready to pass out because he watched Tom fall through the ice caves. He said, "I don't think I'm going to make it, Steve!"

"Ray, don't think like that, or you won't make it. Just try, we'll make it!" said Steve.

Finally twenty-four hours later, Steve and Ray made it to the frozen mountain at the end of the ice caves. It was 9:00 p.m. Tuesday. Ray set up a big weather tent with a heater in it, and the two boys got something to eat, then they crashed for fifteen hours of sleep. They were so tired. By noon Wednesday, it was time to go on.

"Hey, Steve, the sea level surface is only thirty-eight miles north, the rock says here!" said Ray.

"That's not bad. Another twelve or fourteen hours, we'll be home," said Steve.

By midnight Wednesday, Ray and Steve were only three miles from sea level. Shortly the devil grabbed Ray and took him away.

"Steve, help! Steve, help!" Ray hollered.

When Steve turned around, Ray was gone. "Holy shit! Ray's gone, I hope I'll make it!" Steve cried. Steve crawled through a rock, and he had to swim away to the hole he dug, then the devil grabbed him and pulled him under the water.

Steve broke loose under the water because the devil only got his shoe, and he managed to climb up through the hole he dug in the Moodus Caves, then he put a big stone to cover the hole so the devil couldn't get through. It was 3:00 a.m. Thursday. He had to wait until nine for police to open the gates. Steve saw orange glows flying around the caves during the night, then he saw orange sand on the ground, then he heard the devil roar. Then he woke up. Steve was lying in bed in the log cabin, saying, "The orange sand was only a dream!" Steve told Nick, Tom, and Ray his dream, and they laughed and laughed. Steve was sleeping for a few hours, while the other three campers were getting wood to build a weeklong campfire for their vacation at Camp Indiana. Later the campers went in the caves with shovels and dug a hole about an hour and a half before the cave closed.

Nick said, "Steve, we're gonna make your dream come true right now!" The other campers laughed hysterically. Nick and Steve had shovels, and they dug a hole about five feet deep.

A policeman walking by surprised them, and he said, "What the hell are you two doing?"

"Tom is a wiseass" he said. "We're digging a hole to hell to find all my friends in Steve's dream!"

"Well, you boys come with me, we're going to the police station. You are under arrest!" said the policeman. After the boys got in trouble with the police, they went back to the camp.

For a week, nothing had happened in Camp Indiana. All of a sudden, on the last day, the Indian chief saw weird colors and strange glows coming from the caves, so he went to the caves with a blowtorch, and he burned a hole in the bars to get in the caves. Midnight on a Saturday night and a full moon, the Indian chief was in the cave doing powerful formations with his hands to find out if there was really a devil. The Indian heard weird sounds in the cave. He knew those sounds, so he lit a torch. The devil tried to grab him from under the ground. The Indian torched the devil's movement. Suddenly the Indian chief heard the devil. He jumped from rock to rock with his blowing torch! Then he saw the animal in the cave. The Indian chief was ready to fight the animal. He didn't know that this animal was the devil!

The devil with its bright eyes, strong rays came out of the devil's eyes. The Indian chief had trouble functioning. Suddenly the devil grabbed his foot again and clawed his leg. The Indian chief burned the devil claw with his torch, and then he jumped into the water, and he swam from rock to rock. The Indian chief swam away from the devil to nurse his injured leg. Minutes later, a rat bit the Indian chief's neck. A second rat took a chunk out of his shoulder. The Indian chief was in shock, while the rats were eating him up slowly. The Indian chief was suffering and screaming hysterically. A giant rat grabbed the Indian chief by the arm and dragged him. Three more big rats, monster rats, were biting the Indian chief alive! The rats started ripping the Indian apart, by eating at his chest, pulling his guts right out of him, and eating his flesh and slopping up his guts! Then the devil plunged into the action to really finish him off. There was nothing left but bones and lakes of blood. The devil started sucking up the thick Indian's blood and eating its bones. Then a bat flew into the cave, and it bit the devil in the face. The devil grabbed the bat and smashed it up against a rock, and it ate that for breakfast too.

Daybreak, the police came to open the caves' gates. The cop saw a hole burned in one of them, through the bars. Then the police found human bones and saw blood. The policeman wrote a report on possible animal bites. The following Sunday, a bunch of crying Indians had a funeral in front of the cave for the chief Indian. Then the police closed the caves for a week to investigate what happened. The police searched the camp and put up signs, "Beware of wild animals."

Tom had a dream the devil choked him to death one night. Steve had his long dream, the orange sand. Nick had a dream that the Indian chief tortured him by burning him alive. Finally, Ray had a dream that he was possessed by the devil, and he did everything wrong all the time. Ed, the camp master, was killed by the devil.

CHAPTER 8

Caves Hill House

AVES HILL HOUSE WAS A boarding house for girls. Mrs. Chaimber was in charge of nine girls. Karen, Stacy, Everlyn, Robin, Chris, Joy, Machelle, Carolyn, and Betsy. It was a weekend and a full moon. Mrs. Chaimber gathered all the girls together; they all got off the bus in line to get their clothes and got settled in their new home, with Mrs. Chaimber, a very nice lady. (This house was possessed!) The house had been vacant for years. The bus left. All the girls had their suitcases, and Mrs. Chaimber showed them to their rooms.

"Okay, girls, let's get together and gather around the campfire outside," said Mrs. Chaimber. Mrs. Chaimber inspected the nine girls before she spoke. "Okay, girls, my name is Mrs. Chaimber, and I am your group leader. This house is ours for the rest of the summer. It's a nice house. It doesn't look it from the outside, but the inside is nice. This house has been renovated, and it looks pretty new inside. Years ago, the cavemen use to board this house. They believed this house was possessed by the devil, but we don't have to worry about that because there's no such thing as the devil. We have to live here because it's the only house in this area I could find, and we'll be safe here, I promise you!"

GROUND OF THE DEVIL

The girls had a big dinner around the campfire, some wine, and a few laughs for most of the night. These girls were runaway girls. The girls were having a great time.

"I'm going to bed now, Mrs. Chaimber," said Stacy.

"Do you know where to go?" said Mrs. Chaimber.

"Yes, upstairs," Stacy said.

Stacy was walking down a spooky hallway on her way to bed. She saw something shining very brightly straight ahead. Stacy looked out the window. The rays disappeared, then she went to bed.

Awooooooo!

"What in the world is that?" said Karen.

"Okay, girls, let's get inside now," said Mrs. Chaimber.

"Mrs. Chaimber, what is that noise?" said Karen.

"I don't know, and I don't want to find out, so let's get inside!" said Mrs. Chaimber.

The girls were frightened about the noise.

Awooooo!

"There it is again!" Karen cried.

Awoooooo!

"It must be someone playing games," said Mrs. Chaimber. Tracy got up out of bed, spooked out from hearing that noise. She walked around the spooky hall upstairs.

Awooooo!

"It sounds like there's a wolf out there!" said Everlyn. Mrs. Chaimber got all the girls in the house, and she locked all the doors.

"Stacy, where are you?" said Mrs. Chaimber.

"I'm upstairs, Mrs. Chaimber," she said.

"Okay, I just wondered," said Mrs. Chaimber.

Stacy opened the window upstairs in the spooky hallway, and a gust of wind came in and blew leaves in the house all over the place. Then Stacy went to the window, and she looked out up at the moon. The moon started changing colors. Stacy was on drugs, and she had some with her. Stacy popped a couple of uppers! And she looked out the window up at the moon, then she began laughing. The colors she was seeing were all in her mind. Stacy started staggering and laughing hysterically. She was feeling good!

105

"Stacy, what are you doing?" said Mrs. Chaimber.

"I'm looking at the moon outside," she said.

"Why don't you come downstairs and join me with a glass of wine?" said Mrs. Chaimber.

"Okay, I'll be right down," she said. Stacy washed her face, and she went downstairs for some wine. Then later, Stacy took some wine upstairs with her. She went to the window in the spooky hall to watch the moon again. She started laughing again, then the moon disappeared, and a storm was coming. Suddenly she couldn't see the moon anymore. Stacy was drinking her wine, then she heard a noise, then she heard thunder. Stacy was scared of thunderstorms. She watched the trees blow in the wind. The wind got stronger, then she saw a bright flash of lightning, then the trees were moving very fast in the wind. Stacy screamed hysterically when she saw the lightning! Stacy ran downstairs and jumped into Mrs. Chaimber's arms. Mrs. Chaimber held her until she stopped crying. Then Stacy went in another room to get drunk with the other girls.

It was late at night, and all the girls went to bed. Mrs. Chaimber was up most of the night, drinking her wine. She heard all kinds of howling noises throughout the night. Then she finally went to bed. Mrs. Chaimber was scared. She waited until sunrise before she went to bed. Mrs. Chaimber wasn't sleeping very long. She heard *crack, crank, snap,* etc. She got up, and she looked out of the spooky hall window, and she saw some weird animal eating parts of a tree, and it had a long tail rapped around another tree, then the animal took off! It happen so fast. First you see the animal, now you don't. Just like that! The animal howled once after it disappeared. "Oh my good God!" Mrs. Chaimber cried. Mrs. Chaimber went through the whole house to make sure all the windows were closed and the doors were locked before she went to bed; she did it twice, to double check.

The next day was bright and sunny. One of the girls got up, and she went for a long walk out in the woods. She tried to wake up Mrs. Chaimber to tell her she was going for a walk, but she couldn't wake her, so she went outside on her own. The sun was shining brightly through the trees as she walked through the woods. The girl looked down at her shadow; her shadow got bigger and bigger! The girl noticed a tail-shaped thing in the woods, so she kicked it. The tail backfired and grabbed her, and it started pulling her into the ground. She screamed and screamed and screamed! She was too far out in the woods for anyone to hear her scream. The devil got her!

Mrs. Chaimber had a big head this morning from drinking her wine last night, so the girls got up to fix their own breakfast. The girls noticed Stacy was missing! Finally Mrs. Chaimber got up, and the girls were downstairs eating. "Good morning, Mrs. Chaimber!" said the girls.

"Good morning, girls!" she said.

"Where's Stacy?" said Karen.

Mrs. Chaimber yelled, "Stacy! Stacy! Stacy! Stacy, where are you?" There was no answer. "Girls, stay right here, I'm going in the house to look for Stacy," said Mrs. Chaimber. Mrs. Chaimber went in the house, looking for Stacy. She looked throughout the house, and she couldn't find her! "Okay, girls, Stacy is not here. We have to find her!" Mrs. Chaimber cried. The girls and Mrs. Chaimber searched the woods for two hours and still couldn't find Stacy. Finally Mrs. Chaimber called the police.

The police came, and they searched for Stacy and couldn't find her either. Mrs. Chaimber was telling the police about the girls, while helicopters were flying around looking for Stacy.

"Officer, we have a serious problem. Stacy has been missing since early this morning. I saw this strange-looking animal about five o' clock this morning eating a tree, and it had a long tail wrapped around another tree. Then all of a sudden, it made a noise, and it disappeared just like that! I saw the animal, then I don't know, I was so scared," Mrs. Chaimber said.

"What did this animal look like?" said the policeman.

"It looked like a bear with horns on it, and it had a very long tail. It also had pointy fur!" said Mrs. Chaimber.

"It could have been a cactus horse. It's a very rare breed, and it might be a dangerous animal, I don't know anything about them," said the policeman.

"Officer, what the hell is a cactus horse?" said Mrs. Chaimber.

"What I suggest is you to stay away from this animal. If you see it run and hide, try to get to a phone and call the police and tell us where it's at, and we'll come over and kill it!" said the policeman.

"One problem, Officer, if I sent my boarding girls out to find Stacy, how are they going to react if they see this animal!?" said Mrs. Chaimber.

"Well, tell the girls it's a bear, and walk away from it and try to hide or get away. Don't run, because you might excite the animal, and it may come after you! Just get away from it. Secondly, a cactus horse only comes out between dusk and dawn, the animal usually comes out at night," said the policeman.

"Officer, suppose it's not a cactus horse?" said Mrs. Chaimber.

"Mrs. Chaimber, I told you it might be a cactus horse, but it may not be. I'm just saying, it looks like one! Maybe it could be the devil!" the policeman joked. Mrs. Chaimber laughed. "Mrs. Chaimber, if you're gonna go out at night, I would suggest you have people with you until this thing is captured," said the policeman.

"Officer, would it be safe to send my girls out looking for Stacy in the woods during the daytime?" said Mrs. Chaimber.

"I can't see why not. To be on the safe side, maybe you better go with them!" said the policeman.

"Before you go, Officer, this animal also howls like a wolf!"

"It sounds like it maybe a cactus horse. Just stay away from it, and if you see this animal, get to a phone as fast as you can and call us!" said the policeman, then he got in his car and left the area.

The Moodus Police was riding around town, putting up warning signs alerting of an unknown animal roaming around town. (It was the devil!) It was late afternoon, and Mrs. Chaimber gathered all the girls around the campfire, and she said, "Girls, the police is warning the town of Moodus a curfew from dusk to dawn. That means no one goes outside between sunset and sunrise. We have to be in the house by seven thirty this evening, because by eight thirty, it's dark outside! We have this warning because a strange, unknown animal has been running around here at night, so let's eat fast and get inside before it gets dark. Now tomorrow morning at seven o'clock sharp, we're going out to look for Stacy. The National Guard and the Moodus Police will try to find her during the night!"

"Mrs. Chaimber, will the animal come in the house?" said Everlyn.

"I hope not!" she said.

The girls had a big dinner and talked about this animal, then they went in the house just before it got dark. By 8:00 p.m., the sun was going down. The town looked like a ghost town all right. There were no cars on the road at sunset! The girls were in the house, getting ready to have a party. Mrs. Chaimber was searching the house again to see if Stacy may have come back. No Stacy, but she found Stacy's necklace in the spooky hallway. She called for her out in the woods two or three times, but there was no answer, so she gave up. The girls wondered and blamed the animal for getting Stacy.

The Caves Hill House was located on top of a mountain, directly over the Moodus Caves. It got pretty chilly up there even in the summertime. It was early May when the house was rented out. The girls and Mrs. Chaimber were enjoying a late-night snack, finishing the rest of the food left over from the cookout and drinking wine and beer and enjoying a warm, cozy fireplace. Suddenly the fire in the fireplace turned green!

"Mrs. Chaimber, look at the wood, it's green!" said Carolyn.

Mrs. Chaimber laughed, and she said, "That's funny, maybe it's the wood, the way it's burning!"

Then the fireplace exploded. The fire burned out of control and started burning the walls!

"Girls, get back!" Mrs. Chaimber screamed. "Let's get some buckets of water quick!" Mrs. Chaimber got trash barrels from the cellar. She filled them with water, and she put the fire out fast. Then a little while later, the fire came back in the fireplace, the same color, green! Then Mrs. Chaimber threw another bucket on the fire to put it out for good. One of the girls turned the TV on, and the TV blew up.

Midnight, the girls were in bed. Mrs. Chaimber fell asleep downstairs. The fire relit itself in the fireplace. Mrs. Chaimber woke up, and she saw a red-and-green flame burning in the fireplace. "I don't believe this!" Mrs. Chaimber said to herself. She got up to turn the light on, and there were no lights! Mrs. Chaimber grabbed a flashlight, and she went downstairs in the basement to look for the circuit breakers. When she found them, she flipped the switch a little, and the lights came back on. Meanwhile the fire kept relighting in the fireplace. The girls kept throwing buckets of water on it to put it out upstairs! Finally the flame disappeared. Every time the fireplace smoldered, the girls threw water on it.

Mrs. Chaimber searched the basement with a stick. She saw nothing unusual, then she went upstairs to bed. Mrs. Chaimber was in bed sleeping. She had a dream about her husband, who was in the Navy, and he was out at sea. In her dream, her husband had been out to sea for ten years! One day he came home. He didn't look the same. His face was red, and he looked as if he was turning into the devil, and he started breaking everything in the house! Then horns popped out of his head, his face turned gory, and his clothes started ripping off him like it would on a werewolf! While Mrs. Chaimber was having her nightmare, a great big bang that woke her out of a sound sleep ended it. She was screaming for a minute. The loud bang was thunder, and she saw lightning flashing through the windows in the Caves Hill House. She still didn't know where she was! She got up to put the lamp on. No lights again. Mrs. Chaimber went downstairs in the basement to flip the circuit breaker back on, and she saw sparks flying out of the electrical box. The lights blinked on and off a few times, then the lights finally came back on. Mrs. Chaimber looked around the basement again, and she saw a hole in the wall she didn't see before, then she heard rocks crumbling inside the walls. She heard thunder sounding very loudly in the basement, then she went upstairs with her stick.

After Mrs. Chaimber went upstairs, a big rock flew out of that hole Mrs. Chaimber saw, and it landed in the basement. Mrs. Chaimber was in the kitchen, listening to strange noises; she looked out the kitchen window, and all she could see was rain pouring out there. Water came pouring in that hole in the basement in their broken wall. When Mrs. Chaimber was on her way back to bed, she saw a bolt of lightning, followed by a big crash of thunder. Then the cellar door blew open, and Mrs. Chaimber screamed, then she went back downstairs to find out what the noise was. Mrs. Chaimber grabbed her flashlight, and she looked down the cellar; it was flooded down there. Mrs. Chaimber said to herself, "Oh my god, the cellar is flooded!" Mrs. Chaimber went upstairs, and she grabbed the basement door from swinging, then she bolted it shut.

Once in a while the devil got in the broken hole in the wall; no one ever knew about it! It was just before lam. There was a very bad thunderstorm going on outside; the thunder was pounding away, and the lightning was flashing constantly. While the wind was blowing hard outside, Mrs. Chaimber heard a howling noise downstairs. Mrs. Chaimber ran upstairs to bed like a bat out of hell After Mrs. Chaimber fell asleep, the dining room floor was breaking up, and the paint was peeling off the walls. The kitchen cabinets were beginning to fall off, with the winds outside so bad. A loud bang woke Mrs. Chaimber up again. She heard a noise in the bedroom closet. She got up to investigate the noise in the closet. It was a bowling ball rocking on the floor. She picked up the bowling ball, and she put it on some clothes so it wouldn't make noise during the night. She found a blanket to wrap the bowling ball in, then she went back to bed! Girls were awakened by a howling noise coming through the fireplace downstairs in the living room!

The howling noises got worse and worse. The girls woke up screaming and crying. There was a tornado-like storm outside moving through the area. The winds were so strong it blew the windows out in the Caves Hill House. The kitchen cabinets fell and broke, then the front door blew through. The refrigerator moved, and it tipped over on its side, and all the food fell out of it all over the kitchen floor. All the furniture was moving around in the house like the exorcist. The closet door blew open in Mrs. Chaimber's bedroom, and the bowling ball came rolling out of the closet, and it went rolling down the stairs. It bounced off the bottom step and went smashing through a wall, then it rolled out of the wall it went through, and it rolled outside into the woods, and it caught fire! A big tree broke off, and it went smashing through the window in Mrs. Chaimber's bedroom. She woke up screaming hysterically, then the girls woke up screaming. All the windows in the house were busted; the wind was sucking the bedclothes off the bed and out the window.

It was 3:00 a.m. and the storm was getting worse. The wind was blowing well over one hundred miles per hour. Mrs. Chaimber ran downstairs when the tree came in her bedroom, then after she left, the wind pushed the entire tree into Mrs. Chaimber's bedroom, and part of the tree chased Mrs. Chaimber down the stairs. Mrs. Chaimber grabbed the railings as she watched the tree coming down the stairs. The branches were even moving strangely on the tree. Mrs. Chaimber was horrified! A bolt of lightning smashed the window in Everlyn's room, and the strong winds sucked her out of her bed and out of the house.

The rest of the girls were upstairs, screaming in their bedrooms, holding on to something so the storm won't take them away. They were screaming, "*Mrs. Chaimber, help!*" The big tree was in the girls' way. They couldn't get downstairs.

Mrs. Chaimber yelled, "Girls, hang on to something up there!" Mrs. Chaimber was hanging on to a post at the bottom of the stairs to avoid getting sucked out of the house. The girls were screaming in fright, watching the branches move on the tree that came in the window in Mrs. Chaimber's bedroom.

Bats began flying around the house, biting all the girls; the girls screamed and cried hysterically, swatting the bats away. A funnel cloud took Everlyn away, no one knew where. The wind was so bad it was coming in the house, breaking things! Then the wind started to die down. Mrs. Chaimber said, "Where's Everlyn?" No one answered. Mrs. Chaimber was able to get the girls to hang on tight. Then when the winds died down, Mrs. Chaimber told all the girls to be in the basement.

The next day was a sunny day. Mrs. Chaimber was looking for Everlyn. "Everlyn! Everlyn! Everlyn!" She couldn't find her. She went upstairs and looked for her. She still couldn't find her. Mrs. Chaimber went downstairs, and she said, "Is Everlyn down here?" The next day was a bright and sunny day. The girls and Mrs. Chaimber went looking for Everlyn and Stacy. But before anyone dressed up, Mrs. Chaimber checked the girls for bats or rat bites from last night's horror! Some of the girls were bitten, but not bad. "Mrs. Chaimber, I think Everlyn might have taken off, because she told me last night's storm frightened her too much, and she didn't like the looks of this house!" said Betsy.

"I would say so too, Betsy. I think we had a tornado last night, the way this house looks. I was hanging for my life!" said Mrs. Chaimber. Mrs. Chaimber called the police, while the girls were getting ready for church.

"Mrs. Chaimber, do you think Stacy and Everlyn might have gone to the office?" said Betsy.

"Maybe, that's possible," said Mrs. Chaimber.

Sunday morning, the lights were working. The big tree was stuck on the stairway. The windows and doors were blown through. Dead bats were lying all over the place, from when part of the roof was blown off the house. The house was a mess. Mrs. Chaimber had all the girls dressed, and herself, for church when the police came.

Mrs. Chaimber was outside, and the police car drove next to her, and the cop said, "Are you the lady who called the police?" said the policeman.

"Yes, sir. My name is Mrs. Chaimber. Last night we had a terrible storm. The wind was so bad it blew all the windows out of this house, and a tree came in my bedroom and in the house, the front door, look! It's busted right through. Look at the furniture, the shingles, all the windows. This house is a mess!" said Mrs. Chaimber.

"Mrs. Chabba, do you own this house?" said the cop.

"Number one, my name is Mrs. Chaimber. C-h-a-i-m-b-e-r, not Chabba. I'm the boarding lady here, I take care of nine girls. Two are missing, I don't know if they're dead or left Caves Hill House!" said Mrs. Chaimber.

"Mrs. Chaimber, I'm sorry I said your name wrong. My name is Officer Chief Junior, from the Moodus Police Department," said Junior.

"No shit, Junior. What happened here last night!" Mrs. Chaimber joked.

"We had reports of tornadoes in last night's thunderstorms with 140-mile-an-hour winds. I think you're doing pretty well compared to what most of Moodus went through. Several people are reported missing this morning. I'm surprised your house is still standing. Take a ride later on over to the west end of town, all the foundations were ripped out of the ground! You're not the only ones suffering. The whole town is in bad shape. This is the worst storm we ever had since I've been in Moodus. In fact, I don't think Moodus has ever had a tornado before!" said Junior.

"Officer, I have two girls missing. Their names are Everlyn Nimp and Stacy Like, as in, 'I *like* you.' Stacy disappeared yesterday, and Everlyn has been missing since last night's storm. Now Everlyn said to one of the girls she thinks that Caves Hill is haunted, and she wanted to leave. If she did, she did, but maybe the storm could have taken her away, or I don't know, because everyone was here last night but Stacy!" said Mrs. Chaimber.

"Okay, Mrs. Chaimber, we'll find the missing!" said Junior.

At 7:30 a.m., the bus came to pick up the girls and bring them to church. Mrs. Chaimber told the bus driver about last night's horror on the way to church.

Mrs. Chaimber and a bunch of angry girls were in church this morning.

"Good morning, welcome to St. Ray's Church in Haddam, Connecticut, overlooking the Connecticut River. My name is Father Shawn, and this Mass is to bless the people living in Moodus, Connecticut, this morning, where tornadoes blew people out of their homes from last night's storms. How come Moodus gets these vicious storms, and we never get touched! The town of Moodus has been possessed by the devil for years. The devil's powers always seem to take over! We ask the Holy Almighty Jesus Christ in heaven to help that poor town and take out all the horrors!" said the priest.

Mrs. Chaimber and the seven girls left the church crying very loudly. The priest continued on with the Mass.

"Please stand for the confession of faith. We confess to Almighty God and to you my brothers and sisters and to the blessed Virgin to pray for me and to the Almighty God, pray for us. We pray for the possessed and the murderers in that town lately. Let us pray to the Lord," said the priest.

"Lord, hear our prayers."

"We pray for a girl missing from Caves Hill House yesterday. Let us pray to the Lord," said Father Shawn.

After church, the bus took the girls back to Caves Hill House. Mrs. Chaimber met with more police coming home from Mass. The cop said, "Mrs. Chaimber, Everlyn Nimp and Stacy Like are nowhere to be found. They're not in the caves either. I'll report them missing."

"Jesus Christ, that's all I need, goddamn. It'll be okay, girls, get your belongings, what's left of it, and put it on the bus. We're getting the hell out of here. By 3:00 p.m. if we don't find the two missing girls, we're gonna leave without them!" said Mrs. Chaimber.

Mrs. Chaimber and the seven girls left, and the police looked all over and couldn't find Everlyn or Stacy. Mrs. Chaimber spotted a burning black rock in the woods. It looked like a meteorite! The girls ran over to help Mrs. Chaimber push the rock into the water. The girls used sticks to remove the meteorite. Then a fire started in the woods. The meteorite drowned. Then *bang*!

The rock went *puff!* A big cloud formed, then it went *bang* again! Then the rock rolled back into the water and sunk, then it made another puff noise, then the water started boiling around where the meteorite was underwater. Then the water shot sky high into the air, like a geyser, then an orange flame appeared where the rock was underwater. The meteorite started shooting steam out of it, then it was making noises, like rumblings, howling, explosions, etc. Then it floated above water, and it floated down the river and disappeared! The woods caught fire while Mrs. Chaimber, the police, and the girls were looking for the missing girls. The fire got stronger, and it chased Mrs. Chaimber, the police, and girls away.

"Girls, go back to the house!" said Mrs. Chaimber. The police and the fire department found a way to get around the forest fire to the river. Mrs. Chaimber and the rest of the girls ran back to the house. The police was investigating the rock; the rock was resting up against the riverbank. The police was studying the rock, taking reports on it.

"The police reported a meteorite!" The fire department grabbed tools and pushed the rock into the water; the rock made noises.

Divers grabbed the meteorite from underwater and tied it to another rock below, then the meteorite sank.

Mrs. Chaimber and the girls ran back to the house safely before the fire got them. The girls helped Mrs. Chaimber get supper ready. Then they packed all their clothes and belongings on the bus, ready to go, then Mrs. Chaimber started putting the food on the table. When all the food was out on the table, the fire started burning toward the house. Mrs. Chaimber and the girls started screaming to death. But the fire department put the fire out just in time, so the girls could sit down and eat. Mrs. Chaimber gathered all the girls around the campfire, said their dinner worship, then she pulled the foil off the vegetables and then the potatoes, the bread and butter, the salad, and then here comes the beef! As Mrs. Chaimber pushed the beef with the blood pouring out of it to the center of the table, she pulled off the foil, and there was Everlyn's head resting on the beef platter instead of the beef!

"Ahhhhhhh!" All the girls and Mrs. Chaimber screamed till they were sick. Mrs. Chaimber passed out!

The girls went running for the bus, screaming hysterically. Finally the police came after a short while. Mrs. Chaimber was lying on the ground when the police arrived. The girls ran out of the bus, yelling for help.

Lieutenant Licker and Junior were in one car, then more police arrived. Lieutenant Licker picked up Mrs. Chaimber, dragged her over to a stream nearby to wake her. While he was doing that, Junior was looking at the head on the beef platter. He jumped back fast, and he said, "Jesus Christ, who the fuck would have a human head for dinner!"

Maggots, flies, bees, and all kinds of bugs were eating this head until it deteriorated. Lieutenant Licker saw it. He shit his pants! He said, "Junior, take the bus with the girls and take them to the Connecticut State Mental Health Center and meet Mrs. Chaimber right there, please."

"Yes, sir!" said Junior.

Lieutenant Licker investigated the area. Caves Hill House looked a wreck: the windows were all busted, the walls had caved in, the furniture was all smashed, a big tree was stuck right through a wall, the basement was flooded under five feet of water, and the floors were all burned!

Nighttime, Lieutenant Licker went back to the police station to change his shitty pants, then he drove his police car to the Mental Health Center. Mrs. Chaimber was resting in sick care when the police came in to see her. Lieutenant Licker, Junior, and Officer Reid came in her room.

"Mrs. Chaimber, how are you feeling?" Lieutenant Licker raised his voice good and loud. "Are you ready to talk now, Mrs. Chaimber?"

"I'm still in shock!" she cried.

"Mrs. Chaimber, you remember me, Lieutenant Licker?"

"Yes, I do," she said.

"Mrs. Chaimber, I understand a tornado hit Caves Hill House last night, totally demolishing it!" said Lieutenant Licker.

"Yes, it did. I think I remember talking to you early this morning about it," she said.

"Mrs. Chaimber, you remember very well. I have Officer Junior and Officer Reid along with me this evening. I know you've been having bad luck at Caves Hill House, but one thing I don't understand is having someone's head for a meal! Can you discuss this, Mrs. Chaimber?" said Lieutenant Licker.

"We were getting ready to have roast beef for supper, and when I pulled off the foil, the roast beef wasn't there! It was Everlyn's head, one of my boarding girls!" she cried.

"Mrs. Chaimber, how did Everlyn's head get on the roast beef platter?" said Lieutenant Licker.

"I think one of two ways: when I was married before, I was married to Everlyn's father, who is in jail now. I always catered to Everlyn most of the time. She was in three boarding schools with me before, including Caves Hill House. She is my stepdaughter. Anyway, her father was a meat butcher at a meat market near my old house. Everlyn was always in trouble. I would help her to get out of it, and Harry, her father, was always raising a knife at her. He used to hit her, punch her, kick her, and he stabbed her a couple of times and threatened to kill her many a times. Everlyn is Harry's stepdaughter too. He was married before me. He was awfully mean to Everlyn, he hated her," Mrs. Chaimber cried. After she stopped crying, the lieutenant asked her the other reason.

"Mrs. Chaimber, what is the second thing that might have happened to her?" said Lieutenant Licker.

"The animal I saw, maybe," she said.

"No, that animal is not going to bite off someone's head and put it on a platter and cover it up like that. Someone did it! Where is Henry's Address, and what jail is he in?" said Lieutenant Licker.

"His name is Harry Goosewhiple. He's in McCormack Prison in Ireland, and his address was 108 Oak Street in Bakersville, West Germany," said Mrs. Chaimber.

"Mrs. Chaimber, why is he in McCormack Prison?" asked Lieutenant Licker.

"Because he murdered people when he got mad," she said.

"Mrs. Chaimber, why did you marry a fuckin' asshole like him?" said Junior.

"I married him when I was thirty, and he was thirty-one. He wasn't bad with me at all! The only thing I didn't like was the way he treated Everlyn. But he didn't tell me much," she said.

"Mrs. Chaimber, I don't want to know your fuckin' lifestyle with him. All I asked you is why you married him," said Junior.

"He had a lot of money, and he owned very expensive hotels and nightclubs. We had a good marriage for two years, until I found out he was going to jail. Then I divorced him!" said Mrs. Chaimber.

"I already know who this Goosewhiple is. He owns the Blackstone Valley Inn, in New Haven," said Lieutenant Licker.

The next day, Mrs. Chaimber was held at the police station for test and more questions. Lieutenant Licker and Junior went to the Blackstone Valley Inn to investigate this man. Meanwhile Officer Reid was at police headquarters connecting with the McCormack Prison in Ireland for fingerprints of this man. The McCormack Prison said he escaped, but his fingerprints showed up on Rick Reid's computer. Officer Rick Reid studied Mr. Harry Goosewhiple's fingerprints and took the photos to the laboratory, and he tested them, and he got copies and later gave them to Lieutenant Licker. The seven girls were still at the state mental health center, getting tests from the murder. Next day, Lieutenant Licker and Officer Reid went to the Blackstone Valley Inn looking for this man. Junior was at the police station in the laboratory, matching fingerprints. His fingerprints matched the one on the butcher knife that was found at Caves Hill House. He did indeed kill Everlyn and stuffed her chopped-off head on a beef platter and covered it with tin foil!

Meanwhile Lieutenant Licker and Officer Reid ran into him face-to-face, by a trick. They were not in uniform and asked for dinner for their wives, who were there with them. Mr. Goosewhiple didn't know who the hell they were, but Lieutenant Licker knew who he was. The policemen and wives were eating a roast beef dinner when Lieutenant Licker asked for the owner, who was standing at the front door.

"Excuse me, Harry, but the gentleman sitting at the fourth table on your right would like to see you, who has the gray hair," said the waitress.

Harry went over to the table where the officers were. Harry kind of stumbled and knew he was in trouble when he saw everyone eating roast beef. Lieutenant Licker stood up, and he said, "You are Mr. Harry Goosewhiple?"

"Yes, sir!" he said with a smile.

Lieutenant Licker shook his hand, then he pulled out his badge, and he said, "I'm Lieutenant Licker, from the Moodus, Connecticut, Police Department. You're under arrest, and you're coming with us. You are to be silent. Any word you say can be used against you."

Harry was handcuffed and taken out of the restaurant. Two weeks later, the Caves Hill House was rebuilt from the tornado that hit it. It was still haunted. A group of Boy Scouts were staying there for the weekend, when suddenly one of the boys drowned in the bathtub the first night! The scoutmaster called the police. The police came, and panicking boys ran to the police cars.

CHAPTER 9

Katy Wixon and the Devil

Ms. KATY WIXON HAD LIVED in Moodus, Connecticut, for years, and she had experienced all kinds of noises. She never paid attention to these noises, but once in a while, she'd get scared or jump when these noises occurred. Katy Wixon owned a home way deep out in the woods, and she owned a craft store a little ways down the road. It was Tuesday morning. Katy got up for work hearing strange noises outside, so she closed the windows in the house, ate breakfast, and went to her store. She was in a hurry! She arrived at her store. She was unlocking the door, and she heard something whispering to her.

Katy yelled, *"Hello! Hello! Is anybody there?"* She waited outside for an answer. After a brief wait, she went in the store, she put her pocketbook down, and she took her sweater off, then she took the trash out. Katy placed the trash cans near the road. She thought she saw something crawling in the woods. It was a giant snake! Katy screamed hysterically when she saw the snake. She ran like a bat out of hell back into her store and called the police. The phone was ringing and ringing.

"Police Department, Lieutenant Licker speaking."

"Lieutenant, this is Katy Wixon from down the road. I was emptying the trash from my store, and I saw this giant snake in the woods!" said Katy.

"Katy, I heard about this sucker too! Just stay in your store, lock all the doors, and keep your windows closed until I get there," said Lieutenant Licker.

Katy did what the lieutenant told her to do, then he arrived. Lieutenant Licker was knocking on the door at Katy's store. Katy let him in, and she said, "Can you help me, Lieutenant? I saw a giant snake outside!" Katy cried.

"Katy, where did you see this snake?" said Lieutenant Licker.

"I saw it about, maybe thirty feet away from the store, heading my way. I just ran like a bat out of hell!" she said.

"Was the snake near the Dumpster, or was it way out in the woods?" said Lieutenant Licker.

"It was out in the woods, sir."

"Okay, Katy, don't leave your store until it's time to go home, unless you have to. Get yourself some kind of a weapon, look out the window once in a while," said Lieutenant Licker

"Lieutenant, are there strange animals around here, you know, like wild animals?" said Katy Wixon.

"Katy, there's some animals in theses woods," said Lieutenant Licker.

"Lieutenant, the noises scare me. I don't know what it is, and I've been living here in Moodus all my life!" said Katy.

"Katy, when you come here tomorrow, park your car as close to this building as you can and carry some kind of a weapon with you, a baseball bat, steel pipe, etc. because there might be wild animals in these woods." said Lieutenant Licker.

Lunchtime, Katy made a ham sandwich. She grabbed the bread and mustard from the fridge. She had a small fridge in her store. After Katy finished eating her sandwich, she put the bread and mustard back into the fridge, and an egg popped out of the egg box and struck Katy on top of her head, and the yolk poured down her face. She said, "Oh shit!" Then she wiped the yolk off her face. Katy was talking to her cat, "That's funny, an egg comes flying out of my refrigerator and hits me in the head! I must have pushed the wrong button somewhere!"

At 1:30 p.m., a drunk came in Katy's craft store. "Can I help you?" she said. The drunk was quiet for a minute.

"Give me twelve of these, six of those, and twenty of them," said the drunk.

Katy gave the drunk a dirty look, and she said, "Could you repeat that please, I can't understand you?" said Katy.

"I want twelve of these, and how much it cost?" said the drunk.

"Two hundred forty-three dollars," said Katy.

"Oh, forget it, give me six of those and twenty of them," said the drunk. Then the drunk started knocking things over in the store.

"Be careful, mister, you're knocking things all over the place!" Katy screamed.

"Sorry, miss," said the drunk.

"Now what do you want, sir?" said Katy.

"I want six of these," said the drunk.

"They're five for a dollar," she said, and she sold them to him.

"Now I want twenty of them," said the drunk.

"This here, sir?" said Katy.

"No, not them! You see where your hand is? Not there!" said the drunk.

"Hey, mister, don't you get smart with me or you're gonna leave! Now what the hell do you want?" said Katy.

"I want twenty of them," said the drunk.

"They're eighty dollars apiece," said Katy.

The drunk left the store staggering and drooling all over the place. Katy was scared to death of this guy. She locked the door until the next customer came. About 3:00 p.m., a storm was coming; the sky darkened up quickly, and it was beginning to rain. The wind picked up, then lightning started. The drunk didn't close the outside properly. The wind blew it open! Katy jumped out of the way. Katy closed the door of her store, and she saw a bright bolt of lightning strike a tree in half. Katy screamed when she saw the lightning, then she ran over and locked the door. Then she saw another streak of lightning strike part of her store. Did she scream! Katy shut the curtains in the store. She saw lightning flashing out in the foggy woods. Katy had to put a blanket over one window. It was really lightning then!

She saw something weird out in the woods that made her scream. She couldn't describe what she saw. A big crack of thunder came, and the fog in the woods disappeared. Katy watched the storm outside her window. She saw bolts of light striking constantly in the woods followed by very loud cracks of thunder, as the lightning kept flashing several times. She saw some weird animal run from tree to tree. Suddenly it disappeared in the fog. The rain was really coming down, and the thunder and lightning was bad! Katy went through her store to check all the windows and doors to make sure it was locked. Minutes later, the sun came out, but it was still thundering outside. Just before quitting time, Katy got on the phone to call the police. The phone was ringing. Then it went dead. She tried three more times on her phone—still no luck. She tried the operator. Still no luck. The phone was dead. Katy grabbed a baseball bat from a closet before she left her store for the night. She locked up, and she made it to her car safely, with her baseball bat with her.

Katy drove home, and it was still thundering and lightning! Minutes later, the sun came out, and the thunder was getting louder, and patches of fog was forming; the fog patches was broken thunderstorms. Broken thunderstorms usually occurred during severe thunderstorms or from a tornado. Katy made it home okay. She had a baseball bat with her when she got in the house. She put the baseball bat near the kitchen door. Katy was frightened. She didn't think real thunderstorms were going on. She called the police, and the phone was dead. After the storm, Katy cooked a steak out on the porch. While she was cooking a steak, the sky darkened up again, and the storm came back. Out went the electricity. Katy ran to get her baseball bat. The storm was getting bad!

Katy was paranoid now. She thought something was after her, or she thought the devil was taking over her beliefs! Just after Katy finished eating, a severe thunderstorm was just overhead. The lightning was flashing like a discotheque! Katy said to herself, "Oh my god, this storm won't go away!" Katy grabbed a bottle of wine, and she sat out on the porch to drink it. After the storm let up some, she saw a bolt of lightning strike her garden. She screamed so loud she dropped her wine.

Finally the storm was over, and the sky cleared up. Katy saw a rainbow outside, just before dark. Katy was watching the rainbow, when suddenly the ground moved. Katy lost her balance, and she fell and swore. Then she looked up at the rainbow as the sky was getting darker. The rainbow disappeared into a fiery orange glow. "Oh my god, a fire in the sky!" Katy cried. Then she saw this weird-looking animal running through her flower garden, and she screamed hysterically! The animal disappeared quickly, Katy ran to the phone to call police; the phone was still dead! She slammed the phone down, grabbed the baseball bat, and she ran to her car and drove to the police station. She arrived at police headquarters, and she yelled, "Is there anybody here?"

One of the policemen said, "Can I help you, lady?"

"Hi, my name is Katy Wixon, I live up the road here. I saw this weird-looking animal in my yard, and I'm complaining about hearing strange noises and seeing weird things near my house. I have no electricity in my house. I know I'm not haunted, but this is ridiculous!" said Katy Wixon.

"Okay, Katy, I'll send another officer up to see you at your house," said the policeman at the station. Katy went home, and a cop followed her. The cop went through the house. He searched everywhere. The cop sat down to have a word with Katy.

"Katy, what's this animal you saw? We're looking for it too!" said the cop.

"It looks like a bear with a tail. I was too scared to find out what it was. I saw it, then it disappeared just like that! Officer, what animal could it be?" said Katy.

"Lieutenant Licker told me it might be a cactus horse. A cactus horse is a rare breed. It only comes around when we get a lot of rain. It lives in a tropical forest, and it comes out at night. The cactus horse is an unknown animal. Some people call it Big Foot," said the cop.

"Oh my god, does it bite?" said Katy.

"According to Lieutenant Licker, he told me nobody knows if this thing bites, but the warning is to stay away from it," said the cop. The cop and Katy had a long chat about this thing. Soon after, the lights came on, and the phone was working. The cop left. Katy locked all the doors and windows, then she took her bath and went to bed. The next day, Katy was driving to work at her craft store. She saw lumps moving under the ground quickly, and a big boulder rolled up against her car, then the rock stopped! Katy screamed, and she screamed! Katy managed to shimmy out on the passenger side of the car, and she ran to the store screaming! Katy heard very loud heartbeats in the background. She quickly opened the door, and she made it safely to the store. She shut the door fast, and she locked it. Then she ran to the phone to call the police.

"Police! Police! I need help. I saw the ground move, and a big rock hit my car, down here at my store, come quick!" Katy cried.

"Who's this?" said the cop over the phone.

"It's Katy Wixon from the craft store."

"Okay, Katy, stay in the store. We'll be right over!" said the police. Officer Reid said to Junior, another policeman, "I think Katy Wixon is on drugs, don't you?"

"I think she's full of shit!" said Junior.

"She's weird calling us and saying the ground is moving. She must be on something!" said Officer Reid.

"And rocks are fuckin' chasing her!" Junior laughed.

Then Junior drove his police car on another call. Lieutenant Licker came in the office, and he said, "What's the problem here?"

"I have to take a ride over to Katy's Collections to see what bug is crawling up her ass! She's a strange lady," said Officer Dick Reid.

"Why, what's the matter with her? I thought she was a nice lady," said Lieutenant Licker.

"She's always calling here, complaining that she's possessed on noises, the ground is moving, or the fuckin' devil is going to get her or something!" said Officer Reid.

"Look here, just go take care of her problem!" said Lieutenant Licker.

Officer Reid went over to Katy's Collections store. On the way over, the radiator overheated in Officer Reid's police car. Officer Reid got out to check his radiator. It was making a hissing noise and started boiling over. Officer Reid got back into his police car to call for help, then the road burst, and a giant snake came up from under the road with blood all over it! Officer Reid was shocked when he saw this giant thing, so he called back at the station.

"Car 190 reporting to headquarters over," said Officer Reid.

"Car number 190, go ahead please!" said Lieutenant Licker.

"Lieutenant, this is car number 190, we have a serious problem," said Officer Reid.

"Why, what happened?" said Lieutenant Licker.

"I was on my way to Katy's Collections store, when the road opened up, and a big long snake came out. I need help, the snake is making its way through the ground!" said Officer Reid.

"A snake! How big is it?" said Lieutenant Licker over the PA system at the station. "Get some help, Lieutenant, this thing is enormous! Car number 190, over," said Officer Reid.

"Car number 190, we'll get some help. Lieutenant Licker, over."

"Ten-four, Lieutenant, car number 190, over."

Officer Reid stayed in his car until the police arrived. Traffic was backed up. The fire department, the rescue, and several police cars rushed to the scene. The police jumped out of their cars and gunned down the giant snake! This snake was so big that it was a horror for people to watch.

The police was shooting thousands of bullets into the giant snake to kill it, as spectators cheered the police on.

"Where did this fuckin' thing come from?" said Junior.

"It's unusual, huh?" said Officer Reid.

"It's probably the fuckin' devil!" said Junior.

The police escorted the spectators back to their cars. The police then went to Katy's store.

Knock! Knock!

"Come in, Officers," said Katy.

"Katy, what happened?" said Officer Reid.

"I was driving down the road this morning, and I saw the ground move. Then when I parked my car, a giant rock came crashing up against my car. I had to get out on the driver's side," she said.

"Katy, show me the rock that hit your car," said Junior. Junior went out to look at Katy's car, while the other policemen were inspecting the store. Junior was talking to Katy Wixon outside.

"Katy, you're right, you did see something around here. I was called to an emergency to come here with Officer Reid, but unfortunately, a creature broke through the road, and the police had to kill it to get by. This creature was an unusual snake covered in blood and burning in fire. It was one of the scariest things I'd ever seen! Now you shouldn't have any more trouble with ground movement, Katy. We cleared your problem. Now if you have any more, you know where we are. Just get on the phone and call," said Junior. The police left. Dick Reid and Junior were riding because Dick's car was disabled. Dick was talking to Junior.

"Junior, you shouldn't have told Katy Wixon about the snake. She'll really be frightened now!" said Dick Reid.

Junior said, "That's true, now she will call the station every night. 'Help! Help! Now the fuckin' boogie man is coming after me!'"

Moodus, Connecticut, was quiet for about three weeks. Suddenly Katy Wixon woke up one foggy morning. She got up to go to the bathroom, and she picked up a glass to get a drink of water. The glass was dirty and slippery, so she went out into the kitchen to get a clean glass. Katy washed her hands and face with a face cloth.

Katy ran cold water for a while. She washed her face with the cloth to wake her up, then she dried up with a big bath towel. Then she grabbed a glass of water with the clean glass, and she drank it. While she was drinking the cold water, she looked in the mirror, and she saw the devil's face in the mirror! She screamed hysterically, and she threw the glass at the mirror. Katy ran out of the room, screaming. After she threw the glass and shattered part of the mirror, she went back into her room, and she looked into the mirror again, and she saw herself this time. Katy ran her hands across the shattered mirror. The devil's face appeared. When it flashed three or four times, she screamed, "No! No! No! No!" Then she started throwing things at the mirror until she broke it into pieces. Katy threw wine bottles, shoes, glasses, and a chair. She threw anything she could get her hands on, and she smashed the mirror. Then she called the police on the telephone. She was in the house, crying, when the police came.

The policeman said to Katy, "Katy, what's the matter!"

"I saw the devil's face in my bedroom mirror," she cried.

The policeman said to her, "Katy, I think you had a bad dream."

"Officers, I saw the devil's face flashing several times in my bedroom mirror. If you don't believe me, come and look!" she cried.

The policemen saw the broken glass in her bedroom. They wrote down a report, then one cop said, "Katy, I think you had a bad dream. There's no devil around here!"

"Officers, I will show you. Come in the bathroom," said Katy. Katy looked in the bathroom mirror with the lights on and off. She ran her hand across the mirror the same way she did in her bedroom. All she saw was herself. "I saw the devil, Officers, I did!" she cried.

"Katy, did you lose any sleep worrying about this devil you keep seeing in your mirrors?" said the policemen.

"Yes, every night!" she cried.

"Katy, I'm going to send a rescue over here to take you to the hospital and have a doctor look at you. Meanwhile, the police will keep a close watch on your house all night long to find out where this devil is coming from," said the policeman.

Katy Wixon was in the hospital for a couple of days, and she was normal. Sunday morning, Katy was discharged from the hospital. The rescue drove her back home. Then she went straight to church. It was a beautiful afternoon, not a cloud in the sky. Katy set up a grill to cook outside, then she called a friend on the phone. She told her friend about the devil's horrors and going to the hospital. Then she asked her friend over for dinner. Katy was cooking outside while she was waiting for her friend. She saw a funny-looking fog forming. The fog formed into a cloud, and rays were shining on it from the sun in the woods, then it disappeared. Katy said to herself "I must be seeing things!"

Ding-dong! the doorbell rang. Katy's friend arrived.

"Hi, Lindsey, come on in. How have you been?" said Katy Wixon.

"I've been terrific, I hit the Connecticut State lottery! I played 209 straight and boxed, and I won $800 last Wednesday with a dollar ticket, then I played the Hi-Lo jack lottery game and won a $1,000, then I won $3,000 at the horses on Friday night. I'm on a hot streak!" said Lindsey.

"I haven't been so great. I think I'm possessed by the devil. I saw strange movements in the ground. Plus clouds from a storm that looks strange to me, unknown glows or fog and seeing pictures of the devil in my mirrors, the same shit I told you two weeks ago. I been having nightmares every night, and I can't sleep, so I went to the hospital for testing. Now I'm taking medication to help me sleep and stop the nightmares. I really did see flashes of the devil in mirrors and through windows. I don't know if my mind is fucked up or if it's really happening!" said Katy Wixon.

"Katy, do you see what I see? It looks like we're gonna have a violent storm," said Lindsey.

"Lindsey, I think something came outer space and landed in Moodus, Connecticut. I really do. Lately we've been getting violent thunderstorms and tornado warnings. We never used to get storms like this!" said Katy Wixon.

Katy and Lindsey were sitting in front of the fireplace, eating dinner, talking.

"Katy, did you hear on the radio about some unknown animal roaming around town?" said Lindsey.

"Yes, I did. I'll bet it's the devil or has powers like the devil. I heard the animal was a cactus horse. It comes from another country, and it only comes out in rainy weather or at night. This animal has pointy ears, a long furry tail, has horns that look like the devil, and it's shaped like a bear, and the police is looking for it, and they can't find it!" said Katy Wixon.

"Have you ever seen this animal, Katy?"

"Yes, I did, it's the weirdest thing I ever saw Lindsey."

"Oh my god, does it bite?" said Lindsey.

"According to news and police reports, this animal could be very dangerous!" said Katy Wixon.

"Katy, what happened when you saw this creature?" said Lindsey.

"The other day I was going to my craft store to open up. I saw the ground move, then a big rock came out of the woods, and it rolled up against my car. I called the police to help, and they did not believe me. Finally the police came. They told me they killed a giant snake that burst through the road. Then police started to believe something was going on!" said Katy Wixon.

"I heard something about a snake found in Moodus," said Lindsey.

After dinner, a big gust of wind blew leaves through the fireplace all over the room where Katy and Lindsey were sitting in Katy Wixon's home; they screamed hysterically. Katy went outside to get a trash barrel from behind the house, brought it inside, and she and Lindsey raked the leaves into the barrel, then Katy pushed a big couch up in front of the fireplace and later took the barrel of leaves outside. Later toward evening, Katy and Lindsey were drinking some wine and watching TV, then *bang, shangalang!* The devil-like animal got into Katy Wixon's trash.

"What the hell was that!" Lindsey yelled, then she ran to the door.

Katy yelled, "Don't go out there, Lindsey, the devil-like beast might be out there!"

Nighttime, Katy Wixon was carrying a basket loaded with laundry to the basement. She said, "Lindsey, could you come downstairs with me to keep me company while I do my laundry?"

"Sure!" she said.

While they were down there, they heard all kinds of strange noise, noises that sounded like cracks and vibrations coming from the basement walls. Katy was doing her laundry, while Lindsey was listening to the noises.

"Katy, did you hear those noises? It sounded like cracks and rumbling sounds in the walls," said Lindsey.

"I hear all kinds of noises in the basement. It doesn't faze me," said Katy Wixon.

"I wonder what it is," said Lindsey.

"I think it's the sewer outside," said Katy. Lindsey laughed, then they went back upstairs. Lindsey slept over Katy's house tonight, because she had an extra bedroom. A little while later, Katy went down in the basement to put her clothes in the dryer; she stayed down there for a while to see if she'd hear any noises. She didn't hear nothing, so she read a book for a while. The basement was quiet, then she finished her laundry and carried the basket of clothes upstairs, then she went to bed. The next day was Monday, time to go to work. Lindsey had the day off, so she spent the day with Katy Wixon.

Lindsey went with Katy to her craft store down the road. Katy had her best day ever. People were coming in all day, buying, from the minute she started to quitting time. Katy didn't have much time to talk to her friend Lindsey she was so busy. Lindsey helped Katy all day, and they had fun.

"Lindsey, here's $50 for helping me," said Katy.

After work, Katy took Lindsey out to eat and later back to the house. Lindsey and Katy were drinking wine until dark, then Lindsey went home, and Katy Wixon was all alone once again. Katy was nervous for a while after Lindsey left, but she had no problems through the night. She locked all the doors and windows in the house before she went to bed. Tuesday morning was another bright and sunny day. Katy had another busy day at her craft store; she sold almost everything she had, from antiques to furniture. She made thousands of dollars. The store was almost empty!

The next day Katy went to an Orton in New York City to get things cheap to sell at her craft store; she brought all kinds of antiques cheap! Katy left her house at 5:30 a.m. She arrived in New York City at 8:00 a.m. She left at 10:0 a.m., and she arrived back at her store by 1:00 p.m. A line was waiting outside her craft store. She had to sell everything right from her car and a truck loaded with antiques. She had another great day making thousands of dollars! (The possessions had been staying away for a while, but it was on its way back!) Katy closed up early. She had everything she got from New York sold within an hour, then she went out to a fancy restaurant called the Chainwave Inn. It specialized in lobster. Katy had a big lobster meal before she went home. When she got home, she brought plants to plant in her garden outside her house, while she was planting her plants, she saw blood dripping alongside the basement windows. Katy grabbed a hose to wash down the blood on her windows, then she saw a rat run across her yard with a cat in its mouth. She screamed and screamed. Katy really didn't notice if blood was on her basement windows. She just sprayed it with the hose. Katy spent the rest of the day fixing up her yard until it was getting dark, then she went in the house, and she called Lindsey on the phone to tell her what a great week she was having.

Nighttime. Just before Katy was going to bed, she heard a hissing noise. She grabbed a baseball bat, and she went downstairs to see what it was, and nothing was down there, then she went to bed. Katy had a dream about the devil! She noticed the blood on her cellar windows at the start of her dream.

Katy's Dream

Katy's dream was back where she started from, when she noticed the blood on her windows, then she remembered talking to Lindsey on the telephone and hearing the hissing noise, and she went downstairs in the basement. She had laundry instead of a baseball bat, and she was washing her clothes, when suddenly she saw blood dripping down her cellar walls, and the walls were beginning to crack! Then an arm came crashing through the wall. Katy screamed, and she went to run upstairs, and she tripped over her laundry basket, and she got trapped. Katy was screaming for help, then the devil busted through her basement wall, and it went after her! Katy was crawling in her cellar, trying to get away from the devil, screaming to death! Katy made it to the stairs, and she was able to run up the stairs before the devil grabbed her and started pulling her back down into the basement. Katy was screaming hysterically.

The devil kept pulling Katy as she was holding on to a railing. The railing snapped, and the devil grabbed Katy and pulled her into the wall where it came from. Katy woke up screaming her head off. She couldn't sleep for the rest of the night. Thursday morning was a dark and dismal rainy day. Katy Wixon expected a slow day today because of the rain, and she sold out of everything; she grabbed a cloth, and she did some knitting until somebody would come. For three hours nobody showed up, so she locked the door and closed all the shades on the windows and made sure the windows were all locked, then she laid back, and she went to sleep.

Katy's Second Dream

In her second dream, she was dusting instead of knitting. All of a sudden, the wind outside picked up and blew the door in. She ran over to put the door back up, and she heard strange noises out in the woods, then the wind stopped, then she heard a growling sound! After she saw the ground start moving in waves, Katy was so scared she grabbed a bottle and put a rag in it to make a Molotov cocktail bomb. She lit the bomb, and she threw it where she saw the movement. The bomb blew up, and the movement stopped. Then an ugly orange flame appeared, and it turned into a fireball, and it started laughing at Katy Wixon! The fireball got bigger and bigger, and it was laughing louder and louder! Katy ran back into her store to get a gun, then she went back outside to where she saw the fireball, and it disappeared!

Then the ground started moving again, and Katy ran back into the store. Suddenly the devil came right into the store and sprayed fire at her. She screamed and screamed! The store was burning down, and the devil had Katy cornered in the flames. She screamed to death very loudly. A man came in the store while Katy was screaming from her dream, and he shook her, and he said, "Lady, are you all right?"

Katy shook her head a minute, and she said, "I must have fallen asleep. I had a bad dream. Mister, how did you get in here, I thought I had the door locked?"

"No, miss, the door was open. I like those chimes you have, how much are they?" said the man.

"The chimes are $300 a piece." said Katy.

"How much is this china set?" said the man.

"The china is $200 for the set," said Katy.

The man gave her $200 and took the china set, and he left the store.

One month later, the devil got hungry! It was a Friday night and a full moon. Katy Wixon was in her bedroom, combing her hair, when suddenly the devil's face appeared in her mirror. She screamed and passed out! About ten minutes later, her mirror shattered very loudly, waking her up, and she started screaming hysterically. Then Katy ran to the bathroom and closed the door. Then the lights went out, and she saw the devil's face flash on and off seven times in her bathroom mirror. Her hair stood straight up in the air. She screamed, and she kept screaming until the devil's possessions went away. Katy heard thunder outside, and she quickly pushed the bathroom door open, and she ran to the telephone in her kitchen; the phone was dead! Katy screamed, and she cried, then rocks came tumbling down her fireplace into the living room. Katy heard a popping noise after the rocks stopped falling, then she saw a flash of the devil in the fireplace, then she ran out the back door, screaming, to her car. She forgot her keys. "Goddamn it!" she cried, then she went back into the house to get her keys, and she couldn't find them. Katy grabbed a baseball bat, and she ran downstairs to hide from the devil's horrors. Katy searched the cellar, holding the baseball bat, and she was still in fright, wondering if she was going to see the devil appear again. Then she heard rocks falling behind a cellar wall.

Katy Wixon heard bangs, thumps, rumbles, and crashes behind a wall in her basement of her house. The wall Katy dreamed about where the devil came out of was where she heard all the noises. She heard one big crack, and the wall moved. She held the baseball bat and waited. She screamed and ran upstairs when she saw the wall move. Katy Wixon was running around her house with a baseball bat like a madman, looking for her car keys. Finally she found them in her bedroom, and she went out to her car. She put the key in the ignition.

Ra...ra...ra...ra...ra...ra!

"Come on, car, please start!" Katy cried. She couldn't get her car started. Then she went back into the house with the baseball bat in her hands to see if the phone was working; she picked up the phone, no dial tone. Then she dropped the phone on the floor accidently, and she picked it up, and she got a dial tone. Quickly she called the police; it rang a couple of times.

"Moodus Police, Lieutenant Licker speaking."

"Lieutenant, this is Katy Wixon calling. My house is haunted. My car won't start. The devil's in my house! Come quick, help me please!" she cried hysterically.

"Katy, grab some kind of a weapon and hold tight. I'll be there right away!" said Lieutenant Licker. The lieutenant arrived within minutes. Katy was standing in the living room with a baseball bat, crying, when the lieutenant got there.

Ding-dong!

Katy opened the door and let Lieutenant Licker in the house. "Katy, what happened here?" said Lieutenant Licker.

"Rocks came down my fireplace, and I saw the devil! I ran downstairs, and the devil was trying to break through the wall in my basement. I heard rocks falling and strange noises in a wall in the cellar, then I saw the devil in my mirrors, and my mirrors broke!" Katy cried.

Lieutenant Licker laughed, and he said, "Katy, there's no such thing as the devil. You must be dreaming or hysterical!" Then the lieutenant heard rocks falling very loudly and pounding away downstairs at 3:30 a.m. "Holy shit!" said Lieutenant Licker.

"I told you!" said Katy.

Lieutenant Licker went downstairs, and then he searched the rest of the house. It was quiet. "Katy, you will have to spend the rest of the night in a motel. You can't sleep here, you might get hurt. Come with me, I'll give you a ride to Frank Davis Motel. Here we are," said Lieutenant Licker.

"Lieutenant Licker, how come you're working at this hour?" said the motel clerk.

"I work the night shift every once in a while," he said.

"Did you hear about the earthquake? It started about midnight," said the motel clerk.

"Is that what it is? I got a call just after three this morning that this woman's house was haunted, complaining about falling rocks.

Listen, I'm going to leave this woman here for a couple of days because she's in shock. She thinks her house is possessed by the devil, and she keeps hearing the strangest noises, and the police wants her here for rehabilitation, and the police will pick her up in a couple of days. Katy, this is Ms. Rosenberg. Ms. Rosenberg, this is Katy Wixon," said Lieutenant Licker.

Ms. Rosenberg showed Katy Wixon her room. "Katy, if you have any problems, push the orange button on the side of your bed, and I'll come running," said Ms. Rosenberg.

At 5:00 a.m., Lieutenant Licker left orders for the day shift to do. At 6:00 a.m., the first shift started. Lieutenant Licker stated on paper, "Katy Wixon has rocks in her house. She keeps hearing strange noises. Her house is possessed, and she sees flashes of the devil. Please check it out!" Officer Reid and Junior laughed then they went to the scene. Two police cars arrived at Forty North Street. Four policemen went into Katy Wixon's house. A short time later, the fire department arrived with a rescue. The police was searching through the house, and the fire department was testing wires and noises in the house. It was a rainy day. "Last night's earthquakes loosened rocks, and air pressure was causing the weird noises," the police wrote on their report.

The police spent all day and into the evening hours figuring out why Katy Wixon's house was haunted. Nighttime, the police began hearing weird noises so the fire department busted a hole in the basement wall, where police was hearing the strange noises.

"It's only in the night when the fuckin' possessions happen!" Junior said to Dick Reid, another policeman. Lieutenant Licker arrived. He and Junior went through the busted wall; the firemen followed. They had sledgehammers and other tools to bust their way through the opening wall. The police spotted bloodstains on rocks, and blood was dripping overhead. The firemen then led the way through a tunnel. They flashed a flashlight all around in the tunnel. They came to a door that said, "Dee's Tunnel." Junior cocked his gun and blasted the door off Dee's Tunnel, and they went through all the way to the caves. The police and the firemen saw nothing but rocks, pipes, and rats down there. Then they came back. Some got lost in another tunnel for a while, but they found their way back. The fire department boarded up the hole they busted then went upstairs into Katy Wixon's home. The fire department left, and five policemen hung around for a while.

"Lieutenant Licker, did you see all that blood in the cave?"

"Sure, that's the rats eating one another up!" he said.

Katy Wixon's garden was out back. He saw blood on the seam of her cellar windows, so he investigated. About 6:00 p.m., Lieutenant Licker showed up at the house. Katy Wixon was there, drinking coffee with her friend Lindsey.

"Katy, what are you doing here?"

"I came to see if my house is really haunted."

"Well, Katy, I have mixed feelings. The police is trying to find out too," said Lieutenant Licker.

"Lieutenant, what did you find?" said Katy Wixon.

"Katy, if you go back to the motel, I'll tell you," said Lieutenant Licker.

"Okay!"

"Your house may be haunted. We found an old graveyard buried under your house. Some of the bodies may have been buried and tortured, but it's nothing to worry about. The whole town of Moodus is built over graveyards. The noises you heard downstairs were air pockets, and we did have an earthquake last night, that's why you had rocks come in the house. Now there's one more thing to be checked out is where blood is forming around your basement windows. Your foundations is going to be dug up tomorrow to find the problem. So go back to the motel, and I'll pick you up when these horrors are taken care of," said Lieutenant Licker.

The next day, all the foundation was being dug up around Katy Wixon's house to find out where the blood was coming. It was an old torture chamber back in the 1800s where bodies were cut up and placed in its own blood. The tortures were devil worship and possessed anyone who lived over the chamber. The chamber of horrors was cleaned up and moved to the state morgue. The fire department and the police arrived back at Kate's house after the job was done. The fire department went in the house and downstairs, and they saw pieces of the basement wall had fallen on the cellar floor. Then the firemen heard an animal roaring away in there, and the basement wall moved. The police held guns while the firemen busted the wall through again and went inside.

Junior said, "The other night, we went through this wall, as some of you remember. All there is is caves down here, and tight air pockets are causing rocks to break up and making all kinds of weird noises. There's a long tunnel that leads to the caves, behind this wall. It has been closed tightly for years. That's why Moodus keeps getting these fucking earthquakes, because there's a lot of tunnels like this that runs through this area, and it all leads to the Moodus Caves. If we don't break up some of these tunnels, the whole fuckin town will cave in.

"Hi, Lieutenant, we're going through Kate's wall again. Look at this basement! Okay, men, get your weapons ready, we're going through. There's no animals, all you'll find is rats and snakes," said Junior. The firemen and the police went through Dee's Tunnel again, with Lieutenant Licker leading the way.

"Okay, men, listen up, we have to investigate the bloodstains on the rocks. Mr. Poly, the animal roaring you heard was the gas going through the pipes running over your head," said Lieutenant Licker.

Earl Davies was there with the firemen and the Moodus Police. He said, "Lieutenant Licker, I never knew this was here when I sold this property to Katy Wixon."

"Well, you do now, and you're gonna pay the damages!"

"Lieutenant, how can I pay damages when I never knew this tunnel was here or the blood outside?" said Earl Davies.

"Look, pal, if you own property in this town and the police or anyone gets involved for something dangerous like this, you're gonna pay! If not, you're going to jail. It's as simple as that. I don't want to hear no more!" said Lieutenant Licker.

"Sheriff Watts, what's the situation on the broken wall and the messy basement?" said Junior.

"I'm going to have Campinella Construction Co. come down her on Monday to put a new wall in," said Sheriff Watts to the Moodus Police Department.

Lieutenant Licker said, "Mr. Earl Davies, you're gonna pay the bill!"

"Earl, you're coming down to the police station. We need a few questions answered from you, please," said Sheriff Watts.

Police was at the police station questioning Earl Davies, the owner of Katy Wixon's house. The sheriff was writing up a report mentioning Earl Davies and Katy Wixon's names about the murders and the bloodstains found under the foundations and the basement of Katy's house. Early Saturday morning, Earl Davies called Campinella and his workers to come and fix the wall in Katy Wixon's basement. At 5:00 p.m. Saturday, the job was completed; a brand-new wall was built in Katy's basement. The cellar was all cleaned up, and gravel stones of all different colors were installed around the foundation all the way around the house. It looked beautiful! Then Campinella Construction had to dig up some graves in the yard and fill it with stone. Just after the workers left, about thirty of them, a fast-moving thunderstorm came. Lightning struck the side of Katy's house, causing a small fire. The heavy rain put the fire out right away. Blood was flowing down North Street in front of Katy's house during the storm.

Katy Wixon was over at Lindsey's house. She was taking a nap, while Lindsey was in the shower. After Lindsey got out of the shower, she looked in the mirror. She saw herself. She ran her hand across the mirror in her bathroom, and she said, "The devil, what devil? Come on, devil!" Then she laughed, got dressed, and she went to watch TV. Lindsey was enjoying a good horror movie about the devil on HBO, eating frozen dinners, then she fell asleep. Katy woke up at 11:00 p.m., and she shut the TV off because she kept hearing scary music. Katy woke up Lindsey, and they went out on Lindsey's porch to smoke a joint and have a few drinks until sunrise. It was a nice night, and the trees were blowing in the wind, and there was a full moon. Katy and Lindsey were talking about sex. About 3:00 a.m. Katy saw a bright-red color in the woods, then she heard noises that sounded like rocks tumbling.

"Lindsey, do you hear that?" Katy said.

"Yes, I do. I heard it the other night, when we had that earthquake," said Lindsey.

"Lindsey, look out in the woods, do you see a bright-red color?" said Katy.

"No, what is it?"

"I don't know," said Katy Wixon.

Just when it was beginning to get bright, Katy and Lindsey went to bed.

Katy's Third Dream

About 5:00 a.m. was when she and Lindsey went to bed. Katy was at her house in the dream. She went to the bathroom just before she went to bed. She watched the sun rise from her bathroom. It was a bright-red color shining at her mirror. she looked in the mirror, and she saw the devil's face in a bright-red color. It flew out of the mirror, and it went through a tile wall in her bathroom! "You fuckin' devil get out of here!" she yelled in her sleep.

Lindsey woke up laughing her head off. Then Katy put the water on ready to take a bath, and blood was coming out of the faucet. Katy said, "Oh my god!" Then the hot water washed the blood away, then she took a shower. "Earl Davies, you gonna fuckin' pay for this when I see you!" Katy said to herself. While Katy was sound asleep in her dream, Lindsey woke up hearing rocks falling! About 5:30 a.m., Lindsey went downstairs in her basement to see what was going on.

Back to Katy's dream. After Katy took her shower, she went in the bedroom to gather a load of laundry. She checked all her mirrors to see if the devil would appear. Then she went downstairs to do a load of laundry. Lindsey was downstairs too. The devil busted through the wall, spraying fire and chasing them around the basement, then they were engulfed with flames so quickly! Katy woke up screaming her head off.

"*Help! Help! Help! Help!*" Then she threw up all over Lindsey's bed.

"Katy, are you all right?" said Lindsey.

Katy and Lindsey cleaned up the mess and went back to bed. Katy told her about her dream. Lindsey laughed and she laughed and she laughed. Later in the day, Lindsey took Katy back to her house. About 6:00 p.m., her phone rang just as soon she got home. Katy answered it.

"Hello, Katy, this is Lieutenant Licker from the police. Who took you home? I'm at Frank Davis Motel waiting for you. I've been here since 5:00 p.m. to take you home."

"My friend Lindsey," she said.

"Okay, I just want to know if you made it home safely," said Lieutenant Licker.

Katy was shocked when she saw the nice job Campinella did outside in her yard. She and Lindsey had a cookout on Katy's porch until it got dark. Then about 8:30 p.m., Katy heard rocks falling again.

"Lindsey, did you hear that?" she said.

Then she and Lindsey went downstairs into the basement.

"Oh my god, Katy, the wall is on fire behind the washing machine!" said Lindsey.

Pieces of rocks were falling off the wall, and sparks were flying. The devil was beginning to break through the wall!

"Lindsey, let's get the hell upstairs!" Katy said. Just as they made it upstairs, the devil was just starting to punch its way through the wall in Katy Wixon's basement. Katy called the police. "Come quick, my cellar is catching fire!" Katy cried. Then the police, a rescue, and the fire department arrived. Rocks started tumbling in the basement when the police got there!

"Okay, you women stay up here!" said Lieutenant Licker.

The fire department saw streaks of fire in Katy's basement and a broken hole in a different wall this time; the firemen sprayed down the fire in the basement, then the policemen followed them into the broken wall. It was midnight. The police and the firemen did hear some animal roaring in the tunnel.

"Okay, men, let's get this devil or whatever it is! Be careful, because we're going through a different wall this time," said Lieutenant Licker.

"Lieutenant, here's Dee's Tunnel, so the wall goes around!" said Officer Dick Reid.

"Good, we got this motherfucker now!" said Junior. Then Junior kicked the door through leading to Dee's Tunnel, then they went through. The officers and firemen looked if they were going to combat. They had guns, bazookas, tear gas grenades, and bombs. They made it to the caves. The animal was roaring away. Some of the officers were standing guard. Rats were running around like rabbits and jumping at the policemen and biting them. The rats were leaping all over the place!

Lieutenant Licker yelled, "*Get back!*"

The officers started spraying the rats with tear gas because there were so many of them to make a clear path. Junior found a big stick in the cave. He had a can of lighter fluid in his knapsack. He found an old handkerchief. He wrapped it around the stick and poured the lighter fluid all over it to make a torch, then he lit it afire to get some light. Junior then found a bigger stick, and he made a torch for his partner, Dick Reid, and then went around burning all the rats with their torches. Then the animal roared again!

"We got you now, you motherfucker!" said Junior.

"Junior, be quiet, the animal might get away!" said Officer Reid.

The further the officers and firemen went in the caves, there were more and more rats and snakes. Officers Reid and Junior were torching them. What weird noises they were making. Others sprayed tear gas, killing thousands of rats and snakes! There were so many snakes in bunches.

Junior said, "What the fuck is this, *Raiders of the Lost Ark?*"

The police and the firemen went as far as they could go in the caves. Rats and snakes were in swarms. It was so bad police had to throw fire bombs to get rid of them. The rats and snakes were howling while they were getting torched. They ran like a bat out of hell from the flames. The police and the firemen had fire-proof suits on. The men made it to an opening and into a field. They took a break at the field.

"Okay, men, let's go back through the woods. This fucking animal probably lives underwater too! We were very lucky to get through this. I give you officers and firemen a lot of credit! I won't recommend going back through the caves to Katy's house. We'll probably get killed going back. Forget this fuckin' cactus horse. We'll get it another time. Okay, through the woods we go. Follow me!" said Lieutenant Licker.

About 5:30 a.m., the police got back to Katy Wixon's house. Three officers were standing guard with guns and bombs in the basement at the busted wall.

"Listen, ladies, Katy, you're gonna have to go back to Frank Davis Motel or stay at a friend or relative's house for the rest of the night," said Lieutenant Licker.

"No problem, Lieutenant, I'll just go back to Lindsey's house. What happened downstairs?" said Katy Wixon.

"I think some animal, a bear or something, broke through down there," said Lieutenant Licker.

"A bear breaking through a wall!" Lindsey laughed.

"Sure, a bear could break through a wall!" said Lieutenant Licker.

The next day, police gave her a place to stay at BJ's Hotel in Hampton, Connecticut. Katy Wixon had a much better home at BJ's. Two days later, Katy Wixon's house burned to the ground.

CHAPTER 10

The Horrors of Moodus, Connecticut

KATY WIXON WAS WATCHING THE news on TV in her new home at BJ's Hotel in Hampton, Connecticut.

"Good evening, this is the six o'clock news on a Monday night here in Hartford, Connecticut's new TV station, channel 13. The town of Moodus, Connecticut, has been haunted lately. Police reported some kind of strange animal living in the Moodus Caves or underground somewhere in that town. Police believes this animal could be a cactus horse. Other viewers say it looks something like the devil! It could be Big Foot that some animal scientists are looking for out west.

"Lieutenant Licker of the Moodus Police Department says it might be a cactus horse, a very rare breed. The Moodus Police reported seeing a meteorite a short time ago down by the Moodus River. The military said that the possessions in this town of Moodus could be something from outer space, or this freak animal just very well could be deformed!

"Mrs. Chaimber from the boarding house committee has seen this animal one weekend, after reporting two of her girls missing. The incident took place at the Caves Hill house in early May. She said the animal looks like a bear with horns, a very long tail, a big breast, and pricks all over it, and its roar is much louder than a bear. She said its face looked similar, like the devil. Ms. Katy Wixon has lived in Moodus, Connecticut, for years, and she never had a problem until now. She reported being haunted by the devil, seeing flashes of the devil's face many times in her mirrors at home. She also saw blood on the seams of her basement windows. Her and her friend Lindsey reported seeing a wall turning red in Katy Wixon's basement, then the basement caught fire. Katy also reported rocks and bricks falling behind that basement wall and her fireplace. She reported to police that she saw the devil's face in the fireplace too when she lights it up.

"Police has been reporting a few murders in Moodus. They believe this animal might have something to do with them. The Moodus Police twice went through Katy Wixon's basement wall looking for this animal with the fire department and Earl Davies, the owner of the property. Police dug their way to the Moodus Caves. They heard the animal roaring several times but could not see it or find it. Nothing but swarms of rats and snakes were found in the caves. Police believe the fire in Katy Wixon's basement of her home was caused by a gas leak.

"Other residents in Moodus reported to police they have been haunted in many different ways—ways that the police wouldn't believe them! The police reported seeing strange colored glows in the woods, weird bolts of lightning, and seeing unusable weird clouds, clouds that you would see when a tornado is coming! They also reported hearing strange noises. Speaking of a tornado, about almost a month ago, one went through the woods near Caves Hill House, blowing out all the windows there! The winds had to be more than 150 miles an hour. Mrs. Chaimber believes that one of her girls was sucked out a window during that storm. The tornado made a path over one hundred feet wide and tore over a mile in a half stretch of trees. The wind tossed a tree right through the third floor window at Caves Hill House. Mrs. Chaimber was awakened by it.

"It's very unusual for Moodus to have a tornado because it's a hilly country. Tornadoes occur on flat lands. I guess anything can happen during heavy thunderstorms. Here's Lieutenant Licker from the Moodus Police to tell you about the Caves Hill tornado. This is Maggy Green reporting."

"Mrs. Chaimber lost two children during that storm. The tornado touched down somewhere near Caves Hill House tearing the building apart. The storm had actual wind gust of 180 to 240 miles an hour. The tornado uprooted an eighty-foot big oak tree and drilled it like a screw driver into the third-floor window. The tree screwed its way through the window all the way and into the house. The tree climbed in bed with Mrs. Chaimber, luckily missing her, and it was screwing into the wall. Then a strong gust of wind pushed the tree into the house and tossed it down the stairs, ripping up the carpet. All the windows were blown out, and the shutters were blown off. And parts of the roof were ripped off the house. There was quite a bit of damage inside the house too. This is Lieutenant Licker reporting from the Moodus Police."

"Since the horrors in Moodus, Connecticut, has been happening, they'd been getting some horrible thunderstorms lately. Other people reported seeing flying objects and ground movement, things they never saw before. That's the news for this Monday evening. Tomorrow we'll have Katy Wixon for our guest. Good evening and see you at 11:00 p.m., channel 13, Hartford, Connecticut. This is Maggy Green reporting."

The Connecticut State Police drove Katy Wixon from Moodus to channel 13 news in Hartford, Connecticut. Meanwhile Earl Davies went to Katy Wixon's house to get the rest of her belongings to drop off at BJ's.

"Katy, my name is Maggy Green from Hartford's 13 news. Have you ever been on TV before?"

"I have a couple of times, but not to do a news cast!" She laughed.

"Well, tonight's your first chance. Just pull up a chair and sit in the middle of the American flag, and we'll be on the air! Are you ready, Katy?" said Maggy Green.

"Yes, I'm ready," said Katy Wixon.

"Good evening, this is the Tuesday evening news at six, channel 13 in Hartford, Connecticut. Ms. Katy Wixon from Moodus is here with 13 news tonight. Her house burnt to the ground just shortly before 4:00 p.m. this afternoon. Arson is suspected. There was another fire today at Luke's Restaurant. No injuries has been reported. The police in Moodus is looking for that strange animal at this hour. The Moodus Police is thinking of writing a book called *Ground of the Devil* because of all the horrors there! I have Katy Wixon here with me right now. She's going to tell you about her experiences with the pretty devilish town of Moodus. Maggy Green reporting."

"Good evening, I've been living in Moodus all my life, and many times I heard noises that was unbelievable! Noises that sounds like sonic booms, pops, cracks, crashes, sounds like trucks or trains going by! I hear thunder coming from deep under the earth. Or it sounds like a storm coming. Every time I hear these noises, I get scared now! It never used to bother me before, but when I heard there's something out there, now I'm scared. I work at my craft store during the day, and I really hear lots of noises. Sometimes the noises will go away for a while but come back! I see lightning that looks like a disco and weird clouds. People think that I'm crazy or strange because I am possessed. Katy Wixon eporting."

"This is just in from the Moodus Police. Police are reporting fog and strange glows in wooded areas. Police say to stay away from those areas. The Moodus Police Department is giving a $10,000 reward for anyone who finds or captures this animal! This is Maggy Green reporting, channel 13 news in Hartford, Connecticut. We'll see you at eleven o'clock tonight for more updates on the horrors of Moodus, Connecticut."

The next day was Wednesday, about 7:00 a.m. A pickup truck was driving through Moodus, Connecticut, during a heavy thunderstorm. The driver saw an orange glow forming in the woods. Suddenly he saw a bright bolt of lightning, and the thunder sounded very loudly! The driver stopped just past the orange glow, then he backed his truck up to get a good look at it. Then a cop pulled up from behind the truck, and the cop came to the driver's side window, and he said to the truck driver, "May I see your license and registration, please?"

"Yes, sir!" said the truck driver. The truck driver gave his license and registration to the police, and the cop went back to his car. The truck driver sat in his truck, looking out into the woods.

"The reason why I stopped is because you're parked in a restricted area," said the cop.

"Officer, I saw something in the woods!" said the truck driver.

"What did you see?" said the cop.

"I saw this bright glow in the woods, and it looked like it was following me! It was the strangest thing I ever seen, Officer!" said the truck driver.

"Where did you see this glow?" said the cop.

"Right out there!" said the truck driver.

"Okay, thank you! Now don't hang around here!" said the cop.

The truck took off, and the cop went into the woods to check on the glow. The lightning flashed a few times, and the cop was in the orange glow. He heard a hissing noise, and the glow felt quite warm. He ran out of the woods to his police car to call for help at headquarters. The cop turned around, and he looked into the woods, and the orange glow disappeared! About twenty-five police cars raced to the scene to investigate the strange happenings. The police searched and searched the woods until the sun was shining. They found nothing. About 8:30 a.m., one hour and a half later, the sky cleared up like there was never a storm earlier. A beautiful blond-haired girl was riding down the road on a white horse. Suddenly she saw a quick bright flash, and it blinded her, and she fell off the horse. Minutes later, the same truck the police stopped earlier was driving down the road and spotted her.

The man got out of his truck and picked her up, and he said, "Lady, are you all right?"

"I'm blind!" she cried, then she passed out.

Quickly the man from the pickup truck took her to the hospital. She woke up in the hospital. The doctor held her hand, and he said, "What happened, sweetheart?"

"I was riding my white horse when suddenly I saw a bright glow, and it blinded me!" the girl cried.

The man from the pickup truck called the police to report the incident. The police went to the hospital where the girl was at. Other policemen went to the scene where the girl fell. The white horse she fell from was lying dead on the side of the road. Lieutenant Licker was crying. He didn't like seeing a beautiful horse like that lying dead in a gutter. Helicopters flew over Moodus all day, looking for the devil and the strange happenings.

"Ten-four, Lieutenant Licker, this is Junior in car 140, over!"

"Lieutenant Licker at headquarters, go ahead, car number 140."

"Lieutenant, I'm at Hampton Hospital with a girl who fell off a horse. She said she saw something that blinded her, and she fell off the horse," said Junior.

"Ten-four, Junior. I read you, over. Junior, please go to where the horse is and meet me there after you get through at the hospital, over," said Lieutenant Licker.

"Ten-four, Lieutenant. Car number 140, over," said Junior.

The lieutenant arrived back at the scene where the dead horse was; he was depressed. Lieutenant Licker got out of his police car, and he told another policeman to go elsewhere. "Officer Reid, go to Katy Wixon's house and meet the fire department there!"

"Yes, sir, Lieutenant!" said Dick Reid.

Officer Reid met with the firemen at Katy Wixon's burned-out home, moved some burned wood to get into the basement through Dee's Tunnel to look for the devil, the animal. Police didn't know it was the devil yet! Other policemen brought k-9 dogs with them to sniff the devil's tracks. Some of the dogs were attacked by the rats and snakes. The police still never found the devil yet.

CHAPTER 11

The Possessed Zoo
Moodus, Connecticut, Home
for Animals and Zoo

CHOOLKIDS' SUMMER CAMPS AND PLENTY of kids always like to come and see the animals. Mrs. Lang is the caretaker for over two hundred animals. Cats, dogs, birds, horses, cows, pigs, lions, tigers, etc. Mrs. Lang was walking around the zoo, checking on all the animals. She saw one of the gates open, so she closed the gate, and she ran to the office, fearing a wild animal was loose. Mrs. Lang was walking past the dogs. They were pit bulls with horns, and the dogs looked like little devils. Mrs. Lang was shocked. The other caretaker was in the office when Mrs. Lang arrived. He said, "Mrs. Lang, there's an open gate in section 2."

"I took care of that, Mr. Colt, but I don't know what animal might have broken loose. There was only one, whatever it was!" said Mrs. Lang.

Junior arrived at the zoo with his police car. He was a good friend of Mrs. Lang. Junior knocked on the office door at the zoo. "Moodus Police!" he said.

"Junior, how are you?" said Mrs. Lang.

"I'm doing fine, but we got a call that some animal broke loose from here!" Junior said.

"I got the message too. One of the gates was open, and I closed it. The animal broke loose in section 2," said Mrs. Lang.

"Well, I got a call that something large was roaming the streets. Let's go find it," said Junior.

"Junior, look at these dogs. Don't those look strange? We just got them today!" said Mrs. Lang.

"It sure does. It looks like little devils! Did you hear about the strange animal roaming around town lately? Maybe it might have broken into your zoo instead of something breaking out!" said Junior.

"Yes, I did. I hope it's not in here, whatever it is. Mr. Colt will kill it! He's a wiz at killing strange animals! People call the animal the devil. I heard someone tell me a meteorite crashed into Moodus, Connecticut, and the devil came out of it. I even heard about it on TV," said Mrs. Lang.

"Mrs. Lang, if you or Mr. Colt see this animal, just call the police. If you can, shoot the goddamn thing!" said Junior.

Junior and Mrs. Lang went by the dogs again. Mrs. Lang said to one of the dogs, "Here, Poochie!" The dog ran to the fence and started growling very strangely. "I know you don't like uniforms, but it's okay, Poochie!" Mrs. Lang said to the dog.

"Mrs. Lang, make sure you keep these little devils locked up. These little things could be deformed, you never know!" said Junior, then he drove off.

At 8:00 p.m. on a Sunday, the zoo was closed. Mr. Colt was on duty. One of the dogs was barking like hell! Mr. Colt was walking around the zoo with a flashlight. A wolf was roaming around loose. Mr. Colt heard a noise, so he flashed the light, and he saw a tree swaying back and forth and side by side, then he heard scratching and howling noises; the noises got louder and louder, and the tree was moving faster and faster! Then a big cloud formed, and it got very foggy. Mr. Colt lost his sight in the fog. He kept flashing the light around—he was in fright. He heard howling, but he couldn't find the animal! He shined the light on bricks of some building. He was able to find a fire escape on the side of the building. He was able to climb up the fire escape to the roof. The fog was beginning to disappear, and he saw a dog roaming around. What dog! It wasn't! What Mr. Colt thought was a dog was a wolf because he heard it howl, then he shot at it with his rifle, but he missed. The fog came back, and Mr. Colt lost sight of the wolf. He waited a half hour for the fog to clear; the fog cleared, then he spotted the wolf again. He fired three shots directly at the wolf, and the wolf disappeared again. Then the fog came back to stay. Mr. Colt couldn't see nothing! So he gave up and climbed down the roof, loaded his rifle, and he went walking through the zoo again, looking for the wolf. Mr. Colt heard a loud scream, then the dogs started barking like hell. So he went over to where the dogs were. He was aware of the wolf running around loose, so he looked in front of him, back of him, and he kept looking in all directions. He had his gun beside him. Mr. Colt got to the dog cages okay. He saw one of the dog cages had been bitten through, and he saw a dead dog with puncture holes in it, and another dog was torn apart! There was blood all over the place! "Holy shit!" Mr. Colt said, then he went searching for the wolf. The dogs were screaming and barking like mad!

Finally Mr. Colt spotted the wolf a short ways down from the dog cages. He cocked his gun, and he shot the wolf three times before he killed it. Then he walked over to the wolf to make sure it was dead; the wolf was still moving, so Mr. Colt pointed his gun to the wolf's head, and he let go of the trigger and blew its head right off! Then he saw parts of a dead dog coming out where he blew the wolf's head off. The wolf looked like the devil!

Monday morning, Mrs. Lang came in to relive Mr. Colt. "Good morning, Mr. Colt."

"Good morning, Mrs. Lang."

"Any action last night, Mr. Colt?" said Mrs. Lang.

"Yes, I had a lot of action! I killed a wolf last night. It was running loose, and the wolf killed three dogs. One dog was torn apart, and the second one was bitten alive, and I found the third. One in the wolf's stomach when I killed it! I had to fire four shots to shoot the bastard. Finally I blew its head off on the last shot!" said Mr. Colt.

"Oh my dear god, I think we better get rid of the dogs because they look like little devils!" said Mrs. Lang.

"The wolf I shot did a job on three of them!" said Mr. Colt.

Mr. Colt and Mrs. Lang were talking for a while. Finally midday came, and Mrs. Lang was feeding all the animals. When she got done, a police officer tapped her on the shoulder, and he said, "Are you the zoo caretaker?"

"Yes, I am. Why, what can I do for you, Officer?" said Mrs. Lang.

"My name is Lieutenant Licker."

"How do you do? My name is Mrs. Lang."

"Mrs. Lang, it's nice to meet you. The reason why I'm here is because I got a call that three wild animals broke loose from here last night. They were wolves that went through this town like a tornado! The wolves were biting other dogs and cats, jumping up on cars, chasing cars down the street, ripping up scrubs and small trees, jumping through windows of people's homes, and attacking young children. You're gonna have to do something with these animals or the town of Moodus is going to close you up! I will not tolerate this again!" said Lieutenant Licker.

"Lieutenant, I wasn't here last night. The night man told me he killed one wolf last night, but he didn't tell me three were loose!" said Mrs. Lang.

"What's the night man's name?" said Lieutenant Licker.

"His name is Mr. Colt, he'll be in at six tonight," said Mrs. Lang.

"Okay, we're gonna search the zoo. If there are any animals we have to kill, we're gonna kill them!" said Lieutenant Licker.

"Yes, sir," she said. Mrs. Lang was finishing up what she had to do, and the police waited at her office.

"Mrs. Lang, could you take a seat, please," said one of the other police officers.

"Mrs. Lang, just what the hell kind of animals you have in this zoo, they all look like devils?" said Lieutenant Licker.

"I know, but those were the animals that were brought in here!" she cried.

"Mrs. Lang, you don't have to cry every time we ask you questions. It's not your fault that you have a zoo full of demons. All I'm here for is to find a little information from you, that's all! But I have to say, a lot of these animals have to be killed!" said Lieutenant Licker.

Later in the day, the police began shooting some of the animals dead. Helicopters and the police captured over ten wolves in Pickerel Field and killed them. Later the police left Mrs. Lang's office at the zoo. She had a pet parrot in her office. The parrot said to Mrs. Lang, "Hey, lady, you better do your fuckin' job. All of us are getting killed in here, asshole!"

Mrs. Lang was stunned. She couldn't believe what her parrot said to her. Mrs. Lang said to her pet parrot, "Don't you say that again, that's not nice!" She was pointing her finger at it. Then she went into the greenhouse in back of her office, and she saw that all her birds were all dead! She went hysterical!

"See, lady, all the fuckin' birds are dead! How about that," said the parrot.

Mrs. Lang said, "You better watch your mouth before I wash it out with soap!"

"Fuck you!" said the parrot.

Mrs. Lang got mad, and she got a bar of soap and stuck it in the parrot's throat.

"What did you do that for, you fuckin' asshole!" said the parrot.

Then Mrs. Lang gave the parrot a good whack, and the parrot spit at her. Mr. Colt came in at six to relieve Mrs. Lang. Ricky was the parrot's name. Mrs. Lang said, "Ricky, you be nice to Mr. Colt."

"Fuck you!" said the parrot.

"Ricky, be nice!" Mrs. Lang yelled at the parrot.

"Fuck you!" said the parrot.

Mrs. Lang chased the parrot around the office, grabbed it by its throat, threw it in the cage, and she put the cage in the greenhouse with all the dead birds. "Now, smarty, you swear again and I'll flush you down the toilet!" said Mrs. Lang. The parrot kept quiet. Other zoo workers were cleaning up all the dead birds in the greenhouse. "Mr. Colt, the police had to kill a lot of animals here this afternoon because they looked like the devil!" said Mrs. Lang.

"I heard that on the radio in bed, and they captured ten wolves in Pickerel Field," said Mr. Colt.

"The police will be back to see you later, Mr. Colt, have a nice night!"

Mr. Colt was feeding the animals its supper; some of them still looked like the devil! Mr. Colt went to the office after he got through feeding the animals. The police was waiting there for him. The parrot was swearing its head off. Mr. Colt was laughing hysterically in front of the police. The police laughed too.

Midnight, Mr. Colt searched the zoo. He saw animals walking through the woods, so he radioed the police to alert them. Mr. Colt looked up at the moon because he heard a wolf cry very loudly; then he saw fog forming around the moon. The police was at the scene, shooting wolves in the woods. Mr. Colt searched the zoo with his gun. Mr. Colt heard the wolves howl later on, then he heard scratching.

Awooooo!

"That's not a wolf!" he said to himself. Then the dogs started barking like hell, and he saw a wolf coming toward him in the zoo! The wolf ran over to the dog cage and started tearing at it; the dogs were going nuts! Mr. Colt shot it twice and blew the wolf's head off. Mr. Colt went to get a wheelbarrow from a shed near the greenhouse to pick up the dead wolf. He scooped it up in a shovel, and he tossed it into the wheelbarrow. Then the wolf's head rolled over to Mr. Colt's foot. Mr. Colt jumped out of the way. He was frightened, then he picked the head up in the shovel and put it upside down in the wheelbarrow, and he rolled the wheelbarrow over to the incinerator; the head turned around, and its eyes were looking at him in the wheelbarrow, then the head fell out of the wheelbarrow and was rolling with the wind. Mr. Colt shot it and blasted it into pieces! Then he swept the remains of the wolf's head with a broom into the shovel, and he threw it into the incinerator, then he dumped the wolf's body into the big furnace. Then he hosed down the wolf's blood on the pavement.

Awoooooooooooooo!

155

"What the hell, we do not have bears here!" Mr. Colt said to himself. He checked every animal cage in the zoo, because he kept hearing loud howling noises until it was louder than a bear. Finally the police came to the zoo. Mr. Colt was down by the caves where the big animals were.

Awooooooooooo!

The police heard the animal roaring, so they went through the caves to find it, but they couldn't. Then a fire broke out in the cave. The fire department quickly came to extinguish it. The howling was the devil. When the police and Mr. Colt was looking for it, the devil dug itself underground, and it disappeared for the night. The next day Mr. Colt was nowhere to be found. The police was at the zoo in the morning when Mrs. Lang came in.

"Good morning, Mrs. Lang. Do you know where Mr. Colt is?" said Lieutenant Licker.

"No, I don't," she said.

"Don't leave this office until we get back. The police fear the devil might have grabbed him," said Lieutenant Licker.

"You mean the killer animal roaming around in this town?" said Mrs. Lang.

"That's right, Mrs. Lang, now stay here!" said Lieutenant Licker.

Every entrance to the zoo was being guarded by the police. "What in the hell is going on here!" Mrs. Lang said to herself. Later Lieutenant Licker came back with another man, and he introduced him to Mrs. Lang. Mrs. Lang was in the greenhouse. Her parrot was dead; she found it lying on the ground with its feathers torn out of it. She was very upset.

"Mrs. Lang, what's the matter?" said Lieutenant Licker.

"My parrot is dead. All the birds are all dead, my animals are getting killed. What's going on here?" Mrs. Lang cried.

"The wolves is the answer, we have been having a problem with them! Mrs. Lang, this is Mr. Cook, he's a new man here. He was a caretaker at other zoos, so he knows what's going on. Mr. Colt is nowhere to be found at the present time. He disappeared last night, and the police is still trying to find him. He's not at his house or the diner he goes to. He's got to be here somewhere or he might be found dead, don't be surprised! Mr. Cook is going to work with you during the day in case this animal comes around," said Lieutenant Licker.

"I hope he's not dead!" said Mrs. Lang.

"Mrs. Lang, this is Mr. Cook. Mr. Cook, this is Mrs. Lang," said Lieutenant Licker.

"Nice meeting you people," said Mr. Cook.

"Mrs. Lang, show Mr. Cook around the zoo," said Lieutenant Licker.

"God, this place isn't too pleasant, is it? The cats look like different animals, and some animals look like the devil!" said Mr. Cook.

"Mr. Cook, we have been getting a lot of horrors lately since this zoo's been open, worrying about some unknown animal," said Mrs. Lang.

Late in the afternoon, police got a call Mr. Colt was trapped in a well. He's been sitting on a rope way deep in a well to hide from the animal, and he got stuck there near his home. The fire department had to get him out of the well—he was stuck way down there! Then the police took Mr. Colt to the hospital. He was treated and released.

At the hospital, police asked, "What happened last night, Mr. Colt?"

"Officers, you will not believe this. I saw some animal bigger than a bear chasing me! It had pricks all over it, and it runs very fast. The only way I could get away was to jump in a well. I heard this animal roaring all day. I wasn't going to get out of that well," said Mr. Colt.

"Mr. Colt, did this animal look similar like the devil?" said a police officer.

"Yes, it sure did!" said Mr. Colt.

The hospital fed Mr. Colt, then he went back to the zoo at his regular time. Mr. Colt met Mr. Cook and Mrs. Lang. Lieutenant Licker was there also.

"Mr. Colt, what are you doing here?" asked Lieutenant Licker.

"I'm here to go to work. Lieutenant, the police found me trapped in a well because some strange animal's around. I was chased by it!" said Mr. Colt.

"I heard. Listen up, the police and you people are responsible for capturing this thing. We have an unknown animal that looks just like the devil. It has pricks, horns, pointy ears. I believe this animal is a cactus horse or something from outer space. A cactus horse is a very rare breed. They usually come out on foggy, damp nights. Those animals are found in another country. I don't know anything about them, but we have to find it and kill it!" said Lieutenant Licker.

"Lieutenant, I was stuck in that well for eight hours. I heard this animal roaring away. It sounded like a bear, and it had a long tail with prick thorns on it," said Mr. Colt.

"Lieutenant, we have to watch out this animal doesn't get into the zoo or we'll all be dead. I heard on the radio that this animal is very dangerous!" said Mrs. Lang.

"Here's what the police is going to do. We're going to call the military to help just maintain the zoo, and we'll take care of the rest. Mr. Colt, are you sure you're going to be okay tonight?" said Lieutenant Licker.

"Yes, I'll be fine," he said.

Lieutenant Licker and Mr. Cook were talking outside, while Mr. Colt was cleaning the office and the greenhouse. Then he found a sleeping cot, and he went to sleep. He slept through the night until Mrs. Lang came in the next morning. The animals were going crazy! Mrs. Lang came in her office, and there was Mr. Colt sleeping in the cot. Mrs. Lang got some extra food, and she went out to feed all the animals. Finally, the animals kept quiet after. Mr. Colt forgot to feed the animals last night.

"Good morning, Mr. Colt," said Mrs. Lang.

"Mrs. Lang, you're still here!"

"Mr. Colt, it's time for you to go home. You slept through last night," she said.

"Oh my god, are the animals all right?" said Mr. Colt.

"They needed to be fed, but other than that, there were no problems," said Mrs. Lang.

Just before lunchtime, Mr. Cook was bathing some of the small animals. Mrs. Lang was putting new birds into the greenhouse, then she sat in her office to eat her lunch. All of a sudden, the animals started going bananas because the wind was picking up fast outside, and a storm was coming. By the time Mrs. Lang finished her lunch, the sky was almost black as the ace of spades. She heard a rumble of thunder, and she saw a flash of lightning. Quickly she ran outside to get all the animals inside, then the rain came down in buckets, and the wind was really blowing hard! Mr. Cook nor Mrs. Lang had enough time to get the small animals in the greenhouse the storm was so bad! A small twister touched down from the clouds and hit the chicken coop, letting all the chickens loose; then the wind blew cages over, letting the turkeys, the pigs, and the deer loose. The deer ran off into the woods. The animals were being blown around in the wind. All the pigs gathered under a big tree, then a bolt of lightning struck the tree and killed all the pigs! Mrs. Lang watched her pigs get fried by the lightning. She screamed hysterically.

By nighttime, Mr. Cook and Mrs. Lang worked overtime to capture all the animals that broke loose from this afternoon's storm. The police brought three wolves to the zoo from Pickerel Field. About 8:00 p.m., Mr. Colt and Mrs. Lang got back. Mr. Colt finished cleaning up outside. He came in the office, and he said, "Good evening, what happened to you this afternoon?"

"We had a bad thunderstorm this afternoon. The winds were blowing at 105 miles an hour according to the radio!" said Mrs. Lang.

"I see the place looks like a tornado hit it!" said Mr. Colt.

"This storm was bad enough for a twister," said Mrs. Lang.

"I heard on the radio that we had a tornado watch about noon-time," said Mr. Cook.

"I was eating my lunch when the storm came up. I heard thunder, then I looked out the window, and the sky was pitch dark, then next thing you know, everything was flying all over the place. I had to go outside and get the animals inside. The storm was right on top of us!" said Mrs. Lang.

"I was out in the storm, helping Mrs. Lang with the animals, then I went in the office, and I heard on the radio that to be alert for a tornado warning. Then the cages started flying all over the place, and a roof landed here in front of the office. I saw trees busted up,

RICHARD REZENDES

a wired fence twisted in a million pieces. We had to have had a tornado!" said Mr. Cook.

"Jesus Christ, goddam, a tornado!" said Mr. Colt.

Mr. Cook and Mrs. Lang worked overtime cleaning up the zoo
after this afternoon's thunderstorms till midnight. Mr. Colt was taking care of the animals, feeding, etc. Just after Mr. Cook and Mrs.
Lang left the zoo at midnight, the devil entered by jumping over a
tall gate near the horses. A half hour later, Mr. Colt heard the devil
roaring; it was roaming around in the zoo!

"No, no, you cock sucker! You're not going to trap me again, you
fuck!" Mr. Colt said to himself, then he ran to the office and called
the police. About ten minutes later, the police was there. Officer Reid
and Officer Junior met Mr. Colt at the office.

"Mr. Colt, what seems to be the problem?" said Junior.

"I hear that devil-like animal that fuckin' had me trapped for
eight hours the other night. I think it might be here in the zoo!" said
Mr. Colt.

"Okay, let's go find the bastard!" said Junior.

"I hear the motherfucker too!" said Officer Reid.

The police and Mr. Colt searched the zoo all night and couldn't
find the devil. The next day, the police closed down the zoo because it
was not safe. The zoo reopened within three weeks with all new animals. The devil stayed away for six weeks. When the zoo opened up
again, more zookeepers and security were added. Just before school
let out for the summer, Mrs. Chaimber took her boarding girls and
schoolchildren to the zoo to see the new animals. Mrs. Chaimber
showed her girls the wolves first; one of the wolves was turning into
the devil, so one of the girls was watching, and she started screaming.
The devil-like wolf ran to the fence and started biting at the fence,
then all the girls screamed. Then Mrs. Lang turned the hose on the
wolf to cool it down.

The wolf was still going wild, biting at the fence. Mrs. Chaimber
said, "Don't look back, girl, just keep moving!" While Mrs. Lang was
having trouble with the wolves, Mrs. Chaimber took her girls over
to see the monkeys. One of the monkeys ran over to the fence and
spit a peanut at Mrs. Chaimber. The girls broke into a fit of laugh-

ter. Then Mrs. Chaimber took the girls to see the birds. One of the birds looked like the devil too! One girl said, "Oh my god! That bird looks like the devil!" People laughed walking by. Then a giant devil-ish-looking eagle came crashing out of the sky to the ground. Mrs. Chaimber's girls were frightened! The eagle was caged in. The girl started to run because the eagle was trying to bite its way through, and it did, and it started chasing people all over the zoo. Mrs. Lang was able to get the bird. She got a needle, and she jammed it into the bird to put the bird to sleep. Mrs. Lang told everyone to move back.

Ms. Chaimber then took the girls over to see the bobcats, lions, and the tigers. They looked like the devil! "Let's go see the horses," said Mrs. Chaimber. Even the horses looked like the devil! Then Mrs. Chaimber took her girls to see the bulls. Suddenly one of the bulls got mad at a horse. The horse jumped over the fence and went for the bull. The girls watched the bulls and the horses fight! The bulls was tearing up on the horses. The fight was so bad Mrs. Chaimber said, "Come on, girls, we can't see this." The bulls were ripping up the horses so bad it jabbed its devil-like horns into the horses and tore the guts right out of them! The fight was so bad by the time Mrs. Lang and other zookeepers got there, all the horses were all dead!

"Come on, girls, let's go see something else!" said Mrs. Chaimber.

The police gathered the crowd away from the bloody massacre between the horses and the bulls; there was blood everywhere!

The police shut the zoo down for an hour to kill all the bulls. Gunshots were heard for miles. Mrs. Chaimber took the girls to get something to eat before they go back to the zoo. Mrs. Lang passed out when she saw the mess with the horses and the bulls. (This story needs a short intermission!) The hawks looked like the devil. Mrs. Lang had to kill all of them with a spear gun then burn them. The bucks looked like the devil: she had to kill them too! The police were arresting people outside the zoo when kids were trying to break in while some animals were being killed. The zoo closed down for the day.

The next day Mrs. Chaimber took the girls to the zoo again. She went to see the snakes. The snakes were scary looking. There were about ten of them—boa constrictors, rattlers, and other giant snakes. The girls were banging on the window, teasing them.

"Don't bang on the windows!" said Mrs. Chaimber. The girls continued to tease the snakes by banging on the window. The snakes all jumped at the window, shattering the glass, and everyone ran out of there like a bat out of hell, screaming and crying! Even the snakes looked like the devil! Then Mrs. Chaimber took the girls over to see the lions and the tigers, and she told the girls, "Don't go near the fence or these animals will leap out. I now stay away from the fence!" The lions and tigers were roaming back and forth in separate cages. Mrs. Chaimber watched one of the lions turn into the devil. Horns started popping out of the lion's head, then it started growing pointy ears, then it showed its teeth, and blood was pouring out of its mouth. The lion leaped from one rock to another, then it got sick and threw up a big dead rat with puncture holes all over it, then the lion ate the rat after throwing it up, then it threw up again, and five dead rats came out of its mouth in a waterfall of blood! Mrs. Chaimber and her girls watched the horror. She said, "Oh my god!" Then she passed out. The girls screamed, screamed, and screamed.

The girls and other people went over to rescue Mrs. Chaimber. Meanwhile the lions started fighting with one another, tearing each other in pieces. The zookeepers and the police told everyone to leave. The rescue squad came to take Mrs. Chaimber to the hospital. The zookeepers killed all the lions. At midnight, Mrs. Lang was working the night shift. She was working with Mr. Colt. She and Mr. Colt were walking through the zoo, and the animals were still acting up. The devil was roaming around the zoo. The devil tore a hole in the wolf cage and let them loose. Mr. Colt and Mrs. Lang were at the other end of the zoo. They heard a cage rattling, then they both drew their guns, and they searched for the rattling cage. The rattling stopped after a few seconds, so Mr. Colt and Mrs. Lang had to look for it.

"I'll bet it's the wolf cages!" said Mrs. Lang.

"Let's go check, maybe the devil could be in the zoo!" said Mr. Colt.

"Jesus Christ! The goddam wolves broke out of the cages!" said Mrs. Lang.

"Mrs. Lang, go to the office and call the police, and I'll stand guard!" said Mr. Colt.

"Hi, sir!" she said.

The devil wandered off into the woods toward Pickerel Field as the wolves followed. While the devil was on its way to its hiding spot, a police car was racing to the Moodus Zoo, when suddenly the devil crossed the street in the path of the police car. The police car hit it and burst into flames, then the police car exploded! The devil stayed in its rocky shell until the accident was over, then it wandered off into the woods, just like an armadillo! The police arrived, not knowing one of their men was killed on the way! The next day, all the zookeepers had to kill all the animals and burn them, and the zoo closed up for good.

CHAPTER 12

The Red Canyon
Finding the Devil!

"ONCE AND FOR ALL WE'RE gonna find this son of a bitch! The zoo is closed as of today and forever until we get this goddarn devil!" said Junior. The police was writing up reports at the police station on what happened at the Moodus Zoo.

"Junior, we're going to the Red Canyon next. The devil may hang down there!" said Lieutenant Licker.

The National Guard and the Air Force were called in to search for this devil roaming around in town. The search began at the Red Canyon and the Moodus River. Helicopters flew over the Moodus River. Orange clouds and thunderstorms were spotted. The helicopters flying over was the military.

The copilot said to the pilot in the chopper, "Look at this! Have you ever seen an orange thunderstorm before?"

"I'm gonna drop down at eleven o'clock into the clouds to investigate," said the pilot. When the chopper flew lower, the orange storm looked like a fire in the fog! "We better not go into the storm, we'll fly around it!" said the pilot. Then the pilot lowered the helicopter as low as he could down on the storm; the orange fog spread wider and moving fast from the wind of the helicopter rotors. Then the chopper went back up in the air, and the fog disappeared into the water. Then an explosion! Water shot way high into the air.

"Jesus Christ! something must have landed here from space!" said the copilot in the same chopper. Other choppers sent divers down to see what was happening. The orange storm and the explosion was the meteorite the devil was in activating; the devil was inside it. As scuba divers were diving into the water, the devil's shell dug into the sand at the bottom of the river to hide. The meteorite! The divers searched the Moodus River for hours, and they found nothing. The National Guard Investigating Swat Team (NGIST) was searching the town of Moodus all day and night for this stupid unknown animal. The Coast Guard went into the river with boats and divers throughout the night.

About 4:00 a.m., Lieutenant Licker got a call at the police station. He was sleeping in the barracks.

"W-357-190 Coast Guard, come in please." *Beep!*

"Go 'head, W35-l90 police," said Lieutenant Licker.

"This is W35-l90, we spotted a very powerful thunderstorm with dangerous lightning bolts and orange-and-blue cloud cover over the Moodus, Connecticut, River, Police W35-190 over!"

"I read you, W35-190. Moodus Police, over," said Lieutenant Licker.

"Be advised, we also found an active substance in the water near the Red Canyon. Please warn all people to stay away from this area. W35-l90 Coast Guard, over!"

"Ten-four, W35-190. Moodus Police, over," said Lieutenant Licker. The Coast Guard and the Air Force sent help to Moodus to find this very powerful devil, with helicopters and more divers. The divers saw nothing but fish, seaweed, and rocks below the Moodus River. Lieutenant Licker and Junior worked around the clock and lots of overtime to investigate this. At the police barracks, they and other policemen were watching the news on TV.

"Good evening, this is the channel 13 news in Hartford, Connecticut, the six o'clock report. The US Coast Guard officials found a minor content of radioactivity in the Moodus River earlier today. They also found an active substance in the water near the Red Canyon. According to the military, they must ask all residents of Moodus, Hamden, Hampton, and Lime to evacuate your homes within the next ten days. All these residents are to report to your local fire department for transportation. The transportation is free. You will board buses to take you to the shelters. The shelters are located in the Holiday Inn in Groton, New Haven, and right here in Hartford, Connecticut. The Coast Guard reported radioactive thunderstorms in those areas last night. Military divers reported mercury iron side substance in the water near the Red Canyon. The mercury iron side substance deforms where it travels, and it causes a blue cloud underwater. When it reaches the surface, it ignites with the air and forms a gaseous thunderhead, then it either explodes or becomes a tornado! The military thinks the causes of these strange happenings lately could be from something from outer space that might have landed in Moodus, Connecticut!"

The Hartford News continues: "This is just in: all residents who live within five miles of the Moodus River and the Red Canyon must report to the fire station in that town. Buses will meet at all fire stations to take you to Hartford, Connecticut. The deadline is twenty-four hours. The military has been informed about a strange, unknown animal roaming around in Moodus, Connecticut. This thing could be deformed or from outer space. Lieutenant Licker, from the Moodus Police, describes this animal a cactus horse. A cactus horse is a very rare breed. It may have come from a desert from Africa, and it feeds off of cactus plants, trees, and greens. This kind of animal comes out only in darkness or in rainstorms. According to Lieutenant Licker, this animal is believed to have bitten animals at that town zoo, and all the animals there had to be killed. Some people call this animal the devil!

"According to the US military, if Lieutenant Licker said it's a cactus horse, he might be very rich and famous someday! There is no such thing, according to the military! The National Guard is on the lookout for the devil. The military believes this strange animal is either something deformed or something from outer space. Residents of Moodus, please beware of the devil! This is Maggy Green reporting from channel 13 news in Hartford, Connecticut."

After the news on TV, people began running for their lives, banging on neighbors' doors and screaming for help. Cars were going down the highways like race cars, and people were overcrowding the buses at the fire stations, it was a mad house! A baseball game was going on when suddenly spectators saw missiles and rockets flying in the air, warning people about the radiation. The baseball players and the spectators ran to the buses like a bat out of hell, screaming, "What's going on!" Shuttle buses were going around town, picking up panicking people and taking them to the Holiday Inn in Hartford. The Holiday Inn looked like an old prison! Most people had to spend the first night in dirty and smelly rooms at the Holiday Inn. Most people were drinking, eating, and getting high on marijuana there. The Holiday Inns were overcrowded everywhere. Some shelters were located in old prison camps. The people who were not US citizens were sent there!

The Coast Guard was testing the water during the night when people were evacuating. Not everyone had left their homes yet. They still had ten days, except the Moodus River and the Red Canyon. About 5:00 a.m., just about daybreak, the military campers saw a white tornado cross the Moodus River with a blue shadow following it.

"Jesus fuckin' Christ! Did you guys see that tornado? We're all gonna get fuckin' killed if we stay here!" one military man said to another. One week later was the Fourth of July, and it was 103 degrees that afternoon. Moodus looked like a ghost town; no one was in town. The first two weeks of July was miserable for vacationers and tourists because the town had vacated. The military was cleaning up radioactive materials. They had respirators and radioactive uniforms on. The first week of July was a hot one. The temperature during the day was over 100 and over 85 at night, heat, lightning, and thunder every night passing through the quiet town. The heat didn't help the radiation much. The second week of July was another hot one. All the trees were dying, and the radiation was getting worse! Then helicopters began spraying the town of Moodus.

The NGIST was riding around in radioactive cars, and they wore radioactive clothes. The riders saw dead squirrels, dogs, cats, and rats. Riding through town was a disaster. Every animal was dead, laying in the street. The NGIST searched the town in radioactive suits; the radiation was so bad. The military searched and found more chemical while they were searching for the devil. The devil was hiding in the woods. Just before nighttime, most of the military and policemen were at an important meeting.

At the meeting: "Good afternoon, police and military, and welcome to Groton Submarine and Navy base. My name is Captain Titus. I'm sorry to inform you that Moodus, Connecticut, and county is a national disaster area, according to the NGIST, the National Guard Investigating Swat Team."

"Moodus, Connecticut, has a high level of radiation at the locations the Red Canyon and the Moodus River. The radiation is caused by a chemical reactor leading from a plant or something from outer space, because there is no chemical waste dumps in that area. Maybe thousands of years ago Moodus might have had chemical waste, but not lately. Number two, mercury was found in the waters in Moodus. Any living thing that drinks this water could die or deform, insects, animal, humans, etc. For instance, insects might grow into an animal, you might turn into a monster, or an animal might be some kind of unknown creature or maybe the devil! Who knows. Mercury is an element known to deform things."

"Captain Titus, do you mind if I interrupt?" said Mrs. Chaimber.

"Yes, you may!" he said.

"I was at the Moodus town zoo about a month ago. I saw animals' faces turn into the devil! I watched these animals' faces turn, and they were ugly! I heard rumors that these animals drank the water before the military found out that it was contaminated," said Mrs. Chaimber.

"Thank you for bringing that up, Mrs. Chaimber. Number three, unconfirmed reports from the military, police, and local television news has reported an unknown deformed animal roaming around in Moodus, Connecticut. This animal is like a bear, and it looks like the devil! Reports say that this animal is either deformed somehow or it came from outer space! Let me tell you how mercury works: on animals, mercury makes them very hyper. They double the amount of strength and greater. Animals will grow horns or other strange deformations. Mercury will deform humans too! The same as it deforms an animal! But humans will get very sick, die, or grow a third eye or a double nose, vampire teeth, horns, or whatever! Mercury makes insects grow much longer than they are."

"I heard a story from overseas about a mosquito deformed from mercury. It was seven feet long!"

"Wow!"

Everyone laughed.

"I can tell you a lot of stories about the hazards of mercury. Orange-and-blue-colored thunderstorms were reported in Moodus, Connecticut. These storms are caused by mixing chemicals such as mercury and radiation molecules doubling over, and it ignites and forms hazards clouds. Other chemicals are triggered into the storm, such as organic substances with mercury mixing with sulfur. Then it hits the water and makes an explosion. After the explosion, the contents develop into stronger storm patterns, then it gets worse and out of control until the lightning burns the chemical reaction out. Tornadoes can form in a storm like this. In toxic thunderstorms, if the chemicals do not release and keeps building the storm, then a tornado is likely just like a normal storm. If you see this type of storm, you better run and run fast!" said US Navy captain Titus.

"Before any questions and answers, there's a few things I have to go over with you. By the way, my name is General Thorp. I lead the NGIST. We're the guys looking for the devil-like animal in Moodus, Connecticut. About what Captain Titus said about the storms and the orange glows: mercury is an ultra-dangerous substance. Also it can form uranium, which is radioactive once it's activated, and it is beyond dangerous! Mercury also is dug up from the ground, and it could be nuclear waste, ashes that has been for over many years. Number two, the mercury we found in the Moodus River is an organic substance, which means something that has been alive or is alive. Mercury can deform anything! Now you may ask questions, and thank you very much," said General Thorp, from the NGIST.

"Captain Titus, about the Moodus horrors. Do you think the animals at the Moodus zoo drank the radioactive water and turned into the devil?" said one of the police officers. The military laughed.

"According to the autopsies on the dead animals, the deformed animal called the devil bit them and made them deformed. If the devil is deformed, we do not know. Mercury could have deformed that animal, and when it bit the other animals, it may have caused some effect," said Captain Titus.

"Captain Titus, what makes the animals look like the devil?" said Mrs. Chaimber.

"I just got through explaining that to you earlier. This animal called the devil must have bitten other animals and made them turn into devils. Mercury is a funny thing. For instance, take a dog deformed with mercury. Mercury can deform a dog into a different animal. It might still act like a dog, but it will be deformed differently! A dog could deform as a monster and grow much bigger than it normally is. Does that answer your question, Mrs. Chaimber?" said Captain Titus.

"Yes, it does, Captain," she said.

"Okay, now I'm going to give Lieutenant Licker from the Moodus Police a chance to talk Lieutenant.," said Captain Titus.

"Thank you, Captain. The conversations about mercury and radiation brought up through this meeting was a good idea. It's getting us through the gate. But the most thing I'm worried about is this strange animal running loose in my town that looks like the devil. I believe this animal is either a deformed bear, a cactus horse, or something from outer space! Now according to the National Guard, there's no such thing as a cactus horse, so my guess is it's deformed or it's something from outer space. I call this animal the devil!" said Lieutenant Licker. Lieutenant Licker stepped down from the stand, and the captain took over again.

"Thank you, Lieutenant. I have a few more things to add about mercury. When mercury mixes with ground soil and water, it will deform trees and make them come alive into living creatures. Now I may sound a little silly, but it's true. Most of the time, living greens will just rot and deteriorate! But mercury could deform a tree to

170

jump right out of its roots, grow legs, and start running! Keep in mind that mercury will deform anything and everything! Thank you very much," said Captain Titus.

"Gentlemen, my name is Aaron. I'm going to talk to you about mercury and rats! Mercury can do a number on a rat. It makes rats grow into monsters, and monster-like rats can live in water and on land, but most rats get killed before they turn into monsters! If a rat is deformed from mercury and it lives in water, it can grow gills just like a fish, and anything this rat bites will turn into a rat. I hope everyone here is in the military or a policeman because I'm not supposed to let out any information from the military. I'm a chemist for the US National Guard, and I study mercury effects. Thank you," said Aaron.

"May I say one more thing before we close this meeting? Any information that was given to you people at this meeting must be kept a secret. It is military rules. No information is to be given out to news reporters, TV, local police, or anyone! If I find out any information about this meeting given out to the public, you will lose rankings, and you'll also be in serious trouble! Thank you, this meeting is adjourned!" said Captain Titus.

After the meeting, the military went back to its duty, and the police went to the police station downstairs in a radiation shelter. Later, Lieutenant Licker met up with the military at the Moodus River dressed in some kind of space suit, and they were wearing respirators.

"A44-455 NGIST, come in, please!"

"A44-455 National Guard, I read you, over!" said Lieutenant Licker. "Please report to the Moodus River. A44-455 NGIST, over!"

"Ten-four, A44-455, I'll be right there!" said Lieutenant Licker. Lieutenant Licker then met with the military.

"Lieutenant Licker, my name is General Kurt."

"Pleased to meet you, General," he said. "Lieutenant, the Moodus River is highly intoxicated. You have Mercury, uranium, sulfuric acid, and laser ultras. These chemicals are acting over 90 percent in the water, and the Red Canyon, we have high radiation levels," said General Kurt.

"Holy shit, how long will this last?" said Lieutenant Licker.

"I don't know, Lieutenant, but we're working on it," said General Kurt.

"Jesus Christ!" said Lieutenant Licker.

"Lieutenant, also we found mushrooms about three to five feet high growing near the Red Canyon," said General Kurt.

"General, did you hear about the strange animal here?" said Lieutenant Licker.

"Yes, I did. We're gonna kill it!" he said.

The military took Lieutenant Licker for a ride around the Moodus River in a boat. They saw nothing.

Later, Lieutenant Licker went back to the police shelter.

"W35-190 Coast Guard, come in please!" said General Kurt.

"This is W35-190 Coast Guard, over!"

"W35-190, did you find any more chemicals in the water over?" said General Kurt.

"Yes, General, we found mercury, uranium, sulfuric acid, laser ultras coming from the Red Canyon and spreading into the Moodus River. We also have another problem. There are some ten-foot radiation mushroom spotted near the Red Canyon. The biggest problem is the ultralasers. It activates the radiation and causes CO_2 clouds that fills with acid rain, then a severe thunderstorm develops! W35-190 Coast Guard, over."

"Thank you, W35-190, General Kurt, over!"

The police was in their shelters, while the military was investigating the horrors. Katy Wixon was at her mother's house in New York City. Her mother lived on Park Avenue. She was at her mother's because she'd been evacuated from the hotel she was staying at because of the radiation. Katy Wixon and her mother lived in a skyscraper overlooking the Empire State Building on the twentieth floor. Katy turned the TV on to channel 13. The news was on, and she was eating pizza!

"Good evening, this is the 6:00 p.m. news on channel 13 in Hartford, Connecticut. The following areas of the state of Connecticut must evacuate right away! Moodus, Haddam, Hampton, and Lyme must leave their homes because there's a severe radiation watch for those areas. Any people who are still staying at these areas will be moved by the police. If you fail to leave your homes, you may not wake up tomorrow. The military is doing a great job cleaning up the chemicals in the Moodus, Connecticut, River and the Red Canyon. The military found ultraviolet lasers, mercury, and sulfuric acid in the Red Canyon. Also, five sets of military troops came to Moodus to find the strange animal roaming around in that town. The military found out why orange- and strange-colored glows were found in Moodus. It's from ultraviolet radioactive thunderstorms! This is Maggy Green reporting on 13 news."

"This is world news tonight, Major Mud reporting. The State of Connecticut has been experimenting some strange happenings. Ultraviolet rays have caused violent thunderstorms in that state, in a town called Moodus. Strong chemicals were found in the Moodus River, according to the military, that might have triggered these thunderstorms, such chemicals as mercury, uranium, and sulfuric acid mixing together. The military believes Moodus, Connecticut, has a lot of earth shift movements and could have activated some of these chemicals underground. The police and the military have reported leaves dying on the trees and animals found dead. The military has also reported a possible animal from outer space. The look of this animal is ugly and hard to explain. The military is out looking for this animal before it bites or hurts someone. This is Major Mud, reporting on 13 news."

During the evening hours, the NGIST was searching for the animal during a heavy thunderstorm over the Moodus River. The thunder was very loud, and the lightning was very bright. The military had some kind of space outfits on watching the colorful thunderstorm. Meanwhile, helicopters and airplanes flew up and under the clouds in the storm. A tornado tore a path through the woods during this storm. The storm had hundred-mile-an-hour winds. It was a bad one! The storm tore up a small village, and it was heading for the Red Canyon. Trees were uprooted, roofs were torn off the little villages, broken windows and broken pieces of wood all over the place. The next day, the Coast Guard reported the storm beginning somewhere in the water.

"W35-190 Coast Guard, to Lieutenant Licker, Moodus Police, come in please."

"This is Lieutenant Licker, over."

"Lieutenant, an overreaction of chemicals deep down in the water seem to have caused a severe thunderstorm during the night. The Red Canyon Village looks like a tornado went through it! I got the storm on radar starting from the middle of the river where we're investigating the chemical reactions. W35-19O Coast Guard, over."

"Ten-four, I read you, W35-190. I'll send the fire department over to the Red Canyon. Lieutenant Licker, over."

"Ten-four, thank you! W35-l90, over."

The Coast Guard had pictures of the storm and showed the police and fire department the damage. The reports of the storm went to the national weather service for testing. The results came back the next day to the police station saying that the radiation was not as bad as they thought it was, and everyone could return back to their homes. The military patrolled Moodus and the towns that was evacuated and kept things quiet until the meeting tomorrow was all over. The meeting was cancelled for two weeks for more tests to find out if there were any dangerous chemicals. Everyone was still in shelters until the meeting was at stake for safety. Finally the two weeks was up, and the military held a meeting at the US Naval Base in Groton, Connecticut.

"Good morning, I'm General Kurt from the National Guard. Test results from the contaminated areas, Moodus, Haddam, Hampton, and Lyme, Connecticut, is not as bad as we thought it would be, according to a storm in Moodus that the Coast Guard recorded by radar. The chemical blew out of proportion from that storm, and according to the test on this storm, it is not contagious! Everyone may report back to their homes. Thank you," said General Kurt.

The admiral took the stand, and he spoke, "Good morning, my name is Admiral McCarthey. All service men must be here, news reporters, TV reporters, the FBI, and all officials that's investigating the Moodus Horrors must be here at this meeting this morning right now!" said Admiral McCarthey. The general spoke again for the rest of the meeting. After the meeting was held by the eleven o'clock news tonight, everyone was able to go home. Katy Wixon and her mother was watching the 11:00 p.m. news in New York.

"Good evening, this is the channel 13 news in Hartford, Connecticut. Severe thunderstorms ripped Moodus, Connecticut, last night. A possible tornado may have gone through the Red Canyon Village," the Coast Guard reported. "The chemicals found in the Moodus River and the Red Canyon is not as bad as the NGIST said it was. You may all go back to your homes except those people who live near the Red Canyon and the Moodus River, who must wait for two or three days. The military are still testing that area. No one was hurt in last night's storms, thank God! This is Maggy Green reporting."

About a week later, the small villages were being torn out by the military because of the tornado damage in the Red Canyon. Jose and Tanya, the couple from the haunted house, moved into a little yellow cottage in the Moodus valley near the river. The yellow cottage was surrounded by forest and hills. The day they moved in a thunderstorm was coming, and you can see the lightning in the woods. Earl Davies owned the Yellow Cottage. He was there showing the place. Tanya was scared when it was lightning, then it began to thunder. Jose said to Earl Davies, "Is this place haunted too?"

"Of cause not! You people are gonna love it here!" said Earl Davies.

Earl left, then Jose and Tanya finished moving in the little yellow house. Army helicopters were still spraying and flying around all day. Jose and Tanya lived right in the devil's path. The devil hid in the valley and in the hills of the forest. Before nighttime, Jose and Tanya finished unpacking, then they had a drink. Suddenly a big crack of thunder sounded very loudly! Jose and Tanya both dropped their drinks. Tanya screamed, and she was scared.

"Jose, I think we're going to be haunted here too!" said Tanya.

"Tanya, nothing could be as bad as that other house we lived in. That was haunted!" said Jose.

Tanya made two more drinks, and they went for a tour around the house. The thunder was banging away, and the lightning was flashing constantly! Tanya was very frightened. The house was shaking, the dishes were rattling, and the wind was blowing hard outside. It looked like the windows were gonna blow through. The devil buried itself near the yellow cottage. Jose & Tanya sat down for a while to wait out the storm. They had a couple of more drinks, and they looked out of the windows into the spooky forest after the storm. The devil was roaming around outside, but they didn't see it.

Jose and Tanya were walking around the house. Tanya walked into another room, and she looked out of the window. Suddenly, a flash of lightning came, and she saw something out there. She screamed half to death!

"Tanya, what's the matter?" said Jose.

"I saw something out there when the lightning flashed!" she cried.

"What was it, Tanya?"

"It looked like a man out there, a big man standing outside!" Tanya cried.

Jose looked out the window where Tanya saw the man. A big crack of thunder came followed by flashes of lightning. The lights in the house started blinking on and off, and Tanya was frightened! Jose sat by the window until the storm was over. He didn't see nothing out there! He said, "Tanya, you must have seen a broken tree out there. That's all I can see." Tanya started crying. "Oh, Tanya, let me hold you. Stop crying, it's only a thunderstorm, everything is going to be all right!" said Jose.

"Jose, this is the third time we've moved, and everywhere we go, we get haunted!" Tanya cried, then she fell asleep in Jose's arms. A little while later, the storm let up, and they finished walking around their new house.

"Look, Tanya, we have a gas stove, wood stove, and a microwave oven combination. We have a fireplace in the dining room, and we have yellow sinks with gold faucets and a glass table. This kitchen is beautiful!" said Jose. The kitchen and the dining room were together. The house also had a large bathroom and a bedroom. The windows were stained glass like a church and cathedral ceilings. The house had Oriental rugs from wall to wall and a sliding glass door leading outside. The house had a marble kitchen floor and antique furniture in every room. The house was beautiful!

Jose and Tanya were in love with their new home. Finally they went to bed about 3:00 a.m. The thunderstorm came back and woke them up. The wind was blowing the trees like a hurricane. The storm was at its peak. Trees were getting blown over. Jose got up to close all the windows in the house, and he sat up to watch the storm. Jose lit up a marijuana cigarette, and he walked around the house, getting high. The lightning was flashing through the shades. Jose liked to watch storms; Tanya was frightened of them. The thunder started pounding away, and the rain was coming down in buckets. Finally one great big bang sounded. Tanya jumped out of bed screaming! Jose went into the bedroom, laughing.

"Tanya, the storm came back!"

"No shit! It woke me up!"

Then Jose and Tanya made love, then Tanya went back to sleep, and Jose went back out in the other room to smoke another joint. Jose was getting high and enjoying the storm.

Roar!

"Holy shit, this is not only a storm. Something is out there!" Jose said to himself. Jose looked all over the house to find out where he heard the roaring noise. He looked out of every window in the house, and all he saw was the wind blowing the trees and flashes of lightning.

Roar!

Jose heard it again, then a strong gust of wind came! "It must be the wind!" Jose laughed. Then he went to bed. After Jose finally went to bed after getting high all night, he had a dream about a man with big hands. Jose dreamed he was in a submarine. The submarine was on a journey to hell; he was in the Navy, and he was going to war in the middle of the earth with the man with the big hands.

"Where the hell am I?" Jose was saying on the ship.

"Hello, I'm Captain Hands. Welcome aboard the USS *Moodus* submarine!" said the man with the big hands.

A sailor came along, and he said, "We're going to war in the center of the earth to a place called hell to kill the devil!"

"How do you do, Captain Hands? What the hell am I doing here? Where's Tanya, and do you mind telling me what the hell is going on here?" said Jose.

"Jose, your wife is home. You joined the Navy now. You're gonna fight the war!" said the man with the big hands.

"I have to fight the war? I was in World War II, and you think I'm gonna fight another war?" said Jose.

"That's right!" said Captain Hands.

"You want to fight! Put them up, you asshole! I'll kick your fuckin' ass! Come on, let's go!" said Jose.

Captain Hands hit Jose with a fast sucker punch and knocked him out cold. Later Jose woke up, and Captain Hands was standing there, and he said, "Come with me, Buster Brown, you're going to work. I want all these bombs polished and put in its fitters, the torpedoes too! I want the floors swept, washed, and waxed. I want this area to be spotless. When you're done, then come and see me!" said Captain Hands.

Captain Hands was standing by the doorway, watching Jose work. After Jose finished cleaning the bombs, a fire started, and Jose was frightened! He ran and got a bucket of water to put the fire out, then he washed the floor and waxed it. After about eight hours, he was finished.

Captain Hands said, "Okay, come with me. Now I want you to climb down to the lowest deck and polish more bombs and torpedoes. I want them to go in each slot as you did topside. They're twenty-three torpedoes and thirty-six bombs. There's numbers on each bomb, I want them in their correct fitters. Don't drop any, you'll blow the whole fuckin' ship up!"

"Tw-01, what number is that, Captain?" said Jose.

"Tw-01 is the first torpedo. It goes in the number one slot way up above!" said Captain Hands.

Poor Jose spent twenty-four straight hours with the man with the big hands, polishing bombs!

Jose was polishing bombs, and Captain Hands was smoking a cigar watching him. "Get yourself a ladder, you'll need it!" the Captain laughed. Then the captain made him polish some small rockets before he put the torpedoes away. After he was done, he put the torpedoes away. He finally got to the number 23 torpedo, the biggest one! He couldn't hold it right, so he lifted the front end very carefully. The torpedo slipped, and it fell and blew up. Jose woke up screaming to death, jumping up and down on the bed!

Tanya said, "Jose, are you nuts!"

It was 4:00 a.m. Jose said, "I had a terrible dream that I was polishing bombs for the Navy, and my captain had big hands. The last bomb slipped out of my hands and exploded!" Jose told Tanya his dream, then she laughed. Jose sat on the edge of his bed. He was listening to the wind blow outside. The storm was still going on. Then Jose got up to go to the bathroom, and he turned the light on, and the bulb blew! Jose laughed. A big crack thunder came, then bright flashes of lightning, bright enough to turn night into day! The rain was really coming down. Jose walked around the house for a while to shake off his nightmare dream about the man with the big hands.

Roar! Nice and loud!

"Oh shit, we have bears running loose around here!" Jose laughed. Jose searched the house, and he looked out every window, and he didn't see anything. Then he went back to bed. Tanya woke up about seven in the morning to make some coffee, then she watched TV for a while, then she fell back to sleep on the couch in the living room.

Roar!

Jose heard it again, and he woke up, and he got out of bed quickly! It was 9:00 a.m. He looked out every window, and he still didn't see anything! Then he went in the bathroom. He heard the roaring sound coming from the bathroom. He opened the closet, and he could hear the roaring sound coming from under the bathroom. Jose changed the bathroom light, and he heard the roaring sound a couple of more times, then he saw a foot-long worm coming up from the drain in the tub, and Jose killed it!

After Jose killed the worm and flushed it down the toilet, the tub started gurgling, and mud was coming up through the drain. Jose turned around, and he said, "Jesus Christ!" Then Jose was washing the mud down the drain.

Tanya came in the bathroom to take a shower. She said, "What in the Christ is in there?"

"It's mud and shit, the sewer lines must be plugged up!" said Jose.

The mud came back in the tub. Then Tanya called Earl Davies, the landlord, to come and fix it! While waiting for Earl Davies, Tanya got breakfast ready, and Jose was flushing out the tub. Then Earl Davies came while Jose and Tanya were eating breakfast. Earl fixed the tub, and he said, "Last night we had a bad thunderstorm, that's why the tub was jammed. It's okay now. If you have any more problems, call me," said Earl, then he left. Jose went to take a shower, while Tanya finished cleaning up after breakfast.

Roar!

"Aaahhhhhhhhhh! What was that!" Tanya screamed. The roaring noise was coming from the cellar. Tanya ran around the house with a knife. Jose came out of the shower, and he and Tanya searched for that noise. "Did you hear that, Jose?" Tanya cried.

"Yes, I've been hearing that noise all night!" he said.

"What could it be?" said Tanya.

"It sounds like a bear," said Jose.

"Oh my god, will it come in the house?" Tanya cried.

"No, it just roams around outside," said Jose.

"You've got to be kidding!" Tanya cried.

Roar! It was loud enough to wake up the dead!

"Aahhhhhh! Jose, it's coming, it's in the cellar. Call the police, hurry!" Tanya cried.

Jose heard it too. Then he called the police. Before the police came, Jose was trying to get down to the cellar, but the door was bolted shut, and he was trying to pry it open with a cutting board.

Tanya said, "Jose, no! Jose, no! You're gonna get us killed!" Tanya screamed.

About five police cars arrived. Junior ran to the house, and he said, "Police. What's the problem?"

"We have bears in our cellar!" Tanya cried.

"Okay, get out of the house and get in my car, is there anyone else in the house?" said Junior.

"No, just us!" said Jose.

Jose and Tanya ran to the police car. Junior was trying to kick the door through leading to the cellar. It was still raining, but soon it cleared up, and the sun came out. The police officers busted the door and went into the cellar, and they looked around, and there was nothing but spiderwebs and spiders crawling around down there. Jose noticed a man outside going over to the house, and the police chased him out. The man was Chinese, and he had a cabin next door up in back of the woods. He went over to the police car to talk with Jose and Tanya. The Chinaman said to them, "Are you the people who just moved into the yellow house?"

"Yes, we are," said Jose and Tanya.

"Why don't you come over and visit me, you'll be safe there!" said the Chinaman. Junior came to the car, and the Chinaman said, "I'm going to take these people with me."

"Okay, Mr. Chang," said Junior.

Jose and Tanya went over with the Chinaman to his log cabin. He gave Jose and Tanya some Chinese tea and some food. "I'll be right back," said the Chinaman. He went outside to break some wood by karate-chopping it to put under the campfire.

"Sir, could you help us? My name is Tanya, and this is my husband Jose."

"Hello, my name is Mr. Chang, how do you do!" Mr. Chang shook their hands. After lunch, Mr. Chang poured Jose and Tanya more tea, and they talked. "Well, what's wrong my friends?" said Mr. Chang.

"We were bothered by a roaring sound all night long. It sounds like a bear," said Jose.

"Well, let me get my tools and we'll go over and take a look!" said Mr. Chang.

The three of them returned to the yellow cottage after the police left. The police dead-bolted the house up, so Mr. Chang had tools and a shovel with him, and he shoveled dirt away from a hidden bulkhead to get into the cellar. They got into the cellar. Tanya was scared. They saw Oriental faces drawn on the rocky spiderwebbed walls in the cellar.

RICHARD REZENDES

"This place looks like an old Chinese tomb where the Chinese were tortured years and years ago," said Mr. Chang.

"Look here, Mr. Chang, a coffin!" said Tanya.

"No, that's a tomb," said Mr. Chang.

"Mr. Chang, do you think this house is worth a lot of money?" asked Jose.

"No, because there's dead people living under the stones!" said Mr. Chang.

"Oh my god, Jose, we can't live here! Let me call Earl," said Tanya.

The police came back to the house. Mr. Chang, Jose, and Tanya ran like a bat out of hell into the woods! Then they went back to Mr. Chang's place, and Jose called Earl Davies on Mr. Chang's phone.

"Hello, is this Earl?" said Jose.

"Yes, sir, what can I do for you?"

"This is Jose from the yellow house. You haunted us again! Mr. Chang, Tanya, and me got into the cellar by the back of the house through a hidden bulkhead. There's skeletons, tombs, and caskets down there! They're spiderwebs, holes in the cellar walls, and faces painted on the walls, and a bear lives down there somewhere! I'm gonna get my money back!" said Jose.

"A bear! I thought I heard the police right. Listen, I'll meet you in front of Mr. Chang's log cabin in fifteen minutes," said Earl Davies over the phone. Fifteen minutes later, Earl Davies showed up. The police was at the yellow house.

"Hello, Mr. Earl Davies, how are you?" said Mr. Chang.

"I'm so-so, let's go see this graveyard under the yellow house," said Earl Davies. Then the four of them went to the bulkhead and went down cellar. The police was inside. They heard people talking outside. Lieutenant Licker went outside to the back of the house.

"Holy shit! Look at this cellar, Lieutenant. I didn't know this bulkhead was here!" said Earl.

"Neither did I," said Lieutenant Licker. Then he went down the bulkhead, and he saw nightmare city. He came back upstairs, and he said, "Who's Jose and Tanya?"

"We are!"

182

"Pack up and prepare to leave. You can't live here!" said Lieutenant Licker.

Lieutenant Licker, the police, and Earl Davies went through nightmare city. Earl Davies was so frightened he pissed his pants. The police was breaking holes into the cellar walls and found a tunnel of skeletons. The skeletons started falling and breaking all over the place. The policemen screamed. Mr. Chang laughed and laughed!

"Junior, contact the military to have these caskets, tombs, skeletons, and dead people removed from a basement at the yellow cottage in the Red Canyon. There have been decayed bodies down here for years! Mr. Earl Davies, you're coming with me. You're under arrest!" said Lieutenant Licker.

The next day it was eighty-nine degrees at six o'clock in the morning. The NGIST, military, and police arrived in army trucks parked on a street near a bank that led to the Red Canyon Creek, where the yellow house was. The military inspectors were already there! Here comes the Army right by Mr. Chang's little log cabin. He was an early riser! The military and Earl Davies had a long day removing dead bodies all day as the temperature soared up past one hundred degrees. Mr. Chang was sitting under a waterfall, cooling off and laughing at them.

One of the men said, "Go 'head, laugh! Why don't you come and help us, you fuckin' Chink!"

Mr. Chang got up and chased the man that swore at him, and the man ran away. Jose and Tanya loaded a U-Haul truck, and Mr. Chang helped them. About one week later, Mr. Chang was all alone. Now he has to hunt for rabbits and scraps!

"For about forty years, someone nice always lived in the yellow house. Now no one lives there!" Mr. Chang cried. Mr. Chang had nothing to do but investigate a little more on the yellow cottage. He was asking for trouble. He got a flashlight, and he went to the house. The door was wide open, so he went inside, walked around the house to see what he could find, then he went into the basement. Mr. Chang was in the basement. The basement was clean. He flashed the light, and he saw a rat running into a tunnel. He went into the tunnel, and he found a water pocket, like a small pond. Mr. Chang jumped into the underground pond, tying his light to his belt. He saw fish swimming below him, and he swam into a cave. The cave kept going down. There was no up, just down, down, and down! At the end of the cave, Mr. Chang saw a fire burning. He crawled through a small, tight tunnel until he reached the fire burning. Snakes were crawling all over the place! When Mr. Chang got to the fire, he was in a giant smoke stack. He grabbed a rope from his knapsack, and he put a grappling hook at the end of the rope, and he tossed it way up in the smoke stack until it hooked on a rock. Mr. Chang grabbed the rope to make sure it was safe. Then he took a drink from his canteen, then he began climbing the smoke stack. Mr. Chang had to throw his rope about four times, and he climbed three hundred feet. He was almost there. Suddenly the rope snapped, and he fell to his death! Mr. Chang landed in the fire below, and he burned to ashes. It was the devil! People were walking through the Devil's Hop Yard, and they saw a human's leg in the woods and a decayed body next to the waterfall in the park. The police was there reporting the victim was killed by an animal.

CHAPTER 13

The Devil's Hop Yard

HE POLICE PATROLLED THE PARK during the day, and the military patrolled it at night. The military searched the Devil's Hop Yard for some wild animal for over two weeks, and they came up empty-handed. The military did find old skeleton bones, dead animals, blood on rocks, but no traces of the devil-like animal! The Moodus Police found giant footprints tracking through the deep-green forest below, and the search went on from there!

"TL-105 MT chopper, come in please!" said Lieutenant Licker.

"This is TL-105 Military Police, over!"

"TL-105, send some men down to the deep-green forest below the Devil's Hop Yard. I found some large footprints! Lieutenant Licker, Moodus, Connecticut, Police, over."

"Ten-four, Lieutenant, TL-105 Military Police, over."

The military and the police swarmed the Devil's Hop Yard forest to find the devil-like animal. Then as police and the military dug deeper into the forest, they found more! The military found trees split into and ripped right out of the ground and blood puddles on the ground, some footprints, rocks that had blood on them. Some of the rocks looked like it was split in half. The next day, police closed the Devil's Hop Yard because of the strange happenings. Lieutenant

Licker and Junior were walking through the forest, and they saw this couple murdered! The man's head was chopped off with an ax. The ax was next to a rock, the man's head was found in a brook, and the woman had a post driven through her heart! Lieutenant Licker wrote the report down in shock. "Jesus fuckin Christ!" said Junior. The military put the bodies in bags, and it was lifted out of the forest by a helicopter. The next day early in the morning, the military saw blood pouring down the Devil's Hop Yard waterfall. Wild unknown birds was flying around all day. The military searched the waterfall to find out where the blood was coming from.

The military searched the waterfall from top to bottom; the waterfall ended way deep in the forest at a pool full of mud. It looked like boiling mud with thousands of rats and snakes swimming in it. Just before evening, the military noticed colored fog and flashes of lightning. The military tested the storm. It was nothing, just a little strange. The military searched all night until daylight and found nothing! About 7:00 a.m., the police met with the military PTs at the entrance of the park.

"Good morning, I'm Captain Cory from the military police."

"Pleased to meet you, Captain Cory. My name is Lieutenant Licker and my partner, Junior, from the Moodus Police Department. Have you found anything during the night?"

"Yes, sir, Lieutenant, we found large footprints in the forest. It's probably from some large animal. And it doesn't look like footprints from a bear!" said Captain Cory.

"It wasn't a bear?" said Junior.

"No, sir, the footprints look like some unknown animal," said Captain Cory.

"Show us the footprints," said Lieutenant Licker.

"Hop aboard my jeep, Officers, and I will show you where they are," said Captain Cory. Captain Cory drove Lieutenant Licker and Junior to the footprints.

"I know what it is: it's Big Foot!" said Junior.

"What's Big Foot?" said Captain Cory.

"Big Foot is some kind of a deformed animal that has been running around for almost a year now, and we haven't been able to capture it yet! It comes and goes every once in a while. We call it the devil!" Lieutenant Licker laughed.

"We also spotted a bloody waterfall this morning. We still don't know where the blood came from. There was blood on some rocks. We found rocks split in half. We found trees torn from the stumps. It may be this animal biting them off. But the blood, I do not know.

"We also saw these wild-spotted birds, rats larger than normal, swimming in a pool of mud way deep in the forest. Finally we spotted funny-looking fog in the forest. Other than that, That's all we've seen," said Captain Cory.

"Okay, Captain Cory, we have the same reports back at headquarters. If you find anything else that the police don't know about, get back to me right away!" said Lieutenant Licker.

"Ten-four," said Captain Cory as he saluted to the police lieutenant. Then Captain Cory drove away, and the police walked back to their cars. Just about sunset, the military took over. They spotted a thick fog forming deep in the forest way below the Devil's Hop Yard park.

"Jesus Christ, I can't see a thing!" said one of the military policemen. Then he fell off a cliff, screaming to his death, yelling and crying, "*Help! Help! Help! Help!*" Then no more, just like that!

"Oh my god, what are we gonna do? We have to find him!" one of the NGIST men cried.

"There's nothing we can do. He's dead! We'll find the body tomorrow morning," said another military cop.

General Foley was in charge. He said to his men, "We lost Paul Bailey. He slipped off the high cliff to our left. We can't do a thing because the difference between where Paul fell and the ground is well over one hundred feet deep in the forest!" said General Foley. Then the general and his men searched the rock where Paul fell. Sure enough, Paul's stuff was there, and he was gone! Then general slipped off the same cliff, but he was able to grab on to a tree branch and pull himself to safety, yelling, "*Help! Help! Help!*" Then the men helped the general. "You can't see a fuckin' thing! Don't go near the edges, stay in the woods!" said General Foley.

The MTs set up tents and gave up searching for the night because the fog was too bad! The general radioed to Moodus Police in his tent. "L10-11 General Foley to Moodus Police, over."

"L10-11, I read you, go 'head please! Moodus Police, over."

"I lost Paul Bailey in the fog. He fell from the left bank of the Devil's Hop Yard as deep as one hundred to one hundred fifty feet deep into the forest. L10-11 General Foley, over."

"Ten-four, General, but we can't do nothing until morning. We'll send a helicopter. Moodus Police, over."

"Ten-four, L10-11, over."

The next day the fog didn't lift until noontime. A helicopter landed in the park and waited for the fog to burn off. Then the sun came out just before noon. The MTs and the Moodus Police searched the forest canyon where Paul fell. The police found his body. His head was split wide open. You could see his brains, and the bugs were eating it on a big rock. There was a pool of blood splattered all over the rocks and trees. His arms were busted up, and one of his legs were chopped off!

"I'm not surprised the devil had a peace of him!" said Junior.

The park was getting ready to open, but the military had to look for more murders and find this devil! The horrors were not over in the Devil's Hop Yard. Some of the NGIST and military police met at the Moodus Police station before nighttime. Captain Cory had a meeting with Junior and Lieutenant Licker in Lieutenant Licker's office. Captain Cory sat down before he spoke.

"Captain Cory, welcome to my office," said Lieutenant Licker.

"Lieutenant, our MTs and the NGIST military men took fin-gerprints and other tests on most of the horrors we discovered, and here are some of the results. Number one, the large footprints is believed to be an unknown animal, not a bear!" said Captain Cory.

"Captain, the footprints may be a cactus horse. The NGIST says there's no such thing, but I think there is. A cactus horse is a very rare breed and we're looking for it. It looks like a bear, but it's not! This animal has a shape of a bear with horns, pointy ears, with pricks all over it. It has a long pricked tail with a stinger like a scorpion. I heard unconfirmed reports that this animal sprays fire, and it has dangerous claws. It's full of pricks and has big tits, and it also looks like the devil. We call it the fuckin' devil!" said Lieutenant Licker.

Captain Cory laughed, and he laughed. Then he said, "This animal sounds like it comes from space or it's some kind of dinosaur!"

"Captain, the police has been searching for this animal for a long time now. It pops up every now and then and tortures things, then the motherfucker runs and hides! That's why we called the military. Finish up what you have to say because I don't have much time," said Lieutenant Licker.

"We found human blood on rocks and found human flesh and bones in the Devil's Hop Yard. This animal you're talking about is very vicious. It's probably the murderer! We found blood that came from humans and other animals, test shows! That's all I have to say," said Captain Cory.

"Captain, we sent police, the state police with K9 dogs and wolves to get this animal, five dogs and three wolves, and I never saw them again. The animal must have killed them! The town zoo we had to close. We had to kill some of the animals and close the zoo up because this animal was getting in there somehow and torturing the animals. Some of the animals were deforming when this devil, or whatever it is, bit them! We call the town zoo the possessed zoo! We had many animals killed there," said Junior.

"Another thing, Officers, we found trees in the forest that have been ripped out of the ground or has been bitten from the stumps! It had to be an animal of some kind to do that. It couldn't have been a tornado in the deep forest. These trees look like it was bitten by something! We found rocks split in two caused by lightning bolts. We also found unknown species of birds flying over the park. They look vicious!" said Captain Cory.

"The birds Captain Cory is talking about, Lieutenant, are bigger than eagles and it could determine why some of the trees were torn out of the ground and snapped off!," said Junior.

"Junior could be right! One more thing we found was a pool of mud sitting in the forest at the end of the waterfall. It looked like boiling mud. we saw snakes and rats swimming in it. Military test shows that the mud is bubbling from a hot spring. You could have a possible active volcano brewing in the Devil's Hop Yard!" Captain Cory laughed.

"Captain, do you really believe that red birds are vicious enough to snap trees and rip them right out of the ground?" said Lieutenant Licker.

"All I know is that military test shows that some kind of animal is eating up the trees in the forest," said Captain Cory.

"Jesus Christ!" said Junior.

"Captain, what do you think about opening the park this weekend?" said Lieutenant Licker.

"Lieutenant, in my words, you do what you want to do because we have to rule the park regardless what police say. You may open the park, but you policemen, the US military, the park police, and the NGIST have to watch the park twenty-four hours a day, because if someone gets hurt, we're not responsible, you are! If we tell people they can't go here or you can't go there, we have to tell them! The Devil's Hop Yard is declared under a state of emergency. The town of Moodus can do what they want, but if someone gets killed, don't blame the military. Don't say we didn't warn you," said Captain Cory.

The weekend was here. The military set up trailers with radars on them to track this devil roaming around, but the devil hid deep down in the forest in the Red Canyon caves. Helicopters flew around all day, searching for this animal. The police was going to open up the park. The military was on guard. It was Friday morning, and the police and the military were prepared.

Friday night, the night before the park was ready to open. This couple jumped the fence in Chapman Falls, and they snuck by the military and walked down into the deep-green forest, the couple decided to camp in the forest on the Red Canyon cliffs, where the devil was; it was too far deep in the forest for the military to guard. The two lit a campfire, and the devil was roaming around near them. The campfire attracted the devil! The devil came over with no warning. The man went over in back of some rock to go for a pee, when suddenly the devil clawed him from behind and ripped his ribs out of his stomach! The man screamed and bled to death. The girl ran over to see what was wrong, and when she saw her boyfriend's guts splattered all over the rocks, she screamed hysterically. The girl ran to the campsite to get her boyfriend's gun. Then she saw the devil coming for the tent. She shot at the devil several times, and the bullets were bouncing off the devil because it had a hard rock shell. The screaming girl kept firing away at the devil until the devil slipped off the cliff and into the Moodus River!

The devil splashed into the water unharmed, and it swam to the shore, and into the woods it went. The boy was dead laying on the rocks. The girl went to the tent to get a broom they used to brush the ashes away after a campfire, and she swept her boyfriend's dead body over the cliff, and she poured a bucket of water on the blood to wash it away so it wouldn't stink. She swept his bones off the cliff. The devil heard splash, and it plunged into the water and found the body swept off the cliff, and it finished it off!

Later in the day, the girl wrapped herself in a blanket inside the tent to hide from the devil. Then the devil surprised her as it tore the tent, and she screamed and ran! The devil then chased her, and she fell off the cliff, and she landed on a rock just before the water; her blood dripped off the rock into the river. Three Boy Scouts saw it, and they watched.

"Look up there, someone got murdered!" one Boy Scout said to another. The Boy Scouts went up into the woods by climbing rocks and saw the girl's body in pieces mangled on the rock across the river.

"Let's get some help. Some animal must have got her!" one Boy Scout said to another. Then the devil was right there where the Boy Scouts were. The devil chased them. Two got away, and one was eaten alive!

Three more campers were camping in the forest. One of them ran to the cliff, yelling, "Dick! Dick! Dick!" Because he heard his friend Dick crying. The devil grabbed him and choked him. Dick was kicking his legs back and forth, as the devil was choking him. Then the devil bit his head off, then it was tearing his chest and ripping the insides right out of him, piece by piece, then it ate him alive! One of the other campers was bringing some wood back to the campsite, and he saw the devil chewing Dick's leg like a chicken bone. He screamed and screamed and screamed! Then he picked up a big stick, then he poured lighter fluid on the end of the stick. He torched it in the campfire, then he started chasing the devil with it; the devil ran, and it slipped again off the cliff into the Moodus River.

The third camper saw Dick's pants and shirt, but not the body. Blood was pouring down the rocks where Dick was attacked by the devil. The blood was pouring from the area of the attack down on another rock below. The devil was down there waiting! The third camper walked through the forest with the torch. The other camper was watching over the cliff to make sure the devil was dead! Then he saw a girl's body lying on the rocks in a pool of blood. "Jesus Christ!" he said. The third camper saw Dick's head rolling on the cliff, and he kicked it off the cliff into the water. The second camper found the girl's gun at the girl's campsite. The third camper saw eyeballs in a tree looking at him. He screamed and fell off the cliff into the river, just missing a rock! Quickly the devil swam underwater and killed him!

Two girls were rowing a canoe down the Moodus River; they heard someone scream. Then they saw a helicopter flying up above, then a police boat pulled up alongside the canoe the girls was in and told them, "Please pull the canoe ashore. Come with us!"

"WCY-9 MT Chopper to Moodus Police, over."

"Lieutenant Licker from Moodus Police, I read you, WCY-9, go ahead please!"

"Lieutenant, I'm flying low over the Moodus River, and I spot a lot of red on the rocks below. I guess the devil-like animal was hungry last night! WCY-9, MT Chopper, over!"

"We got danger, thanks for the warning! Lieutenant Licker, Moodus Police, over!"

"Our troops are moving in, Lieutenant. WCY-9 MT Chopper, over."

"Ten-four, I read you, WCY-9. Lieutenant Licker, Moodus Police, over."

Later in the morning after last night's nightmare in the Red Canyon, the Devil's Hop Yard reopened. It was a beautiful Saturday morning. Buses and cars from all over came to visit the grand opening of the Devil's Hop Yard! Thousands of balloons were let off into the sky and cannons going off! People were taking pictures of the park, the mountains, the trees, and the beautiful color of this park. Extra police, park police, and the military were on duty in case the devil came near! It was fun and games for everyone. Plenty of food was being served.

Katy Wixon arrived at the Devil's Hop Yard in a Rolls-Royce cornice she brought on an insurance case about the devil haunting her, and she parked her car next to these bikers. Katy Wixon knows some of the bikers as she watches them when she was parking her car. She overheard one of the bikers say, "She's the girl that told police she saw the devil in town!"

"Ar ha ha ha ha!" they laughed.

Katy got out of her Rolls-Royce cornice, and she buttoned up her sweater, and she just looked at them dirty bikers! One of the bikers said to her, "Hey, babe, you're looking good today, nice car!"

She smiled at them, and she walked into the woods.

One of the bikers said to her when she went in the woods, "What's the matter, miss? Do you see the devil in there?"

She came out of the woods and took her sexy hat off, and she said to the one that was yelling at her, "I know you. You're the drunken punk that came into my store one day, trying to rip me off, asking me questions and not buying anything! And you broke my door when you left too! Smarten up, buddy, and stop acting like an asshole!" Katy Wixon put her sexy hat back on and she walked away.

The bikers said, "Tough lady!"

Another biker yelled to her, "Hey, honey, do you want to fuck?"

She turned around and she said, "Go fuck yourselves!"

Junior came over Katy, and he said, "Are those bikers bothering you?"

"Yes, they are," she cried.

Junior went over to the bikers, and he said, "All you bikers get the fuck out of here right now!"

One of the bikers started pushing Junior, and a fight broke out! Then the park police and Moodus Police jumped in to break it up! The kid who started it got his ass whipped! Katy Wixon laughed hysterically.

Katy Wixon was still laughing, watching all the bikers get arrested one by one! Katy was walking in the woods, and when she came to a bridge, she passed out near Chapman Falls. Suddenly people ran over to help her. She almost fell into the waterfall! The powers of the devil made her faint because she was possessed by the devil. Later Katy got something to eat, and she was all right. Then she went back into the woods. Suddenly she saw the ground move just a little, then she saw a flash of light. She screamed, thinking it was lightning. A Boy Scout heard Katy Wixon scream, so he came over to her, and he said, "What's the matter, miss?"

"I saw something in the woods," said Katy.

"What did you see?" said the Boy Scout.

"I saw the ground move a little, then I saw lightning!" she said.

"I think I saw lightning too!" said the Boy Scout.

"I think I'm possessed by the devil," Katy said to the Boy Scout.

"The devil! There's no devil here. The name of this park is the Devil's Hop Yard, but there's no devil here," said the Boy Scout.

"Let's go for a walk in the woods and see how spooky it is," said Katy Wixon.

The Boy Scout looked at her, and he said, "Okay!"

The Devil's Hop Yard Tour: "Good afternoon, ladies and gentlemen, and welcome to the Devil's Hop Yard, national park and resort area. My name is Jerry, I'm the tour guide of this park. If you look down to the left a little, you'll see Chapman Falls. Look to your upper left and you will see the bridge we're going to cross soon. Look down on Chapman Falls and see the wonderful red stone with crystals in it. Look at the footprints on the stone, it is believed to be the devil's footprints, thousands of years before Christ! This is why we call this park the Devil's Hop Yard. In the wintertime, Chapman Falls never freezes, and the stones turn red at night. It gets cold here at night in the Devils Hop Yard because we're on top of a mountain. It gets cold up here, but it's warm during the day. Now let's walk along the Chapman Falls and follow the waterfall."

"Let's stop here on the bridge," said Jerry the tour guide.

One of the tourist guides stepped up on the bridge, and she ran her hand across the railing of the bridge, and she had blood on her hands. She quickly washed them off in the waterfall, and the blood disappeared. Then she saw a big dead fish on the rocks with its guts hanging out! Then something grabbed her hand in the water. She screamed, horrified! Then she saw the devil's face in the waterfall, and blood was pouring down the waterfall and over the rocks, then the blood disappeared, and the girl was screaming to death. The park police had a hard time handling the girl because she was screaming so much.

"Everyone get back! Everyone get back! I said everyone get back, she's going to be okay!" said the military MTs. Then a rescue came to pick the hysterical girl up and take her to the hospital. The tour guide continued his tour after the excitement.

"Okay, everyone, on the bridge. Okay, look straight down the waterfall as far as you can see. Notice that the waterfall follows way past the forest. That is Chapman Falls. Chapman Falls is five and a half miles long. This waterfall follows through this park, way deep into the green forest and into the Moodus River. It ends at the Red Canyon. The Red Canyon is a cliff that leads to another waterfall, also flows into the Moodus River.

"Look down at the dark green treetops. That's the Dark Green Forest of Moodus, Connecticut. The dark green forest also ends at the Red Canyon. Everyone look at the crystal stone in the waterfall. The crystals come from burnt rock. During the winter, these rocks heat up, and in the summer, the crystals get rays from the sun, and it reflects off the stone. Sometimes these rocks will activate and cause ultraviolet rays and make the waterfall turn red, but that rarely happens. The waterfall is a hot spring, the only hot spring on the East Coast. We could be on a possible volcano. The crystal rocks you see in the waterfall is called the devil's feet. Let's take a five-minute break before we finish the tour," said Jerry the tour guide.

After the five minutes were up, Jerry spoke and continued the tour. "The devil's feet is believed that many years ago, the devil lived in this park, and the devil hopped from rock to rock. Everyone step off the bridge and follow me, please. Ladies, gentlemen, let's stop over here. Here are some large footprints which is believed to be the traces of the devil years ago! The devil's feet are so hot it planted it's feet into the stone, so the devil would hop from stone to stone. That's why we call this park the Devil's Hop Yard!

"Now we're on Devil's Cliff. Look straight ahead of you. You'll see the mountains, the valleys, beautiful colored flowers and trees, and the lakes below. We will see the dark green forest later," said Jerry.

The crowd enjoyed the tour, taking pictures of the beautiful scenery and looking through binoculars and telescopes. Then Jerry continued the tour.

"Okay, everyone, we're heading for the trails. The trails widens and turns, but there's beautiful scenery throughout the park. These trails attract joggers, bikers, campers, and Boy Scouts, etc. Trails are a big thing in this park. If you look to the right, you'll see some beautiful scenery. You can see everything here! Be careful because we're on a two-hundred-foot cliff with no railings! Just stay back and look. You can practically see the whole park," said Jerry.

"What's this coming?" said one of the tourists.

"It's a gondola. We're going on that next," said Jerry.

The crowd screamed with joy. Everyone wanted to ride the gondola.

"Everyone listen up. The gondola ride is $6. Pay at the ticket booth!" said Jerry.

Everybody got their tickets and boarded the gondola. Then the gondola left Devil's Cliff.

"Good afternoon, ladies and gentleman, my name is Rick, your tour guide on the gondola. Please fasten your seat belts!" said Rick. The gondola was flying over the Devil's Hop Yard park. The crowd was loving every minute of it! Rick, the tour guide on the gondola, said, "Welcome aboard the Devil's Gondola. We're now flying over the Devil's Forest. Everyone enjoying the ride?"

"Yeah!" the crowd roared.

"Now if you look straight down, we're flying over the Moodus Canyon. The Moodus Canyon is a very deep opening in the forest! Now we're flying over the Red Canyon," said Rick. Then the gondola jolted right over the Red Canyon. Everyone screamed for their lives. "Don't worry, ladies and gentlemen, the gondola ride gets a little bumpy once in a while, it's nothing to worry about, don't be afraid!

We're now flying over the Moodus River and Caves Hill House. Everyone hang on, we're dropping into the dark green forest, called the Devil's Forest! Look how spooky it is in here. It's dark like this twenty-four hours a day in the deep forest! This forest gets almost no sunlight at all during the day. This forest is believed to be where the devil lived years ago," said Rick.

The crowd couldn't get over the darkness of the Devil's Forest. The gondola flew fast out of the forest, from darkness to daylight in three seconds. The crowd on the gondola stood up, clapping and cheering. The crowd gave a standing ovation before Rick spoke again.

"Ladies and gentlemen, we're new flying over the camp ground and picnic areas of the Devil's Hop Yard. If you look up and straight away, you'll see the famous great castle of Connecticut. The castle is on Mt. Sherlock," said Rick. The crowd was clapping at the view. "Okay, we're new approaching a stop. There's another Gondola going to the castle and Mt. Sherlock tours. Whoever wants to go, it's a separate $6 admission round trip through the Devil's Hop Yard. There will be a ten-minute break before we finish our tour. Thank you," said Rick and he got off the gondola to get a cup of coffee, then he came back. Some people got off, and some got on the gondola. "Ladies, gentlemen, the next gondola is going to the great castle. It's a two-hour ride, one way ticket for six bucks. You'll see the great castle, then you will fly high over the Connecticut River, high enough to see the polar caps on the Canadian mountains. And you will see New York City! Whoever is staying on my gondola is on their way back to Devil's Cliff!" said Rick. The gondola was filled and ready to go.

"Ladies and gentlemen, we're now flying over Chapman Falls. Get a good look at it. Everyone look down quick, there's people skinny-dipping in the water fall!" said Rick. The crowd looked down and laughed. "Now we're flying over the Chapman Falls Bridge. Look below and you will see a nice view of the Devil's Hop Yard. Now, ladies and gentlemen, we're now flying over a mountain. If you look down, we're flying over a crater that might have been a volcano years ago. Look down in the crater and you will see a village, there's Indian camps there! If you look to the right, you will see the Moodus Caves and Camp Indiana. Look around the rim of the crater, you will see walkways for viewers to look down into the villages. The crater attracts thousands of tourists a day during the season. This crater is really a valley splitting between mountains. It's beautiful, ha?" said Rick. The crowd cheered. "Now, ladies and gentlemen, we're flying over the trails in the park. Look at all the joggers below. We're now coming to a stop, and this was where we started from. This is the end of our tour, and thank you, ladies and gentlemen," said Rick, the tour guide on the gondola. The crowd gave a standing ovation, then they went "Booooooooo!" because the tour was over, then everyone got off the gondola.

About ten minutes later, the gondola was filled and ready to go. Katy Wixon was on the gondola this trip. She was having flashbacks of the devil! A thunderstorm was forming in the mountains. The Boy Scout was with Katy Wixon. The gondola was flying through the dark forest. Suddenly, Katy Wixon saw a bolt of lightning, and she screamed and screamed. The Boy Scout held her, and he said, "It's okay, it's only lightning!" Then the gondola got stuck in the forest. Katy Wixon started screaming to death, then a nurse came over to her.

"May I have your attention. We're stuck in the forest because the power went off from the thunderstorm. Don't panic, the power will be restored shortly. Thank you!" said Rick, the tour guide on the gondola.

An hour later, the gondola was still stuck in the deep green forest. Everyone was screaming because the gondola was jolting, and sparks were flying all over the place!

"Ladies and gentlemen, I can't help the delay. We have a bad storm going on and we have to wait until it passes before we can get out of the forest. Please don't panic, and stay calm. There is a nurse for further assistance, she will get to you, thank you," said Rick.

It was aggravating, a gondola full of tourists stuck in a gondola in the deep forest during a heavy thunderstorm. Katy Wixon said to the nurse she kept seeing the devil in the woods through her flash-backs. Everyone on the gondola was laughing because they thought she was nuts! Then the gondola lifted out of the forest into dark black clouds then into sunlight. Katy didn't enjoy her trip much because of her flashbacks. The gondola stopped at the castle stop, Everyone stayed on because the storm looked like it was coming again! It started to rain and thunder. The gondola was passing the Devil's Hop Yard and Chapman Falls, then by the time the gondola reached the crater, it got stuck and jolted again. People screamed for their lives. Rick's talk box was not working because of the storm. The nurse even screamed her head off! Then a cable snapped, and the gondola slid almost sideways over the crater. The people were practically having a heart attack until the ride was over. Everyone was glad to get off that ride!

Nighttime, the military heard strange noises in the forest, but they couldn't find anything. The devil was eating trees, bushes, and animals in the deep dark forest, mostly snakes and rats. The NGIST were working their way into the Devil's Forest; the MTs were patrolling the streets in town with the Moodus Police. The National Guard was in the Devil's Hop Yard and Chapman Falls National Parks at night searching for this devil! The NGIST found dead dogs, horses, deer, wolves, birds, any animal you could think of was tortured by this devil roaming around the deep forest. The military heard someone screaming far away in the forest; the devil got one of their men near the Moodus River. The military searched all night until daylight and couldn't find this devil-like animal.

CHAPTER 14

Chapman Falls

WO COUPLES WERE CAMPING FOR the weekend in Chapman Falls Resort, Bob and Lori, and Rick and Jan. Rick was driving. "Rick, slow down, you're driving too fast!" said Jan.

"Don't worry, Jan, I want to get there as fast as I can!" said Rick.

"Rick, if you don't slow down, the police is gonna get us, and we'll never get there!" said Jan.

Sure enough, here comes the flashing lights, and the cops were following him, and he had to pull over.

Jan said, "Rick, I told you, but you don't want to listen to me!"

"Jan, shut up, ha?"

The cop knocked on the window, and he said, "May I see your license and registration, please?" The cop went back to his car with all the police lights flashing. Then the cop came back to Rick's car, and he gave Rick his license and registration back, and he said, "All of you get out of the car, please." The cop searched all four of them for drugs, then he searched the inside of the car, except for the trunk, which had a pound of pot in a garbage bag! "Okay, everyone can get back in the car. The reason why I'm stopping you, Rick, is because you were driving sixty-one miles per hour in a thirty-five-mile-an-hour zone. You were driving twenty-six miles over the speed limit!

Now I'm going to have to write you out a ticket, and the fine will be $260 plus a court appearance. If I catch you driving over the speed limit again, I'm gonna put you in jail," said the cop.

"Officer, how do we get to Chapman Falls from here?" asked Jan.

"Chapman Falls. Okay, follow this road down about seven until you see a sign the says 'The Devil's Hop Yard!' Take a right and go down seven more miles until you see a sign 'Chapman Falls,' bare left and you will run right into it! Now drive slowly because the Connecticut State Police will screw you to the cross if you don't!" said the cop.

"Jan, you're an asshole! After the cop gives me a $260 speeding ticket, you ask him for directions to Chapman Falls? I know where the fuck Chapman Falls is!" said Rick.

"Rick, if you didn't drive so fast, you wouldn't have to pay a $260 fine!" said Jan.

"Jan, fuck you!"

"Rick, luckily the cop didn't make us open the trunk or we really would have got screwed!" said Bob.

"I know we were very lucky, I thought sure the fuckin' asshole was gonna check, but he didn't! If he did, we'd be up for a good twenty years! I didn't see a car on the road until that asshole state trooper came out of nowhere! A $260 speeding ticket, I swear he must be the fuckin' devil!" said Rick.

Bob and Lori laughed and laughed.

"Rick, just drive a little slower next time!" said Jan.

"Jan, if you don't shut up, I'm going to stop this car and you'll walk to Chapman Falls!" said Rick.

"Go 'head!" Rick slammed on his breaks and stopped the car, and he told Jan, "Get the fuck out now!"

"Come on, you two, stop arguing and let's go!" said Lori.

"Jan, get the fuck out of this car!" said Rick.

"No!" she cried.

Then Rick grabbed Jan by the throat, and he said, "If I hear one more peep out of you, you're gonna walk!" Jan cried and cried.

"Come on, Rick, leave the poor girl alone!" said Lori.

Rick drove down the road a little.

"There's the Devil's Hop Yard!" said Lori.

"Okay, now we make a right and drive seven more miles, and we should be there!" said Rick.

While Rick was driving to Chapman Falls. Here comes the flashing lights again! Rick stopped the car, and he said, "What's the fuckin' problem now?"

"Rick, stop your swearing!" Jan yelled at him.

Then Rick slapped Jan in her face. Jan hit him back, and the two of them were hitting one another when the cop came to the car! Rick rolled down the window, and he gave the cop his registration and license, then the cop went back to his car. While everyone in the car was ready to shit their pants. The cop was gonna make us open the trunk now! The cop came back to the car and gave Rick his license and registration back.

"The reason why I'm stopping you is because you're swerving all over the road from side to side," said the cop.

"Sorry, Officer, I just had a big fight with my girlfriend. I'll watch my driving," said Rick.

"Could you step out of the car, please?" said the cop. Rick got out of his car. "How many drinks have you had?" said the cop.

"None, sir!" said Rick, as he was shaking like a leaf!

"Why are you shaking so much?" said the cop.

"Because I don't get stopped by cops very often," said Rick.

"Rick, take a deep breath!" said the cop; he was having a Breathalyzer test. Rick was sitting in his car, practically crying! Then the cop came back to the car, and he said, "Where are you going?"

"We're going to Chapman Falls," said Rick.

"Okay, Rick, you're okay, have a safe trip and drive carefully," said the cop.

Rick WAs driving down the road, and he said to his friends, "Boy, if I knew Connecticut had so many staties, I would have never come here!"

Rick kept driving, and Lori said, "Rick, stop, here's Chapman Falls!" Rick stopped the car, and he pulled into a roadway to read the sign, what direction it was pointing, then here comes the flashing lights again!

"Another fuckin' cop!" said Rick.

The cop got out of his car, and he flashed the light in Rick's car, and he said, "This is a private area. You cannot enter."

"Officer, I'm looking for Chapman Falls Resort Camping Area," said Rick.

"Okay, turn around and go to the intersection you just passed and bare right and you will run right into it," said the cop.

"Thanks a lot," said Rick. Rick turned his car around, and it stalled; he tried to start his car, and it wouldn't start. He pumped the gas a little, and he got it started, then he drove off! Finally Rick found the place where the four of them were staying. "Okay, this is where we're staying, in a log cabin. Get our things and let's go! Now listen up, this cabin has two floors, sleeps six. There's four of us. We have a wood stove up and downstairs and a big fireplace! We have plenty of wood, and we can cook inside or out. Let's light a fire now because it gets cold in the mountains, get fuckin' high, and enjoy our Labor Day Weekend!" said Rick.

It was 5:30 a.m. before everyone was in bed. The four of them enjoyed watching the sunrise over the great Chapman Falls, smoking dope before they went to bed for the rest of the night! Meanwhile a cop was out checking Rick's car during the night. The cop saw his license plate: New York, Ks-my-Ass. The cop laughed and laughed!

"Lori, get my bong and we'll get buzzed!" said Bob.

"Hey, gang, there's another asshole cop outside checking out my car. I hope he doesn't smell the pot. Let's shut the lights off and get into bed before he comes!" said Rick.

The cop shined his flashlight in all the windows of the cabin, then he left.

"A pig!" said Jan.

"Another fuckin' cop!" Rick laughed.

"Rick, where should we keep this bag of pot?" said Bob.

"Let's put it in my footlocker. The combination is 06 left, 11 right, and 24 left. We'll keep all our drugs in this footlocker, so let's put all the drugs away before another fuckin' cop comes!" Rick laughed.

"Rick, did you see my bong?" said Bob.

"Yes, I did, I put it in the footlocker."

"How about these *Playboy* books?" said Bob.

"Leave them where they are. Now let's get to sleep. It's almost six o'clock in the morning," said Rick.

Lori and Bob slept upstairs, while Rick and Jan slept downstairs.

"Rick, come to bed and let's fuck!" said Jan.

"Oh! you don't want to fight anymore!" Rick joked.

Rick woke up about one o'clock in the afternoon, and it was a rainy afternoon. There wasn't much to do but party when it was raining. Rick grabbed a couple of beers out of the refrigerator, then he rolled up a joint, and he started smoking it. It was party time all over again! Then Rick blew smoke in Jan's face, waking her up, and he gave her a can of beer. He said, "Come on, baby, it's time to party!" She just rolled over, and she went to sleep. Then Rick went upstairs to bother Bob and Lori. They were moving under the covers, so he left them alone. Meanwhile the devil was roaming near the campsite around the cabin, then it turned back and went out into the woods. Rick thought he heard a noise, but he was not sure, so he lit up a second joint, and he got high! Later Bob and Lori came downstairs and joined Rick smoke dope. Then it was 3:00 p.m. Jan was still sleeping. After the rain let up a little, Bob and Lori went out to see the waterfalls.

"Hey, Jan, get your ass up and come out and join us!" said Rick.

Then Jan got up, and she took a shower, got dressed, and she went outside with the rest of them. Bob, Lori, and Rick were at the waterfalls with a cooler full of beer, wine, and sandwiches. Jan was missing out! Then Jan brought a marijuana bong with five tails from the cabin outside to where the rest of them were.

"It's about time, Jan. Grab a sandwich and a beer or a glass of wine!" said Rick. The four of them had a big party that afternoon overlooking Chapman Falls! "Forget everything, just party!"

"Rick, throw me a beer!" said Bob.

"Here you go!" Rick threw him a beer.

"Do you have some wine in that cooler?" said Jan.

"Sure, baby, here's some Champagne for you!" said Rick.

"Oh, Rick, champagne! Wow, what a classy picnic we're gonna have! Rick brought me some champagne!" said Jan. While Jan was getting excited about her champagne, the bong everyone was getting high out of fell into the waterfall, and they lost a lot of pot. Rick accidently kicked the marijuana bong into Chapman Falls when he was getting Jan some champagne!

Bob was mad, and he said, "Rick, you stupid bastard. You just kicked the bong in the water. Now we can't get fuckin' high!"

"Sorry, Bob, I have another one in the footlocker. I'll go get it," said Rick. Rick got another bong from his footlocker and some more pot, and he went back to the party.

"Now watch where the hell you're going next time, Rick!" said Bob. Rick poured Jan another glass of champagne, and he grabbed a beer, and he started kissing Jan all over. Bob, Lori, and Jan took off their socks and walked to the waterfall. Rick was rolling up a few joints to smoke later. Bob was in the waterfall, and he saw something.

"Rick, did you see what I saw?" he said.

"No," said Rick.

"Look in the waterfall!" said Bob.

"I don't see anything!" said Rick.

Bob said, "Look good!"

"It looks like blood flowing over the rocks!" said Jan.

"Yeah, it does!" said Lori.

"Let's go for a walk, maybe we'll find the body!" said Bob.

"I don't see no blood," said Rick.

"Rick, keep looking, you'll see it! Who's coming with me?" said Bob.

"I will!" said Lori.

"I'm staying here with Rick," said Jan.

"Where's the blood, Bob?" said Rick.

"I don't see it now! The blood is gone!" said Bob.

"Okay, gang listen up, let's put our stuff away. Grab a small cooler to put a few beers and sandwiches in and we'll walk the water-fall. Everyone for it?" said Rick. The rest agreed.

"Rick, did you finish rolling the joints?" said Bob.

"Yes, I did," he said.

"Okay, let's go!" said Bob.

The four of them went back to the cabin to regroup, then they went for the gusto! They walked the waterfall down into the deep forest all the way to the end of the waterfall in darkness.

"The waterfall lights up at night. Oh wow!" said Jan.

As the four of them walked deeper into the forest, the waterfall got more beautiful!

Great big floodlights were planted in the waterfall to see it in the forest because it was so dark down there. Then the four found a sunny spot in the forest, as the sun came out and shined on Chapman Falls. The water pounded the rocks like the ocean, spraying water into the deep green forest below. It was beautiful!

"Look at the giant rainbow the waterfall is making!" said Lori.

"Oh wow, how nice!" said Jan.

Later the rainbow disappeared, and the sky was clear. Then Bob heard thunder as everyone was crossing the waterfall, walking on the rocks down into the deep green forest. Bridges led to the deep forest called the Devil's Forest. Then Bob heard thunder again.

"What's the matter, Bob?" said Rick.

"I hear thunder!" said Bob.

"Bob, you're dreaming, how the hell can you hear thunder when there is not a cloud in the sky?" said Rick.

"Rick, just listen, will you," said Bob.

"I think I hear thunder too!" said Jan.

Later the campers came to a long bridge, and the deep green forest continued way below. It was a long way down. Fog was starting to form in the lower forest. You could see the clouds moving under the bridge. The bridge crossed from one mountain to another. A thunderstorm was forming in back of one of the mountains.

"I still don't believe you heard thunder. It's probably the waterfall, Bob," said Rick.

"Rick, look under the bridge!" said Bob.

"Holy shit! We're way high over the clouds under a bridge. We must be high up there!" said Rick.

All of a sudden—*crack!* Thunder sounded very loudly.

"Rick, if you didn't hear that, you're deaf!" said Bob.

"I heard it, Bob. It sounds like thunder! Gang, we can do one thing or the other, let's head back or cross to the next mountain until the storm passes and hope to find a rock to get under or a shelter, because we're gonna get soaked. We get nasty thunderstorms in the mountains! One minute it will be sunny, then a storm is coming just like that!" said Rick. The storm under the bridge was rising and forming black thunderheads. "Let's cross now, we don't have much time. We're going to the next mountain!" said Rick.

The campers were very frightened because the storm was moving fast, and the thunder was very loud! Then the storm came up so quick it was following the campers to the next mountain, then it was lightning! The clouds rose upward so fast it covered the daylight into night with big black thunderclouds. Lori and Jan were crying as their boyfriends pulled them along. The wind started to blow as the frightened campers made it to the summit on the second mountain. The rain held up.

Then the storm was on top of them. They couldn't find a shelter right away, but they found a big rock to get under at the summit. A snake crawled out from under the rock. Jan saw it, and she screamed to death! Rick grabbed a big stick with a point on it, and he stabbed the snake with it, and he tossed it! More snakes were under the big rock, hiding from the storm, so the campers had to run back out into the storm until they found another rock or shelter. Everyone had to run out in the pouring rain and thunder and lightning!

"Rick, we're not gonna make it!" Jan cried.

"Jan, shut the fuck up, we'll make it!" said Rick. He grabbed Jan's hand and pulled her along. Everyone was soaked as the storm was getting very bad. The lightning was brighter than daylight—it was like being in it! The thunder was so loud their ears were popping; fiery bolts were zapping down the sides of the mountains. Jan and Lori screamed hysterically when they saw the bright bolts hit.

"Here are some rocks. Let's see if we can get under one," said Rick. Finally the campers found a big rock to hide under, because a severe thunderstorm was overhead. The thunder was so loud it seemed like the end of the world. The rain was coming down like a typhoon, and the wind was blowing like a tornado! The campers found a cave around the big rock, and they went in there to wait out the storm. Meanwhile, the devil was in that cave sleeping!

"Let's stay here for a while. The rain is coming down in buckets," said Rick. The campers watched the thunderstorm in the cave. Bolts of lightning struck everywhere, different colored ones too!

"Look at the lightning now, it's green!" said Jan.

"Holy shit! Green lightning means a tornado!" said Rick.

"What?" said Jan.

"My father told me, when the lightning is green, that means a tornado is coming!" said Rick.

"Well, we're not fuckin' leaving here until this storm is over!" said Bob.

The storm got worse instead of better. The girls screamed and cried until it was over. The campers watched lightning slice trees in half, and the rain was washing them down the mountain. Trees were getting tossed and ripped out of the ground from the wind as the campers watched in shock.

Rick and Bob were getting a kick out of watching the storm, laughing, but when trees started to uproot and fly like a bird, they were very frightened. The four campers drank a few beers until the storm passed. Jan fell asleep. It was starting to get dark and cold before the campers left the cave. Finally they made it to the top, where the summit was on the high mountain, then they were in the Devil's Hop Yard, which closed down because of possessions of the devil. The State Police was there at the summit to meet the campers.

"Look there's a spotlight shining on us. *Help! Help! Help!*" said Bob.

"No shit, Bob, we're gonna get arrested too!" said Rick.

The cop shining the light said, "How many are you?"

"There's four of us," said Rick.

"How the hell did you people get into the Devil's Hop Yard?" said the cop.

"The Devil's Hop Yard, is that where we are? I'm trying to get back to Chapman Falls," said Rick.

"How did you get on the grounds without anyone seeing you?" said the cop.

"We're trying to find our way back to Chapman Falls," said Rick.

"Officer, we got lost in a storm," said Bob.

"You mean you guys crossed Chapman Falls!" said the police.

"Yes, we did, over a bridge," said Bob.

"I can't see how. You'd have to have a bridge about a mile long, because no one can't outswim Chapman Falls!" said the cop.

"Maybe some campers built a bridge," said Rick.

"Officer, we crossed from mountain to mountain, and we crossed a high waterfall, and we ended up here!" said Bob.

"I still don't believe you. No one has ever crossed Chapman Falls," said the cop.

"Well, believe us, Officer, because we crossed it," said Rick.

"Well, I'll tell you boys were very lucky, because we have some kind of animal roaming around here killing people and animals. Get in the car and I'll take you back to Chapman Falls. If I catch you campers in here again, you're gonna get twenty years in the slammer! Do you understand?" said the cop.

"Yes, sir!" said the campers.

About 9:00 p.m. the police drove the campers back to their camping area in Chapman Falls. "Now stay on this side of the water-fall!" said the cop.

"Yes, sir, and thank you for the ride back," said the campers. Then the cop left.

About 9:30 p.m. on a Saturday, the four campers went in the cabin and turned on the woodstove to warm up! The campers were in bed by midnight they were so tired. All the campers had a dream. Jan's dream was about the cop meeting them in the Devil's Hop Yard.

"How did you people get here?" the cop said in her dream.

"We got lost in the storm!" said Rick.

"Go back the way you came!" said the cop.

"But, Officer, it's freezing out. I need a ride back, man!" said Rick.

"You people go back the way you came or you're all going to jail!" said the cop.

"Let's go back!" said Rick.

"We can't go back, Rick, it's too cold!" Jan cried.

"Jan, we're going back! Follow me, everyone, stay away from the water and find the trails. Some of them may be flooded. We'll build a campfire in the forest to keep warm," said Rick.

Then the campers were crossing the bridge over the deep forest.

"Don't look down!" said Rick.

Jan looked down, and she saw a big bird flying under the bridge, then crack! "What was that?" Jan cried. Then the bridge collapsed, and everyone fell, Jan leading the way headfirst into a big thunderstorm below the bridge. Trees, rocks, and pieces of the broken bridge flying with her. She screamed at the top of her lungs in her sleep, then she woke up crying and shaking at about 12:30 a.m. Rick grabbed Jan.

"It's only a dream, it's only a dream!" he said to her.

Jan got up to feed the fire, and she told Rick about her dream. "I thought it was really happening, because I don't remember the police giving us a ride home last night," Jan said. Rick and Jan went back to bed, then Rick had a dream.

Rick's dream: The campers were all sitting by the waterfall, eating chicken and smoking dope, then the campers went for a walk alongside the waterfall and down into the forest. It was a foggy day. The campers were crossing the waterfall by hopping from rock to rock and hoping that everything would be okay. Jan and Lori heard strange noises in the forest in Rick's dream.

"Ladies, it's all right, there's nothing to be afraid of in the forest at night. It's just trees and fog!" said Rick. Rick lit a campfire in the woods, and the devil's face appeared in the fire. Everyone screamed and jumped back!

Roar!

"Did you hear that, Rick?" Jan cried.

"Yes, I did, let's head back!"

"Rick, what was that?" she cried.

"I don't know, it might be a bear! Let's get the hell out of here!" said Rick.

Rick woke up, and he put a log on the fire, and he walked around the cabin for a while. It was about 1:00 a.m. Rick went back to bed.

Lori had a dream next. Lori's dream: Lori dreamed the campers were way up in the mountains; they saw snow and ice like it was wintertime. Everyone was dressed warm. The waterfall was still running, with ice and snow covering the rocks. Before the campers went up in the mountains, they were swimming in the waterfall with bathing suits on.

"We're gonna have an early winter this year!" said Lori.

"How cold is it up there?" Bob yelled through a loudspeaker.

"It's twenty-seven degrees!" said Rick, yelling down the mountain.

"Let's head back, it's too cold!" said Jan.

"Yeah, let's go before we freeze to death up here!" said Lori. Then everyone lost directions because a sudden snowstorm came, and everyone froze to death. Lori was screaming, "Rick, help! Rick, help! Rick, help! Bob, help! Bob, help me please! Jan, help! Jan, help! Somebody help me! I'm lost and a snowstorm is coming, somebody help!" Lori was crying in her dream. Then she fell in the snow, sliding down the mountain, and her fingers froze, then she started rolling down the mountain, and she stopped and hit a tree. She kept screaming, "*Help! Help! Help!*" Then she froze solid, and she couldn't move and turned into ice. She woke up so fast she jumped out of bed, and she walked around the cabin for a while. She went to the bathroom, then she went back to bed. It was two thirty in the morning. After Lori went back to sleep, Bob had his dream.

Bob's dream—it was early in the morning, and the campers went on a hike. Bob saw a policeman hiking in the woods. Bob said, "Hey, Officer, is it okay for me to hike here too?"

"Sure, I'm hunting for bears! What are you hunting for?" said the cop.

"Bears? There's bears in these woods?" said Bob.

"Did you hear about the devil roaming around here lately?" said the policeman.

"What devil?" said Bob.

"We have a vicious animal around here killing people!" said the cop.

"Oh my god!" said Bob.

The policeman and the rest of the campers went hiking, and there were weird animals in the forest. Suddenly they were trapped and screamed for help. The policeman started shooting them, and the weird animals leaped at Bob, and it was attacking him. Bob screamed, "*No! No! No!*" Suddenly the animal ate him! Bob woke up breathing heavy. Then he got up, made himself a hot cocoa, then he put another log on the fire, then he went back to bed.

It was 3:00 a.m., Jan woke up. She fixed some hot cocoa, and she went back to bed. It was a very cold night in the mountains. At 9:00 a.m. Sunday, it was a warmer day. Rick woke everyone up.

"Wake up, let's go, time for breakfast!" While the others were getting up, Rick made a big campfire outside near the waterfall. The campers enjoyed breakfast, telling one another about their dreams last night. They laughed and joked. After breakfast, the campers went to church a little ways up the road. There was a 10:30 a.m. Mass in a little church on the camp grounds. After Mass, the campers went hiking for the rest of the day. They walked the waterfall again all the way to the end. It was a nice day. The campers ended up at the bridge. This time the campers took a wrong turn. Instead of going over the tall bridge, they ended up at the Red Canyon cliffs; the waterfalls split two ways. One was coming from the Devil's Hop Yard, the other flowed to the river.

"This is the place we're looking for, the Red Canyon. Follow me!" said Rick.

"According to the map, this is where we take the path to the Devil's Forest. This is where we wanted to go last time," said Bob.

"That's correct! The only way to the Devil's Forest is to crawl down the rocks following the waterfall. We may have to hold on to some trees, but it's no big deal. We cannot cross the bridge. We have to climb down," said Rick.

"Rick, are you nut?! We're gonna get killed!" said Jan.

"Jan, just follow us and you'll be okay. Don't look down, and take one step at a time!" said Rick.

The deep forest was a gorgeous view but a scary climb down. (The horrors were about to begin)}

"Hey, Rick, I have a parachute in my knapsack, and I'm going to jump!" said Bob.

"No, you're not!" said Lori.

"Lori, baby, don't worry, I used to jump from planes all the time. My father was in the Air Force!" said Bob.

"Bob, you're fuckin' crazy! You're not going to jump!" said Rick. Rick and Bob got into an argument about parachuting off the cliff, then they ended up in a fistfight, and the girls were screaming, trying to break it up. Then Rick and Bob started really going at it, fighting; they were almost at the edge of the cliff, wrestling with one another. The girls were yelling at them to stop.

"*Stop! Stop! Stop your fighting, you two!*" Lori cried.

Jan hit Rick with a stick to break up the fight. Suddenly Rick slipped off the cliff and into the canyon below, wrestling with Bob! Jan screamed and screamed, and she screamed and cried, watching Rick fall to his death! Bob didn't see Rick fall. Jan and Lori pulled Bob from the edge to a tree to treat him. He was covered in blood from the fight. Lori took his knapsack off him. Jan used her first-aid kit on Bob to bandage him up. Jan was crying and having a flashback!

"Bob! Bob! Bob! Bob! Bob! Bob! Help!" And that was all Jan heard. The three campers left and cried hysterically. "All I could hear was Bob's voice six times, then 'Help!' Now he's gone!" Jan cried.

"Listen, girls, stay here, I will be right back. I'm going to the bridge to see if I can see Rick's body," said Bob.

"*Ahhhhhhhhhhh!*" Jan went berserk. Lori had to hold her down. Bob saw nothing but green trees below the bridge. The girls ran over to the edge, and they saw Bob running on the bridge.

The girls cried, "Bob, don't jump!"

Bob parachuted over the bridge. Lori screamed to death, then his parachute opened! Jan was hysterical over Rick's fall. Jan and Lori watched Bob float through the air as they were in tears. Bob was yelling for Rick as he landed in the forest. Instead of the waterfall, the wind shifted him into the devil's dark forest. Bob's parachute was stuck in the evergreens, and he unwrapped himself and shimmied down the tree into the forest. The girls saw Bob's parachute lying on top of the trees below.

"Oh my god, he's dead too!" Lori cried.

"Maybe not, Lori, don't think that way, but I know Rick is dead!" Jan cried.

"He might have landed and crawled down the tree, I hope," said Lori.

"Lori, look! Flares! Flares! Flares! He's alive!" said Jan.

Bob made it to the waterfall, and he started climbing up to save his girlfriend and Jan. Then Bob got trapped in the canyon. The canyon was too steep for him to climb. "Oh fuck, how the hell am I gonna get up here, fuck!" said Bob to himself. Bob shot five more flares up in the air for help, and the girls were on their way down. Bob went back into the forest to find another way to climb back up the mountain, but he was in the wrong place at the wrong time.

"Oh my fuckin' god! What the hell is this!" Bob was trapped by the devil. He first saw a rock move in the forest, then the devil jumped out of it and leaped at Bob and attacked him! The devil's mouth opened wide and crumbled Bob in two bites! The girls were more than halfway down, and they heard Bob yelling. He didn't have a chance; the devil attacked him so quick and ate him alive!

Jan and Lori yelled, "Bob! Bob! Bob! Rick! Rick!" The echoes sounded six times then no answers!

"I'll bet Bob's dead too!" Lori cried.

Jan and Lori yelled for Bob and Rick all day long and still didn't get any answers. The girls were on their own. When Rick fell, he landed in the waterfall. The devil ate him up. The devil was chewing one of Rick's legs like a chicken bone in the waterfall. Suddenly a helicopter was flying low over the forest. The devil quickly wrapped up in its shell and froze until the helicopter passed. Later the helicopter came back to remove Bob's parachute from the top of the trees. Lori and Jan waved at the helicopter, yelling, "Help! Help! Help!" Lori and Jan cried when the helicopter just flew by! Finally Jan and

Lori made it to the forest; they were not aware of the devil down there!

It was 6:00 p.m. and getting dark in the forest. Jan and Lori took a break and smoked a joint, and there was a dead, decomposed body near them, but they didn't see it, then the girls went on their business. Jan and Lori kept walking through the Devil's Forest, yelling for Bob and Rick, and still no answers! Finally the girls found the waterfall, but it was a long way up. They saw the bridge up above. It looked like a small popsicle. It was way up there! Lori slipped on a rock, and she ran into a tree, but she was all right; she just screamed.

"Lori, what are we going to do? We have to climb back up this mountain!" said Jan.

"Oh my god! Blood all over the rocks! Ahhhhhh!" Lori cried.

They yelled for Bob and Rick but no answers, so they gave up. Jan saw a big hole in a tree climbing up the mountain; she looked in it, then she jumped back, then Lori went to check it out. She got sucked inside the big tree hole!

"*Ahhhhhhhhh!*" Jan screamed. Jan saw Lori look inside! She was gone! Jan ran up the hill as fast as her little legs could go, screaming to death. The devil grabbed Lori through the hole in the tree and sucked her under the ground! As Jan was running in fright after what she saw, she passed out near the waterfall. About four o'clock in the morning, Jan woke up, and she was lying near the waterfall. She heard the helicopters flying by. There were six of them. She yelled, "*Help! Help! Help!*" The helicopters" lights spotted her as she ran to a rock, and the helicopter saved her.

CHAPTER 15

The Devil in Moodus, Connecticut

ℰARLY MORNING ON LABOR DAY, the National Guard Investigating Swat Team (NGIST) was searching the forest for more bodies or animals after finding Jan alive, thank God, deep in the Devil's Forest. The devil ate everything down there! The NGIST found blood in the waterfall and on the rocks in the Red Canyon Falls. A busload of people were camping near the Moodus River for the Labor Day weekend, when suddenly the devil ran out of the woods and attacked several people. People were running around, trying to get away and screaming! The devil was chasing them to the bus and biting them; most of the people were bitten and stung by this devil-like animal. The devil bit a girl's arm off as she was trying to get on the bus. Another girl had gotten her hair pulled by the devil's claw as it was attacking the first one. Then the devil bit another girl's leg practically off, and a man got bit in the back by the devil and gouged his back, at the same time it bit another man's leg, but he got away! The bus driver was a big man. He was able to wrestle the devil with a big stick so he could get on the bus and close the door and the side door, then he opened the emergency door and stood there with the big stick. The devil chased the rest of the people to the back of the bus; the bus driver got his gun, and he shot the devil when it was trying to get in the bus. Some people made it without a scratch, and some got eaten alive! Three of the passengers were beating the devil with rocks before the bus driver shot it, then the devil backed off so survivors could get on the bus safely! A fourth man tried to get aboard the bus, and the devil chopped him in half with one big bite! The bus pulled away, and the devil chased it, and it busted through the side doors, spraying fire and trying to get in; then after the devil got in the bus, it was spraying fire all over the bus, and everyone was getting burned! People were jumping out of windows and leaping through the emergency exit to safety. The bus driver kept shooting at the devil, and the bullets were bouncing off its shell, and it sprayed fire at the bus driver and burned him alive! The bus was rolling down a hill. Most people jumped out while the devil was trapped in the bus, holding their wounds after getting burned.

Then the bus hit a tree and burst into flames! Survivors clapped and hollered "Ding-dong the devil's dead, the devils dead, the devil's dead! Ding-dong, the devil's dead today!" and ran off into the woods. The bus was engulfed with flames. The devil curled up in its shell and escaped through the emergency exit, and it went back into the woods to go on its business. Arms and legs were laying in the campground in a pool of blood. Big water rats came out of the water for dinner! Then about five police cars pulled up at the burning bus, and the survivors ran over to the police, hollering, "Police, help us! Help! Help! Help!"

Junior was in the woods, going for a leak, when the survivors ran over to them. The police was on the burning bus and saw dead people on it that got burned by the devil! Then the cops heard people screaming. The police got their loudspeakers out and ordered the injured, "May I have your attention, please? Get away from the bus in case it blows up! Please be patient until the rescue squads arrive."

"Car number 105 to Lieutenant Licker at headquarters, over," said Junior.

"This is Lieutenant Licker at headquarters, go ahead, car number 105."

"Lieutenant, a bus loaded with a camping group from New York lost control and hit a tree and exploded, and there are dead bodies on it. Please send the fire department, rescuers, and all the help I can get. There are people here screaming that some animal burned them. Car number 105, over!" said Junior.

"Ten-four, Junior, right away! Lieutenant Licker at headquarters, over."

"Car number 105, where are you located, over," said the police at the station.

"I'm located at the Moodus River near Red Canyon. Car number 105, over," said Junior.

Then help was on the way. The burn victims were in the water. The people who were bitten bled to death and passed out in the woods! The fire trucks were putting the fire out on the bus, and the rescue team went in to remove the dead bodies. They pulled one man's arm off, then stuffed the burned bodies in bags and hauled them away! The police was questioning the survivors, while the rescue workers were throwing up when they saw these burned bodies. Then a tow truck came to remove the bus. Dozens of police cars arrived to the scene from all communities. The rescue took the injured to the hospital and the dead to the morgue. The area stunk like dead rats.

Every survivor was in the hospital, the police was at the Moodus River looking for more bodies, then the military came in with tanks to look for the devil. The doctors at the hospital took the worst survivors in right away to be treated; the ones who were shaken up, the nurses talked to them near the emergency room.

"We have eleven survivors out of forty-one here right now, according to state police. Five are seriously injured now in the emergency room, right?" the nurse said to another one at the receptionist desk.

"That's correct," said the head nurse behind the counter. Then the same nurse took the six unhurt victims into another room and gave them some medication and took their blood pressure, then she asked questions.

"What happened?" the nurse said.

"We were camping in the woods in Moodus, Connecticut, by the river, when suddenly this weird-looking animal came out of nowhere and started attacking us! It sprays fire, and it killed a lot of people! The bus driver had a gun, and he shot it, and it still killed the bus driver spraying fire at him! It bit people's arms off and legs, and it ate some people alive. It was the most horrifying I ever seen!" one lady cried.

"What did this animal look like?" Officer Reid from the Moodus Police asked the lady.

"It looked like a bear with pointy ears, horns like the devil, a long tail, and pricks all over it!" she cried.

"That's all we have to know," said Officer Reid.

"It looks like something from outer space!" one man from the survivors said.

"We have an animal roaming the streets we've been trying to capture. We call it the devil because we don' t know what it is. From all the horrors it's caused Moodus, under my concern, it's the devil! This animal has horns, ears, a long tail with pricks all over its body, and it stings and sprays fire, and it has four legs. The military will get it. This animal has done more damage in this town then the tornadoes out west!" said Officer Reid.

The police and the military surrounded the Moodus River and the Red Canyon for the devil. Fires broke out in the woods, and the military was putting them out.

"Officer, that animal is dead, because the bus exploded, it was on it!" said one of the survivors.

"When I got to the bus, there was nothing but burned bodies, and the interior was demolished. The devil got away!" said Officer Reid.

About 3:00 p.m., helicopters landed on the Moodus River, sending military divers into the water. The Air Force sent out paratroopers over the Moodus Canyons to find this devil. The National Guard Investigating Swat Team, NGIST, followed the devil's footprints from the Moodus River into the deep green forest.

Lieutenant Licker went to the hospital to see the patients. Some of the patients were all banged up, and some were in the emergency room wearing respirators. The nurses worked on the shaken-up patients for scratches and burns. Lieutenant Licker went to the receptionist's desk, and he asked the doctors and nurses, "Who has been working on these patients? We have had several accidents in this town by this unknown animal. Make sure when you take tests on these people to get the results to the lab as quick as you can, because something might deform and come alive! I want to know if this animal is from outer space or if it's the devil from hell or if it's a cactus horse or whatever it is! I want you to know this animal sprays fire and bites! It has pointy ears, horns that looks like the devil, and has pricks all over its body. It has a large breast, four legs, and claws like a lobster! Get the results to the lab and send them to Dr. Zipper's office on North Street. This animal is radioactive!" said Lieutenant Licker.

"Lieutenant, this animal you're talking about is a dinosaur!" said one of the doctors.

"Bullshit! How the hell can a dinosaur spray fire! This animal is from outer space, I know that's a fact! There is no dinosaur ever on earth that was radioactive, wake up, Doc!" said Lieutenant Licker.

"Jesus Christ! This town is possessed and going fuckin' crazy!" said the doctor.

"Doctor, I believe this animal came from Venus, according to the military!" said Lieutenant Licker.

Junior came in to the hospital, and he met Lieutenant Licker, and he said, "Lieutenant, more bodies are being brought into the hospital, thirty dead!"

"I know, Junior, it's a disaster!" said Lieutenant Licker.

The policemen went to the hospital cafeteria to eat supper; some nurses and doctors were there too, watching the six o'clock evening news on a giant TV screen.

"Good evening, this is the Monday evening news at six. It was a miserable Labor Day holiday in Moodus, Connecticut. Thirty people are known dead, and eleven others injured when a busload of campers were leaving the Moodus Connecticut River bound to New York, when suddenly they were attacked and burned by this devil-like animal roaming around in Moodus.

"The campers who died were bitten alive and bled to death! Some lost their arms and legs, but most were burned alive! The eleven survivors were being treated at the hospital for radiation diseases. They will be in the hospital for at least a few days because they're in such shock! Some of the survivors describe this animal as having nine legs, horns, a big breast, and a long tail with a stinger at the end. Others said it looks like the devil with pricks all over it! The devil-like animal chased the people on the bus, and the animal broke through some doors on the side of the bus, and it was attacking people and burning them! One survivor said that the bus driver shot the devil with his gun, and it just wouldn't die. Then the bus rolled down a hill and struck a tree, and the devil was in it. According to police, they say that the devil was not in the bus when they arrived! Survivors had to jump from windows and the emergency exit, and they were later found dead! This is Maggy Green reporting from the channel 13 news in Hartford, Connecticut."

Most of the nurses got sick after hearing about the terrible news and saw scenes of what happened. The helicopters continued on searching for this devil, sending paratroopers and military men to guard Moodus. The NGIST spotted the devil running out of the woods and into the river. They shot several shots at it. It leaped into the water, and it dug a hole in the bottom of the river to hide; the devil scooped under the sand with no trouble to hide. Hundreds of divers jumped into the river to find it. The devil hid in a cave under the river floor—that was where the devil belonged! The devil was smart. It knew when someone was after it. It hides where it can't be seen! The military followed footprints down beneath the river, and they never found it! The NGIST was checking for radiation in the area. There was some but not much. The military dug holes in the ground to track the devil but found nothing! Late at night, the devil was out roaming around the Moodus River. The military searched the woods for more bodies. A submarine was placed under the Moodus River with a dummy attached to it for the devil to attack the next morning, The submarine and the dummy were still there.

This couple and their daughter were eating in the dining room. The mother and father had a bowling league to attend later. The last thing the mother said before she left the house was "Cindy, you clean up the dishes because Dad and I are late for our bowling league." On the way to the bowling alley, Cindy's mother was having flashbacks about her. She said to her husband, "Cindy had a pretty dress on tonight." Cindy's father was taking a long time to bowl because he was thinking about her, how good she was in school and she may go to Brown next year when she went to college. Then he bowled a strike, and he shook his head, then he sat down. Mother got up to bowl. The father was still thinking about Cindy. Mother dropped the ball on her foot, and she passed out on the bowling approach! Everyone in the bowling alley ran over to her.

Meanwhile Cindy was at home, eating a dish of ice cream, and her dog was barking up a storm! Cindy saw a flash of lightning, and the dog ran to the window barking like hell! Then she heard a growling noise. The dog sat at the window, barking. The lightning got extremely bright. Cindy ran into the kitchen. She was so scared! Suddenly the devil crashed through the open window at Cindy, and it bit her in half! The dog jumped out a window. The devil swallowed her from the waist down. Then the devil jumped out of the window, and it went back into the woods. Other people in the neighborhood heard glass breaking. They saw Cindy's house with a broken window. Meanwhile Cindy's mother and father were on their way home from bowling. They saw their dog running around in the street. Father drove down the road a little, and he hollered for the dog, "Buttons, come on, Buttons! Did Cindy let you out? Goddamn her, I told her not to let the dog out at night when were not home!" said Cindy's father. The dog jumped into the car, crying and acting strange, then Cindy's Father pulled into the driveway of his house with his car, and he turned the key off.

He saw people knocking at the back door. A woman came running to Cindy's parents, and she said, "Mr. and Mrs. Braga, someone must have broken into your house. The front window is busted on your porch," said the women. Another neighbor called the police. The police hasn't come yet. The mother and father entered the house. The father grabbed his baseball bat, and he went looking in the bedrooms. The mother walked into the kitchen, and she saw blood splattered everywhere! Mother saw Cindy chopped in half. She had her hand over her mouth, and she screamed, "*Oh my god!*" Then she passed out and dropped to the floor! The father ran to the kitchen when he heard the wife screaming, and he saw Cindy's body sliced in half with blood and guts hanging out of her! He was about ready to throw up!

The police arrived. Cindy's father was very quiet and shocked. The police came in through the window and saw the body. The fire department and three rescuers and about five more police cars came. Worms and snakes were swimming in the blood from the body. The rescue crew removed the body by putting it into a bag and carrying it to the rescue wagon. The police escorted the father out of the house. He was in the Army. The mother was woken by the rescue workers and taken to a hospital. The father was down at the police station.

"Are you John H. Braga Jr.?" asked Lieutenant Licker.

"Yes, I am," he said.

"Are you aware of some animal roaming around town?" said Lieutenant Licker.

"Animal, what animal?" said John.

"We have a deadly animal might be from outer space that may have leaped through your house, killing your daughter, Cindy," said Lieutenant Licker. Lieutenant Licker got a paper, and he showed it to John. It was about the animal, titled, "The Devil Haunts Moodus, Connecticut."

"Oh my god! We just moved here from Boston, and I never heard of such a fuckin' devil! Whatever it is, I'm gonna burn the motherfucker! How can an animal come crashing through my windows and kill my daughter!" John Braga cried.

The next day, Cindy's parents were at the police station.

"Mr. and Mrs. Braga, I'm sorry to say your daughter was killed by that animal," said Lieutenant Licker.

Cindy's parents went out to eat at some restaurant, and the father picked up a newspaper, and he read about the Labor Day bus horror massacre. He couldn't eat! Cindy's parents moved back to Boston.

The military was still looking for the devil. A search and a curfew watch went on in Moodus. The devil was roaming around in the rain in the deep forest. It stayed down there for a while. The devil was at the waterfall, drinking water, and a bear was about to approach. The bear roared! The devil turned around, and the bear

223

seemed frightened. The bear stood on its hind legs and watched. The devil was a lot bigger than the bear. A seagull was flying over Chapman Falls, and the devil whacked it out of the air with its claw. The bear stood on its hind legs and watched. The sea gull was laying on a rock, flapping its wings, then it died. Then the devil faced the bear, ready to challenge it, then it went after the bear! The bear bit the devil's neck. The devil wrapped its tail around the bear and stung it. The bear was weakened, and the devil ate it alive! The devil tore the bear apart while it was suffering from the sting. Then another bear came along to challenge the devil. The devil sprayed fire at it and burned it alive! And he ate it! Later the devil went back to the waterfall to drink some water. Birds were flying over Chapman Falls, and the devil was sweeping them out of the sky again! Later the devil dug a hole underground, and it crawled into a cave to go to sleep.

The military was shooting at something in the woods, thinking it was the devil, but it wasn't the devil's underground hiding.

This couple was camping in the deep forest near the Red Canyon, and the devil was near. The campers' dog went for a walk in the woods, but it never came back. The campers went looking for it.

"Come, Cocoa. Come, Cocoa. Here, Cocoa!"

Roar!

"Oh my god, a bear!" said the girl.

The boy said to the girl, "Get in the tent!" The boy made a campfire, and the devil got him! It chopped him in half, then it sprayed fire at the tent, killing the girl!

"Help! Help! Help! Help!" The girl ran around burning to death. Finally she died.

The next day, the devil was in for a surprise. The military dropped bombs in the deep forest, forcing the devil to hide underground. The Air Force dropped bombs, and the National Guard carried powerful guns. Then the devil had to run to hide, then the helicopter was landing, and the devil crawled into its shell and froze. The helicopter landed right beside it.

"Air chopper number 200, over," said the pilot.

"At 0500 hours, chopper number 200, I read you loud and clearly!" said the Air Force.

224

"We have captured the animal in Moodus's Red Canyon, Chopper number 200, over."

Just after the pilot in chopper number 200 radioed to the Air Force, the devil sprayed fire at the helicopter, and it burst into flames, killing the pilot and the copilot!

"Chopper number 200, come in please."

"Chopper number 200, come in please."

"Chopper number 200, come in please!"

"Chopper number 200, come in please, this is the Air Force, do you read me! There's no answer, there's something wrong! Lenny, get another chopper out to Moodus right away!" said the Air Force.

The devil ran to hide under some rocks for the day, until the Air Force finished bombing. Lenny was flying over the Red Canyon and spotted the burned chopper below. A second chopper couldn't find a place to land. The National Guard found the burned bodies in chopper number 200.

The next night, the devil crawled through a cave, and it saw a large drain, and it crawled up the drain well, and it ended up in a supermarket—Stop & Shop. The devil went in the meat room, eating all the meats. The alarm triggered, and the police came. Quickly the devil ran to a stairwell, where it hid. The police searched the supermarket. All the meats were missing! The police noticed the drain was broken through, then they heard a crash, and the devil ran into the woods in the back of the supermarket. The police saw the broken doors from the stairs, and they searched every exit in the market and outside! The police searched the light into the woods; the devil was long gone!

"Maybe lightning hit the windows!" one cop said to another.

"No, the devil's been in here, go take a look at the meat counter!" said the other cop.

The police stayed at the supermarket all night until it opened the next day at 8:00 a.m. About 8:30 a.m. business was just getting started. It was a rainy day. The devil got back into the store from the drain underground. When the help came, the doors were chained up, and they had to enter from the stairway entrance because of last night's break; the police was there.

"What happened here last night?" an employer said to the manager of the supermarket.

"The police said some animal broke in from an underground drain and ate all the meats and broke windows trying to get out!" said the manager.

Shortly about fifteen people were shopping for school supplies, when suddenly the devil came up through the drain in the meat room, and it came crashing through the doors and into the supermarket. It was running down the aisles, knocking things all over the place! One lady was coming around a corner in the market, and she met the devil face-to-face!

"Aahhhhhhhhhhhh!" she screamed so loud and the devil chased her out of the supermarket! Others were screaming hysterically when they saw this ugly thing. Then the devil bit one of the shoppers; the manager struck the devil in the head with a brick, then the devil spun its tail around and stung the manager, and he dropped dead right away! Everyone ran out of the supermarket! The devil was heading for the meat room, and the butcher threw knives at its head, and the devil sprayed fire at him and killed him! The butcher looked like a burnt piece of chicken. Then the devil ate him up! Quickly the police and the military arrived to trap the devil in the supermarket by spraying tear gas and poisonous gasses, and the military was gonna blow it up! The devil found the drain and dug its way under the ground like it always did. A B-52 flew over and bombed the supermarket to smithereens! But the devil lives on!

"I think we got it, Officers!" said the MTs after the military cleaned up the debris. After the mess was all cleaned, the military radioed to the police.

"W35-190 National Guard, over."

"Moodus Police, I read you, W35-l90, over."

"We found a crater in the center where the Air Force blew up the Stop & Shop. The crater looks like it leads to a cave! W35-190 National Guard, over."

"Ten-four W35-190, hang tight, we'll be there, Moodus Police, over."

Several policemen arrived with K9 dogs. "What the fuck is this!" said Junior.

"I don't know, but the Air Force is taking test of this scary crater. The devil might still be down there! What may have happened is the devil may have dug another hole into the ground, spraying fire, which opens the hole wider so the devil can keep digging!" said one of the MTs

"Oh my fuckin' god, You gotta be kidding!" said Junior.

"No, Junior sir, I'm not kidding! Look at the color of the crater. It looks like pieces of rock from a meteorite. The devil's shell is from outer space, some of these rocks we're finding matches with the ones on planet Venus!" said the MT guard.

"Jesus Christ! I don't fuckin' believe it, a meteorite!" said Junior.

Later the National Guard went in the crater and caves, looking for the devil, and came up empty-handed! The Air Force dropped another bomb over the crater, and they sent more men into the underground tunnels to find this monster! A high school football game was going on, and the spectators saw fire in the woods. Then the devil roared, and the flames were getting bigger. People started running and screaming! The visiting just scored a touchdown and kicked the extra point, tying the game 21 to 21, then the devil ran out of the woods, spraying fire, and it went on the football field, chasing everyone! Everyone was running in all directions to get away from the devil; the devil tore down the scoreboard and the goal post and dug up the field and ran right back into the woods!

Everyone quickly got in their cars, and the devil came back out of the woods, stepping on cars, breaking windows, and chasing people through the parking lot! Some people got bit by the devil. The football teams threw rocks at the devil to chase it back into the woods. Then helicopters flew by, and the police came. The devil ran off into the woods as fast as it could! A forest fire started and burned the football stadium. The fire department and the military put the fires out in the woods. Rescuers arrived to take the injured to the hospital, and tow trucks came to pick up damaged cars in the parking lot. The military went looking for the devil again! The injured were in the hospital, being treated for the wounds and radiation. The people described this animal.

One man said to the nurse, "I was watching a football game when suddenly a dinosaur-like animal came running out of the woods spraying fire and burning everything! Then it was biting people, jumping over cars, and chasing everyone, trying to kill us! It was a vicious animal!"

"Did this animal look like a giant bear with pricks all over it, and it had a long tail with a stinger at the end, and it had horns and pointy ears?" asked the nurse.

"Yes, Nurse, it was the most worst thing I ever seen!" said the man.

Junior from the Moodus Police came over to talk with a girl who got bit by this thing.

"Miss, how do you feel?" said Junior.

"I have a pretty good bite on my ass!" she said.

"Miss, can you describe this animal that bit you?" said Junior.

"To me it looked like the devil. It's definitely something from outer space! No animal on earth sprays fire!" said the lady.

"It is the devil, we can't kill this son of a bitch!" said Junior.

People were crying and hysterical in the hospital after being attacked by this animal! The military was spraying poisonous gasses in all the caves in Moodus to kill this fuckin devil. The devil was back in the deep forest, hiding in the Moodus River in its shell. A thunderstorm was overhead, and the military tested the storm for radiation by shooting up rockets and found the storm was the devil's power!

The military kept spraying all of Moodus, Connecticut, all night long. The devil still was resting in the Moodus River. The next day the devil was looking for new places to hide. It found a railroad crossing. The red lights were flashing, and a train was stopped; the devil grabbed ahold of one of the railroad cars with its claws, and it jumped aboard. The train was traveling to New York. Suddenly the devil crashed through a back window onto a crowded car. People screamed when they saw the glass break, then the devil landing on its back.

"A big turtle!" some drunk yelled. Then the devil started chopping off heads on the train, eating anybody it could. People were in shock! People were breaking windows and jumping off the train after being bitten. One man tried to get out from an emergency exit, and the devil bit his head right off! People were screaming to their death! One girl was trying to escape, and the devil chopped her in half. Arms, legs, heads, and bodies were getting eaten alive! One man was hanging out the window, and the devil bit his legs off!

"No! No! No! No!" one lady screamed, and the devil bit her head off. Her head bounced on the floor, and the eyes were going round, round, and round! One old man was swinging his cane at the devil, and it sprayed fire at him and killed him. He disappeared into a cooked skeleton! Then the devil threw up snakes, rats, and other animal it ate! Then the devil ate what it threw up as one lady watched in shock! The train was covered in a foot deep of blood with heads, legs, arms, bodies, snakes, and rats swimming in it! The devil was drinking the blood and swishing the blood all over the windows on the train. The driver stopped the train when he saw the blood pouring out of it. The blood was pouring out of the car the devil was on like a waterfall. The driver saw the massacre. He was shocked when he saw all the bodies. Then the devil grabbed him with its claw and killed him! Then the devil jumped off the train, and it went back to Moodus. The train was running with all dead people aboard it. The next day, children were going to school, and the children saw the devil roaming around in the woods, and the kids were screaming! One kid said, "Teacher, teacher, there's bears in the woods!" The school principal called the police. When the police came to the school, the devil in the woods disappeared!

"What did this animal look like, children?" said the teacher.

"It looked like a big bear with horns and pointy ears!" said the children.

The police and the military surrounded the woods near the school. The devil was hiding in there somewhere! A helicopter was flying over a train, not moving, then it landed, and the National Guard troops went aboard the bloody train and found legs, arms, heads, and bodies lying in dried-up, stinking blood; the smell was worse than you can imagine! One military said to the chopper pilot, "Jesus Christ! This animal did all this! How the hell did it get aboard the train?" The pilot called for more help. The Air Force helicopters were flying over Moodus with laser guns, looking for the devil.

Two days later, the devil crashed into a crowded diner in town. Everyone was screaming! One man pulled out a shotgun and shot the devil, and it left!

"What the hell was that?" one of the waitresses cried.

"It's the devil! The man-eaten' killer!" said the man with the gun.

"What!" the waitress cried.

The man with the gun paid his bill, and he left the diner. The devil was in the parking lot running into the woods. The man with the gun shot at it three times before it skipped into the woods! The man ran in the woods, looking for the devil, but it disappeared The man went back to the diner to warn everyone.

"Everybody, watch out for the devil. It bites, sprays fire, and it stings! This animal has killed a lot of people, thirty people on a bus, other animals, bears too! It cleaned out a Stop & Shop, it broke into someone's house and bit a girl in half! Then it went through a football game, chasing people away!"

The police arrived at the diner. There was all busted windows. They were frightened that the devil might be out there, ready to grab someone! The police and the military guarded the diner so everyone could eat in peace. The police sent out K9 dogs to track down the devil and find out where it was. The devil killed a wolf in the woods.

The police found nine K9 dogs and a wolf dead in the woods! The next night, a carnival was going on in one of the Moodus school grounds.

"Ladies and gentlemen, welcome to our fourth annual school carnival here in Moodus, Connecticut. We have plenty of games, rides, and fun!" said the hostess of the carnival.

Three boys were ready to go on the roller coaster. One of the boys said, "I don't think I want to go, I'm scared!" He went for a walk into the woods to go for a pee. The boy heard something moving when he was in the woods. He flashed his light near a tree, and the devil grabbed him by the throat with its claw and bit his head right off! After the other two boys got off the roller coaster, they went looking for the third boy.

"Tommy! Tommy! Tommy!" one of the boys hollered. No answer. The two boys went into the woods, looking for Tommy, the third boy, and both of them never came back. The devil came up from behind the boys, and it bit the head off one and sprayed fire at the other and killed them. The boy torched screamed but not for long; it happened so fast! People at the carnival heard someone screaming in the woods. A fire started out in the woods, and a few people went out to investigate it. Then the devil came into the carnival, and it was chasing people and biting them! A dog went after the devil, and it sprayed fire at the dog and cooked it! The devil then started going mental. It sprayed fire at all the game booths, setting them afire. The devil torched a cat, and it kept chasing people. The devil made the carnival look like the gates of hell, spraying fire at everything! After everything was torched, finally the police and the fire department arrived. The devil had run off into the woods. Most people got away and drove to the police station hysterical! The school carnival was one big ball of fire! The military and the police searched the school grounds and the nearby woods to find the devil; they found the tortured boys, the dog, and the cat, but no devil.

Lieutenant Licker said to Junior, "This work is from the devil!"

"I'm gonna get that motherfuckin', cocksucker, with my bare hands and tear it apart! This fuckin' devil is getting away with too fuckin' much!" said Junior.

The military was on guard for the rest of the night around the school grounds. The military found a hole in the woods where the devil dug to hide. The devil dug very fast and deep into the ground and covered up the dirt, and it kept digging with its claws. The military was sending laser messages under the ground, and the laser rods were going crazy! They knew the devil was near, but they couldn't get to it! During the night, the military staked out in the devil's mine, waiting for it. The next morning the police drove by the diner, and all the windows were busted, and everything was tipped upside down and destroyed; it looked like a tornado hit it! Down the road, the devil broke into an ice cream parlor, and it ate all the ice cream and cones, cups too! The place was torn apart! The owner came to open up the ice cream parlor, and everything was busted up except the phone. No money was missing. There was $1,000 in the cash drawer, but the place was a mess, so he called the police on the phone. The police was there in minutes.

"What's the matter, your place got robbed too?" said the police.

"No money was taken, but look at it!" said the owner of the ice cream parlor.

"Take what you have to, I'm gonna do a radiation check. The devil must have had a feast with your ice cream last night!" said the cop.

"The devil!" The owner laughed.

"You didn't hear? We have an unknown animal that crashed into Moodus, Connecticut, in a meteorite! An animal came out of it, and it looks like the devil!" said the cop.

"Holy shit! You got to be kidding!"

"You better leave, your place is radioactive too!" said the cop.

The owner left the ice cream parlor, and he stopped to get a newspaper at a store down the road. The headlines said, "The Devil Terrorizes Moodus, Connecticut, School Carnival, Leaving 3 Dead and 29 Injured!"

"Holy shit!" were his words.

The devil found a new hiding spot for a few days in a cave under some old hotel. The NGIST, the Air Force, MTs, and the National Guard set up tents at every place in town the devil may be. Airplanes and helicopters flew day and night with floodlights over the deep forest, looking for this dangerous devil!

It was a Monday morning. The custodian was washing the lobby floor in the hotel. The devil came up through the basement floor in the hotel near the boiler in the hotel. The custodian came downstairs with the mop, bucket, and wringer. He wheeled the equipment into a closet near the boiler, and the devil bit both of his legs from under him. He was screaming to death, then the devil tore at his chest! The hotel owner heard someone screaming down the cellar, so he ran down there and put a light on, and he saw the devil eating the custodian alive piece by piece! The owner said, "Oh my fuckin' god!" He picked up a shovel, and he went after the devil. The devil sprayed fire at him and killed him! Then the devil ran upstairs to the hotel lobby. A full elevator stopped to let off people at the lobby. Suddenly when the elevator opened, the devil attacked the people getting off, biting them and spraying fire and killing them all!

"*Aahhhhhhhhh!*" everyone screamed to death as the devil began torturing. People were coming downstairs to turn keys in to check out, and they saw the horror! One man had a gun, and he fired six shots at the devil, then he got on the phone and called the police. The devil wouldn't die with six gunshots fired at it!

Before the police came, the devil ran back down in the basement. It broke a hole in the concrete cellar floor, and it started digging to escape. The police and the military arrived just in time and surrounded the hotel. The police went into the lobby and saw the burning victims lying on the floor near the elevator. Meanwhile the NGIST trapped the devil in the hotel basement. It was digging into the concrete basement floor! The military then sprayed a poisonous gas to choke the devil. A helicopter was flying over the hotel with a loudspeaker.

"May I have your attention, please. Everybody must vacate the hotel immediately! This is a warning from the US Air Force. The hotel is going to be blown up within ten minutes!"

The police got everyone out of the hotel in time. Later the National Guard came with heavy equipment to kill this animal. They had bazookas with big rockets in them and machine guns, an army tank, bombs, and M-150s, and the military raced to the hotel basement with the equipment.

"Okay, open fire in ten seconds! T-10-9-8-7-6-5-4-3-2-1. *Blast!*" The military blast the devil's shell into pieces. The military still was spraying the poison gas to kill the devil. Then the military removed the devil's remains and swept it into a steel box and sent it to the military morgue. Then the Air Force bombed the hotel on North Street.

At the Air Force base, the military brought the devil's remains in a laboratory. The Moodus Police was there. Lieutenant Licker and

Junior flew by helicopter to the Air force base. While they were flying, the pilot introduced himself to the police officers.

"Officers, my name is General Matt from the US Air Force."

"Pleased to meet you, General, we have to talk about this animal when we get inside."

"General, come this way. My name is Lieutenant Licker and my partner, Junior. No reports are allowed out to the public, everything is a secret! That's number 1 until all the autopsies are settled. Please, please note that in mind!" said Lieutenant Licker.

Helicopters were landing at the Air Force base in Hartford, Connecticut. Lieutenant Licker and Junior met with the Air force and the National Guard. They followed General Matt to the morgue.

"Everyone, please take a seat and the veterinarian will come out with a report in a few minutes," said General Matt.

"Excuse me, the results of the autopsies will not be ready in a couple of days, so if you all would come back at that time," said the veterinarian doctor.

The military and the police had some reports on the devil and came back to the lab two days later. By 7:00 a.m. Tuesday, the military and the police came back for the autopsies.

"Lieutenant Licker and Officer Junior, you may come in to the morgue. Please shut the door behind you. Put these uniforms on because the morgue might be radioactive! Thank you," said General Matt.

"Lieutenant, you had a deadly animal in Moodus!" said the vet doctor.

"I know!" he said.

"According to the autopsy, this animal came from the planet Venus. Venus has a hard crust of rock from intense heat on that planet to make meteorites so powerful! It was a meteorite that crashed into Moodus, Connecticut, with an animal in it. Whatever life is on Venus, it's extremely powerful! All Venus is slate and hard rocks. This animal is also radioactive. It was deformed by the chemical mercury on that planet, causing it to build power. This animal attacks in many ways: it has razor-sharp teeth, it bites most of the time! Number two, it sprays fire, because this animal lives in 850-degree heat and cools at night and holds heat buildups inside. You have a very vicious animal here, a lot worse than any on earth, I'll tell you that! Let's take five, and I'll be right back," said General Matt.

"Okay, let's finish up with the autopsy. Number three, it has two claws to defend itself. It uses its claws to dig underground to get away. Its claws are sharp enough to crush rocks! Number four, this animal has a very hard rock shell, and when an attack is coming, it hides in its shell like a parson or an armadillo. Number five, it stings. It has a long tail it uses to sting with. It has a stinger at the end of the tail, and when it stings, it kills instantly! Its venom is stronger than getting hit by lightning!

"Number six, it has pricks all over its body. It's also used to attack. It grabs you with its tail and throws you on your back, and its pricks go right through you! Number seven, this animal has horns like the devil it uses to buck you with or pin you up against a tree, wall, or whatever! Number eight, this animal kicks to defend itself too! It uses its feet to kick rocks or kick trees over so it can eat them!

"I understand this animal did quite a bit of damage in Moodus, Connecticut. This animal attacks eight or nine different ways, and it has killed many people and animals in Moodus. I'm sorry to hear about this, but it's once in a lifetime that a meteorite like this one comes from outer space! I haven't told the bad news yet. This animal is a female! You might have more little devils running around in Moodus, Officer Junior and Lieutenant Licker! It has big tits!" The vet doctor laughed.

"Jesus Christ! We may have another devil roaming around in Moodus!" said Junior.

"That's right, Junior. Test shows that the animal may have been pregnant before we killed it!" said General Matt.

"The reason why this animal went ape all of a sudden is because it may have been pregnant and laid eggs, or it was aggravated!" said the vet doctor.

"Doctor, is there any possibility that this animal could reactivate and come alive again?" said Lieutenant Licker.

"No, this animal was blown to pieces. It's dead!" he said.

"Lieutenant, the poisonous gas we used was enough to kill the animal regards on how much power it had! We had to use special bombs to blast the devil's rock shell. The gas we used will kill any living thing. All we have are pieces of a meteorite, it can't do no harm whatsoever. You have no more worries about this animal. The only thing we have to worry about is if it laid eggs! If it did lay eggs, it won't survive on earth anyway!" said General Matt, from the US Air Force.

"Doctor, what would you call this animal?" said Junior.

"The devil!"

About the Author

_T_HIS STORY IS ABOUT A comet that hit Moodus, Connecticut, and a creature living underground for several months before it went on its attack, and it killed people and animals, and it had magical powers. The creature looked like a huge porcupine with pricks all over it! By the way, this creature is a female with large breasts. It sprays fire like a dragon. It has a large tail and a powerful stinger. It has lobsterlike claws like a scorpion and feet like an elephant.